*Hook Line
and
Sink Him*

# Hook Line and Sink Him

Jackie Pilossoph

Blackhawk Publishing

# Hook Line and Sink Him

Published by
Blackhawk Publishing & Media Group, LLC
888 West 6th Street Suite 1400
Los Angeles, California 90017

Copyright ©2008 by Jackie Pilossoph

Publisher's Note

This is a work of fiction. It is not intended to depict, portray, or represent any particular real persons. The author has encountered many people in life, and this story was inspired by some of the things experienced by the author. The characters, places, incidents, and dialogues are based on the author's imagination, if real, used fictitiously. Any resemblance to actual persons, living or dead, business establishments, events, or locales is entirely coincidental.

Printed in the United States
ISBN: 10: 0-9826378-9-6
ISBN: 13: 978-0-9826378-9-0
LIBRARY OF CONGRESS: 2010901101

ALL RIGHTS RESERVED

No part of this book may be reproduced or transmitted in any form or by any means, electronic or mechanical, including photocopying, recording or by any information storage and retrieval system, without permission in writing from both the copyright owner and the above publisher of the book, except by a reviewer who may quote brief passages in a review.

Dedicated

to My Mom & Dad,

with Love

*Jackie*

## Author Notes

Writing this book was so much fun! Jeff and Dave, my two main characters, are like so many guys I've known over the years. They're sweet and loveable, and really good guys, but in their minds, marriage is synonymous with imprisonment. This was a concept I found hilarious to write about. As I typed away on my computer, taking these guys on a crazy but meaningful journey, I found myself smiling, giggling and tearing up chapter after chapter.

Trying to get this book published wasn't fun! It took a lot of hard work, persistence, determination (which I get from my dad), and the patience and drive to keep trying, even during the times when rejection e-mails flooded my inbox. There were days I wanted to take my computer, throw it against the wall and never log on again. I didn't do that, though. Instead, I kept persevering, hoping someone would eventually recognize my potential. The rejections kept coming. Until one day…

So, the first person I'd like to thank is Kevin English, my intensely hard-working publisher, for believing in me and my ability. I will always be grateful to you. THANK YOU! I'd also like to thank Laurie Smith. Working with you, Laurie, is so enjoyable and always great, thanks to your constant energetic attitude, your sweet, gracious demeanor, and your incredible ability of knowing our audience and what they want. And to everyone at Blackhawk Publishing, I know you worked really hard for me. Thank you so much.

Also, Karen Kleyla, without you, none of this would have happened. Thank you!

A lot of other people helped me along this journey, including my agent, Tina Tsallas, whom I trust immensely and Rachel Siegel, an amazing editor. There were also a few agents who gave me valuable feedback and advice, and who made me a much better writer. Thank you! I'd also like to thank my friends, the ones who took time to read my manuscripts and give me your honest opinions. It means the world to me.

I'd like to acknowledge another group, my fitness instructors: Kathleen, Kellie, Missy, Sheila, Lisa and Ginger, as well as all of the women who work out with me. To each of you, you inspire me on a daily basis with your discipline, your perpetual energy, and the smiles on all your faces.

I'd like to thank my family, my parents, Frieda and Zack, and my siblings and nieces and nephews, Billy, Vicki, Ali, Zackie, Sue, Sara, Jamie, Gena, Robin, Andrew, Jada and Pepper. All of you give me strength and support every day. And through your love, you motivate me to be the best I can be. I love you all.

And Mark, I love you dearly.

Most of all, thank you to Isaac and Anna, for being such wonderful little people. Your sweet personalities and hugs and kisses melt my heart each and every day. I love you more than you can possibly imagine.

Lastly, HOOK, LINE AND SINK HIM couldn't have been written without years of dates that ranged from heart-stopping, over-the-top outstanding, to I'd rather be getting a root canal horrible. So, to all the guys who dated me, especially all the guys who acted like marathon runners the second the subject of commitment came up, thank you! Without you, I'd have no stories, and definitely no characters! I'm sure a lot of you commitment-phobes have caved, and are now in committed relationships, but I also have a feeling some of you are still out there, as single as ever. Two words of advice: watch out! After reading my book, don't be surprised if some girl tries to HOOK, LINE AND SINK you!

*Jackie Pilossoph*

# Prologue: End of August

The hug lasted well over ten minutes. "I'm going to miss you so much," Sheila said through tears, her arms wrapped so tightly around me it felt as if I was being squeezed.

"Me too," I whispered. I really did mean it. After spending a year being her boyfriend and sneaking into her bedroom at least four nights a week for the past three months, our separation was going to be difficult.

She pulled away from me and looked me right in the eyes. "I love you Jeff," she said, her voice serious, tears streaming down her cheeks, "I really do."

"I do too, Sheila," I said with a sad smile.

"Then say it."

"Didn't I just do that?"

"No. You said 'I do too,' not 'I love you too.'"

This was hard for me, as I suspected it was for any eighteen year-old guy. This was the first person to whom I'd ever even come close to saying the "L" word.

I smiled at my sweet girlfriend, the one who I'd spent a semester staring at from across the room in Ms. Prince's psychology class before we even met, the one who my best friend Dave had to pass a note to in study hall to tell her I liked her, the one who had taught me how to kiss the correct way and the one who just a few weeks earlier had taken my breath away when I showed up at her house for the prom and saw her coming down the stairs. My girl looked so beautiful that night, so pure, and more like a princess from a fairytale than a high-school senior.

I took a deep breath and whispered, "I love you, Sheila…"

And then we kissed. And we kissed and kissed and kissed until Sheila's dad's car pulled out of their driveway and he honked the horn. He rolled down the window and said with a smile, "Get in the car Jeff. I'll drive you home before we head out."

Sheila and her parents dropped me off and headed to Indiana University, where the first girlfriend I'd ever had in my life was starting school in one week. I stood in my yard waving to her until the car was out of sight. I still remember, my heart actually physically hurt. The love I felt for Sheila was so real. And so untainted. It was the kind of love only people who have lived under two decades are capable of having.

## Mid-September

A little more than two weeks had gone by since Sheila left for school, but it seemed like two years. Why couldn't I shake the emptiness and the sadness I felt about not being with her? After all, I myself had just started college. Northwestern University…downtown Chicago. There were girls everywhere! Girls from other cities, girls from other countries, girls who were speaking languages I'd never even heard, their voices sounding more like music instead of conversation. So many were beautiful, most were smart, a few were sporty and quite a few sexy. But none were Sheila.

Sheila and I had history. And we were in love. I didn't want anyone else. The newness of everything in my life and the insecurity of the unknown were both causing me to crave familiarity. I wanted to be with my girlfriend so much it was making me unable to eat, sleep, study or have any fun whatsoever.

So one Friday morning as I sat in my Introduction to Broadcasting I class with Dr. Tyler McGinnis, I made the decision to drive up and visit the woman I loved. Even better, I decided I would surprise her.

With Bruce Springsteen blaring from the cassette player, I headed east on Highway 90/94 in my best friend Dave's mom's car. She had reluctantly agreed to loan it to me for the weekend, reluctant not because she cared about the car or was worried that I would wreck it or anything. She had just said she thought I should try to move on and embrace my new life, focus on my studies and my social life, and not grip on so tightly to the past.

"You just don't understand, Mrs. Stein," I said to the woman who I'd known since I was six, "I love this girl."

She gave me a gentle smile and said, "I do understand." Then she hugged me to show her support and told me to have fun and bring the car back with at least half a tank of gas. I loved Dave's mom but she drove me nuts. She really didn't get it. She didn't understand how much pain I was in and how desperate I was to see my girl, the first girl I ever really loved.

I thought about how nice it was going to be to see the look on Sheila's face when I showed up at the door. I would grab her and hug her and kiss her and she would tell me she loved me. And I wouldn't answer, "Me too." This time I would respond, "I love you too."

Four hours later when I pulled into Briscoe Gucker, Sheila's dorm, I was so excited I could barely breathe. I parked the car, grabbed my bag and headed up to the seventh floor. In the elevator a couple was making out and I don't just mean kissing heavily. I'm talking mauling each other. I chuckled. It was only the third week of school. They'd obviously just met.

When I got to Sheila's floor I looked around and saw a sign that read, "702-710 --->." I followed the arrow and when I got to room 706 my heart began to pound. Maybe I should have called, I thought to myself, she may not even be here.

What happened next is sort of blurry because it is so unbelievable to me to this day. That being said, I also remember it as clear as crystal. I put my hand up to knock on the door. Actually, I had already made a fist. A split second before my knuckles made contact with the door, a guy walked by and said, "Dude, I wouldn't interrupt what's going on in there if I were you."

I turned around, completely in a daze and said, "Is this Sheila Brook's room?"

Now the guy's face went from normal color to pale white, as if he had just realized he messed up huge. "Uh...I don't know...maybe... no...I don't think so. Wrong room..." Then he ran off.

I knocked on the door as hard as I could.

"Not now!" I heard a guy's voice shout. I knocked again, even harder this time, my heart pounding and my blood beginning to boil. "Come back later!" the guy shouted.

"No way, fucker!" I yelled, "Open the door!"

I'm pretty sure I heard a woman gasp at this point, who I thought was my girlfriend.

"Open the door, Sheila!" I shouted.

Some of Sheila's neighbors had begun to come out of their rooms for what they all knew was going to be a show. I turned and looked at all of them, unable to speak, the look of a caged lion on my face. A couple of the girls seemed scared, that's how I knew I must have looked pissed beyond belief.

A moment later the door slowly opened. Standing in the doorway was my girlfriend, wearing a big sweatshirt and socks, and the same pale, frightened, freaked-out face as the pussy who had run away from me moments earlier. "Hi," she said sadly, "I'm so sorry, Jeff."

I looked at her for a long time without saying a word and then I pushed the door open and burst into the room and onto her new guy, who was standing by the bed. My weight pushed both of us down onto the bed and I began delivering severe blows onto his face. I could hear Sheila screaming, "Jeff, stop it!" but I didn't.

When the guy was finally able to maneuver himself up a bit, he returned a punch onto my left cheek. I felt sudden pain so severe that my entire body went limp for a second. But I still say, no matter how much physical pain I was experiencing, my heart was bruised a hundred times more.

Eventually, some guys burst into the room and broke up our fight. I could hear all the girls talking loudly and I could hear Sheila screaming at me and the guy yelling at Sheila, but I was so out of it, I had no idea what anyone was saying or yelling.

I walked outside the room, looked back at Sheila, and said in almost a whisper, "I can't believe you." Then I simply put my head down, turned and walked down the hall.

"That's right, asshole!" I heard the guy shout, "Go back to Chicago!"

I never turned around to look at or respond to the guy who had replaced me, but what I remember so clearly is that I couldn't believe he was being such a jerk. After all, what had I done to *him*, besides give him a couple of well-deserved punches? He had stolen my girlfriend! No "Sorry dude, it's not personal" or "Listen man, it just happened"? Instead he was calling me an asshole! Ouch.

I was pretty oblivious to the sympathetic "awws" coming from all of the girls still standing in their doorways, but I remember this one girl saying to her friend, "He's pretty cute, huh?" and that made me chuckle as I walked out the door, even with my freshly broken spirit.

After leaving the dorm, I drove to a nearby Mickie D's and called Dave from a phone booth. "Dude, you're not going to believe this," I said, telling him the very short story resulting in the end of my relationship with Sheila.

His response: "Girls suck." Then he said something that would stick with me for a long long time. "Screw 'em!" Dave said sadly, "Screw 'em all."

At that moment I decided to take my best friend's advice. Literally. I would never let another girl into my heart. Ever again. But I certainly would sleep with girls.

Twelve years later…

# Chapter 1

The first time I ever saw Anna I was sitting on a bar stool next to her looking at the back of her head. I could not see her face but I could certainly hear her annoying voice. She was shouting at the guy who was seated on her other side.

"How can you be so insensitive, Chris?!" she yelled at him.

My buddy Dave, who was bellied up to the bar on my other side, leaned over and began to listen as well.

"I'm just being honest, Anna," replied the guy whose name I already knew, "What do you want from me?"

"Chris is really calm," mumbled Dave.

As I nodded in agreement I noticed Chris was a good looking dude with his Mediterranean skin, big brown eyes, and full head of hair. That's how I knew instinctively that Anna would be a major babe. I could not imagine a guy like Chris involved with someone even remotely unattractive.

I was still unable see Anna's face but all of a sudden I got a whiff of her really nice thick dark hair when she stood up and shook her head. "Unbelievable!" she shouted, "What do I want from you?! I want to be your wife!" Her hair smelled great but I had a strong urge to tap this chick on the shoulder and tell her to back the hell off of this guy Chris.

"I should get a tape recorder," Chris responded, still unbelievably composed.

"And why is that?" asked the good smelling psycho.

"Because I could record this conversation and just keep re-playing it night after night after night." Now Chris was finally starting to lose it. "That's how often the subject of marriage comes up!" He ended his statement with a fake, sort of bitter laugh.

We continued to eavesdrop, trying not to laugh but at the same time concerned for this dude Chris. After all, he seemed like an okay guy. So he didn't want to get married. What was the big deal?

Turns out this conversation was familiar to Dave, whose girlfriend Lori had been on him for at least a year, pestering him for a rock. I think Dave felt comforted by what we were witnessing. It made him feel good to know there was another poor guy out there who had to put up with the same crap.

Anna fired back at Chris. "I guess you think this is funny."

"No," he answered, "I'm just sick and tired of talking about marriage. How many times do I have to say it? I'm not ready! I'm not ready!" He repeated himself very slowly, "I…am…not…ready!"

Anna's reply: she slammed her beer down hard on the bar. "Well, guess what?! I'm ready! Ready to dump you and move on with my life!"

This is where things turn into slow motion, because when Anna turned around to get up and leave and I got a look at her face for the first time, I went numb. I've had this happen to me before. I see a girl and I am so completely awestruck by her beauty that I cannot move or speak. Usually, though, it's because I feel an urgent need to kiss her or to put it more bluntly, to nail her. This has been the case dozens of times for me and if I do decide to make a move, which I almost always do, I end up in her bed the next morning wondering how many beers caused me to misjudge this girl I just had sex with.

Anna was different. There was something about her, something fresh, out of the ordinary. She had beautiful eyes that sparkled and these really pretty cheeks, full but not fat by any means. I found myself having a strong urge to kiss them. And her lips…very full, almost fake looking. I didn't know if they were real but I didn't care. In a nutshell, something about this woman was causing me to feel weak but in a really good way. It was a feeling of vulnerability, like I was exposed for the first time in my life to someone so amazing, it made me believe in angels.

I began to tremble a little bit, and although I hate to admit it, I felt myself struggling to breathe. I wanted to chalk this up to laying eyes on yet another beauty running around Chicago that I had not yet had the pleasure of getting to know in an intimate way. The problem was, I couldn't. I had a strange suspicion right then that seeing Anna had just changed my life.

Dave and I sat and watched her storm out of the bar while Chris took a big chug of his beer and ordered another one. Then my buddy decided to make a move. He leaned over to talk to Chris. "Dude, you okay?"

Chris smiled. "Yeah, thanks man. My girlfriend...she wants..."

When I was finally able to wake up out of my infatuation coma, I interrupted Chris. "We heard," I said with a lot of sarcasm.

"Sorry, we couldn't help overhearing you guys," added Dave.

"Don't worry about it," said Chris before taking a sip of the cold beer that had just been placed in front of him. "Anna...that's my girlfriend...she wants a ring...and I'm just not there yet, know what I mean?"

I was quick to answer, "He does." I pointed to Dave.

"Dude, I'm going through the same shit," Dave said to Chris.

"I don't get it," Chris continued, "Why can't a girl just be happy to have a boyfriend? What's the big deal about getting married?"

"Yeah. What is this, the fifties?" replied Dave.

"I'm Chris, by the way." Chris held out his hand to shake Dave's and then mine.

"I'm Dave. This is my buddy Jeff."

We all shook hands, and although Chris seemed like a cool guy, I had zero interest in the conversation I knew was about to take place, so

I stood up and said, "Be right back." Then I left the two comrades alone to commiserate more with each other while I headed across the room to approach a hot blonde. I had to do something to get Anna off my mind, plus I wasn't in the mood to get into a deep discussion with two suckers who didn't have the guts to end their unproductive relationships.

No more than five minutes later, I was working it with the blonde (whose name was Jessica) and I was feeling the love, especially when I told her I was sure she was in television or movies.

All of a sudden I heard Dave shout, "Jeff!" When I looked up he was waving me over to him and Chris.

"What do they want?" I flirted with Jessica, "Can't they see I'm busy?"

She gave me a playful smile and said, "Hurry back."

I walked back across the room and said to Dave, "What?"

"I was just telling Chris about Lori."

Now I was annoyed. This is why they pulled me away from a woman who may actually be a live Barbie doll? "So?" I asked.

"Do your Lori imitation," Dave demanded.

Now I realized my coming back over here wasn't really a wasted trip, because making fun of Lori was one of my favorite pastimes. It never failed to crack us up when we needed a good laugh to take our minds off something.

"Okay, here goes..." I looked at Dave very seriously and put my hand on his shoulder. Then I spoke in my best Lori voice, "Jeff, why do *you* think Dave won't commit to me? Why is he so afraid of intimacy? Can't you talk to him? He listens to you."

We all got a good chuckle at Lori's expense and then Chris said with a laugh, "Here's Anna." He changed to a high-pitched voice and said, "Remember, if you do buy me a ring, make sure it's a platinum cushion cut diamond."

We all laughed heartily.

"What the fuck is a cushion cut?" asked Dave with a chuckle.

"No clue," replied Chris.

"Now can I go back to the girl I'm hitting on?" I asked them.

Dave replied, "Sure. You just keep picking up the hotties. Chris and me, we'll just sit here and continue to talk about our unfortunate situations." He actually had to yell the last part of that sentence because I had already begun to walk away.

A few minutes later I headed back to the guys, this time with Jessica on my arm. "We're out of here," I said with a wink, "Nice meeting you, Chris. See you in the morning, dickhead." Then Jessica and I were out the door.

Dave and Chris stayed and had a couple more beers and if I had to guess, they continued to tell each other war stories about their enemies, Anna and Lori. I figured they'd probably develop a kinship, which was understandable. But if I'd been there with them, the conversation wouldn't have been about needy girlfriends. We would have talked about important stuff like the Cubs chances of going to the playoffs or the rumors going around that Wrigley Field is getting more bleachers. But I wasn't.

I was with Jessica. Here's the thing though. As the two of us sat close in the back of a taxi, headed to another bar, a name kept popping into my head. Anna.

# Chapter 2

There is a little dive just off the Armitage exit of the Kennedy expressway that has gotten extremely popular. Why? No one really knows. *Marie's Rip Tide* basically consists of a few old wobbly tables and a bar with a lacquer countertop. They don't serve food and the place doesn't even play any music. For some reason, though, *Marie's* is always packed. I guess some guy decided it was cool to hang out there. He told a friend who told a friend who told some friends and suddenly *Marie's Rip Tide* is the place to go. I don't get it. It was even written up in "Suzie's Night Out," a weekly column in *The Sun Times*.

Jessica suggested we go there for a nightcap, so who was I to say no? I had no problem having another drink and doing some people watching. The only thing I cared about was where we were going after *Marie's*. I was very interested in ending up at Jessica's place, so whatever she wanted me to do in the meantime, I was happy to oblige.

The place was a zoo, as usual. A hundred people at least, packed like sardines in a little room not much bigger than my apartment. I grabbed Jessica's hand so she wouldn't get lost in the crowd and walked to the bar with her right behind me. "What can I get you?" I shouted to her.

She yelled back, "A Cosmo."

After a few minutes of waiting for the guys in front of me to order and get their beers, I got our drinks. Of course since there wasn't an empty table anywhere in sight we had to stand and drink. Jessica's martini kept spilling over the sides as people were constantly bumping her arm while trying to inch their way around the crowd.

"So where are you from?" Jessica shouted.

"Here," I yelled. As I shouted to her about where I grew up, I decided I wanted to get the hell out of this dump. Why were we here when we could be back at her place having some real fun?

Jessica must have sensed my dislike for our present venue, because after a minute or so she screamed, "I'm going to use the restroom. When I get back let's go."

I shouted back "Good plan," and off she went. Now I was psyched. I knew Jessica wanted to take me home with her and I was looking forward to that. She really was attractive. Nothing like the angel who just broke up with Chris at the Burwood, but still very hot with a killer body.

While I waited for my date to return I looked around at the crowd. The owners of *Marie's* had really done well for themselves, establishing the place as a major hangout. They were probably the luckiest people on earth, opening a bar without putting any money into the decor and then by some random act of God having it become one of the hottest late-night spots in the city. I noticed that every single girl in this place was gorgeous. And every guy (I'm not gay, by the way, but I have to confess) was a stud.

A tall, dark-skinned, definitely foreign guy with jet black hair caught my eye. For some reason, I became very focused on him. He was smiling and flirting with a woman who was seated across from him at one of the small round cocktail tables. I couldn't see the girl's face but this guy was turning on the charm big time, perhaps better than moi. The way he was grinning at her I could tell he was doing the best job he possibly could to take the girl home.

I continued to watch for another moment and couldn't help but smile when the guy leaned over the table and began kissing his conquest. "Nice move, dude," I thought. Instantly, the girl leaned over and kissed him back and soon they were passionately kissing, to the point of being a little disgusting. I couldn't remember the last time I had seen such a public mauling. The two were all over each other and in my opinion needed to take it somewhere else.

"Get a room!" I heard some guy joke to them as he walked by. Obviously, they decided to take his advice, because a few seconds later they got up from their chairs and the guy grabbed his jacket off the back of his seat.

What I saw next made me gasp. The girl dropped her purse on the floor and when she went to pick it up I saw that it was Lori. Dave's Lori. My buddy's girlfriend was cheating on him! At that instant all I could think of was Dave sitting with our new friend Chris (probably at this very moment) telling him how much Lori wanted to marry him when the truth was, Lori was here, sucking face with someone else.

Was she punishing Dave for not giving her a ring all these years? Or was she just having a guilt-free fling? Was this a one-time deal or did Lori have extra-pre-marital affairs often? I suddenly felt hatred for this chick beyond belief, especially when I saw the hottie put his hand on her butt while they exited the bar.

In my eyes, Lori had just gone from desperate wife wannabe to cheating liar with no morals. I had zero tolerance for dishonesty and deceit when it came to relationships, which is part of the reason I was never in them. After all, why commit to someone and then cheat? Why not just be honest, not make promises, and stay free? I had a lot more respect for people who had that attitude (like myself) then I did for both guys and girls who got into relationships and didn't have the guts to get out before starting something with someone else.

Maybe I was ultra sensitive on the subject. After all, more than a decade had gone by and Sheila's name still popped into my head whenever I thought about infidelity. For me, the name "Sheila" was synonymous with unfaithfulness and I just couldn't let it go. But now, at this moment, old Sheila wasn't even looking half as bad as evil Lori, the woman who now joined the ranks of my high school sweetheart. In my eyes, both of them were the scum of the earth.

"Are you okay?" Jessica asked me. I was so shocked and disturbed by what I had just seen that I didn't notice her return.

"Yeah," I lied, "Let's get out of here." I took her hand and headed to the door but then realized I needed to wait a few minutes before leaving, because what if the horny teenagers were out in front of the bar hailing a cab and saw me?

Don't get me wrong. I wouldn't have minded confronting Lori, the slut, but I didn't know yet what I wanted to do with my new found information. The last thing I wanted was to hurt my best friend. I loved the guy and he didn't deserve what I had just witnessed. Dave was a good person, kind to everyone. And he meant well, even when it came to Lori. My buddy was confused about marriage and wasn't ready yet. That was it. He wasn't trying to hurt her. He just needed to figure things out. My theory for a long time had been that Lori wasn't right for Dave because if he really and truly loved her he would have already headed to the chapel, or in his case, the huppah.

Lori and Dave had met three years earlier at a Jewish singles function. It was the first and last Jewish thing Dave would ever go to. Dave could not stand singles shindigs, let alone those with religious affiliations. He preferred to meet women on his own. And even though he could count the number of dates he had been on with two hands and the number of girls he had slept with on one, Dave had too much pride for blind dates or singles functions. He had always said there was something about them that was humiliating no matter how desperate a guy was to get laid.

He was suckered into going to this particular event by his mother, because her friend Margie had a daughter named Robin who had moved here and didn't know anyone. Dave's mom offered Dave up to take the girl to the function so she wouldn't have to show up there alone. Of course, Dave objected at first, until his mother suggested, "Why don't you bring Jeff, too?"

"Because Jeff's not Jewish, Ma," he answered.

"So what? Does he have something better to do?" Dave's mom was older and sweet and delicate but she was also smart and shrewd. She knew that if I came along Dave would go. That's why Mrs. Stein had called me herself earlier in the day to tell me her plan and to ask me if I would accompany her son and Robin to the thing. Since I could never say no to the woman who had practically raised me, I agreed.

"Jeff probably has plans already, or a date," Dave told his mother.

"Why not call and ask him?" said the sly fox.

"Fine. If Jeff goes, I'll do it."

That night, the Jewish guy and the goy picked up Robin and headed to the function. Robin confessed to us in the first five minutes of the drive that she was going to the party just to appease her mother and that the truth of the matter was that she was a lesbian with a serious girlfriend.

"Great, now the night is a really a complete waste of time," Dave complained, "Hey, I have an idea. Let's blow off the desperado bash and go to that new steak place. Prime I think it's called…"

I told them it didn't matter to me. I was up for anything. Robin, however, insisted we show up to avoid the suicide attempt she knew her mother would make if she found out Robin didn't go.

Once inside, the three of us made a beeline for the bar. We engaged in small talk and scoped out the crowd while sipping martinis. The girl-guy ratio was at least 20 to 1.

"I feel like a guppy in a shark tank," Dave grumbled.

"Shut up and keep an open mind, asshole," I answered.

"I feel sorry for all the desperate women," said Robin, with a concerned look on her face.

I could sense her feelings were genuine but I couldn't resist joking, "I'm sure you'll forget about all these poor girls when we drop you off at your girlfriend's place."

"I'm counting the minutes," she giggled.

A moment later two girls approached us and introduced themselves. Robin instantly made herself scarce.

"So, what do you do?" one girl asked Dave.

"Where are you from?" the other one inquired, looking at me. Dave and I answered the questions and the girls kept firing away. I suddenly felt like I was applying for a job, which I guess they thought I was. The job title: husband. The job description: No experience necessary. Actually, no experience preferred.

"Have you ever considered wearing a shirt that says, 'I'm trying to nail you to the huppah?'" I felt like asking girl number one. "Ever considered the Weight Watchers points program?" I wanted to ask the other one. I felt like a jerk for thinking this way, but it was frustrating that these women were so desperate to find a mate. Why couldn't they just relax, have fun, live their lives, and not worry about it? After all, that's what I was doing and I was extremely happy with life (or at least I thought so at the time.)

I looked over at Dave and I could tell he wanted to scream out for help or run away. You would think Robin would've done something, given the fact that we were there because of her, but when I looked over at her she wasn't even paying attention. She was busy looking at her watch and downing the rest of her drink. It was no use. We were trapped. Trapped like innocent Americans in a Mexican jail.

"So, what do you do again?" my girl asked me.

I suddenly realized that I held a "get out of jail free" card. "Actually, I have to tell you something," I said to her empathetically, "I don't want to waste your time so I'll just say it. I'm not Jewish."

I promise I am not lying when I say that within four seconds the girl was gone. I stood there smiling and now I could feel Dave's frustration. There was nothing he could do. He was headed for a life sentence behind bars. Then all of a sudden, fortunately and surprisingly, help arrived.

"Where the hell have you been?" Lori walked up and asked him. Before Dave could respond to this girl he had never seen before, Lori grabbed him and kissed him hard on the mouth. "I've been looking everywhere for you."

"Uh...don't get crazy honey...I'm right here," Dave replied in his best acting voice.

"Nice meeting you!" Dave's girl immediately said before scurrying away. No time to waste for her. Much like my aggressor, she was on a mission and needed to move on and away from "the guy with the girlfriend."

Once she was gone, Lori gave Dave a big smile. She never even looked at me. "I'm Lori. You can thank me anytime."

As I walked away to give my buddy some space, I checked Lori out. She wasn't particularly beautiful but she was extremely cute and had a nice little body. Plus, what she had just done was amazingly cool and I could tell Dave liked her.

An hour later, I ended up driving Robin to her chick's house and Dave went home with his savior. I didn't hear from the guy for 48 hours, and when he finally did call me, he told me he had a new girlfriend. I was really happy for Dave, first because I knew he got laid, which he needed in a huge way, but also because for the first time in a long time, I knew my buddy was on cloud nine.

Things with Dave and Lori went well for the first couple of years. They had lots of sex, lots of laughs, a pretty good friendship and minimal fighting; that is, until Lori decided she wanted to make things more permanent. The first time she brought up the subject of marriage, Dave got so freaked out he didn't call her for a week.

However, disregarding my advice he ended up at her door with a dozen roses because he didn't want things to end. He just didn't want to be a Mr. and Mrs. He tried to explain to her that if she would wait, he was sure he would eventually propose. So Lori tried waiting, but the arguments on the subjects of marriage, commitment and weddings continued. And for the past year, Dave had found himself walking on eggshells, like the time the two were walking down Michigan Avenue and a bride and groom were getting their pictures taken outside the Peninsula. Lori went off on Dave, stormed off, and didn't speak to him for two days. Then there was the time Lori spotted an invitation to a wedding on Dave's desk. The letter was addressed to "Dave Stein and Guest." Lori went ballistic. It had gotten to the point where Dave could not even watch the movie "Wedding Crashers" with Lori. She told him it was in bad taste to rent a movie like that with her.

"I don't get it," Dave said to me, "It's a comedy. It's not even really about marriage."

"I don't know what to tell you, dude," I replied, "But you really should see it. You should watch it by yourself. Vince Vaughn's hilarious."

"Thanks," Dave replied. My response had made him feel defeated. He wanted advice from me and I had none to give. Actually, I take that back. What I really wanted to do at the time was to tell him to end the relationship. But I couldn't do that. It wasn't my place. Dave had to get there on his own and he clearly was not ready yet.

"Can we go now?" Jessica asked me with a nudge.

"Sure."

As I tried to hail a cab I felt extremely bummed out, so much in fact that I was thinking of backing out of the whole Jessica situation and just going home. What was I going to tell Dave? Was I even going to tell him? Should I call Lori and tell her what I saw? I had to think of how to handle the circumstances, and I quickly realized that no matter what I did, things would turn out badly for my best friend. Temporarily anyway. I knew Dave would be fine in the long run, but the near future was looking grim and I didn't even want to think about it.

"Are you okay?" I suddenly felt Jessica's arms wrap around my waist from behind, "You seem sad about something." I think she was trying to sound sympathetic but it was more seductive than caring.

I turned to face her.

"Because if you're sad, I know a way to make you verrrrrrrrrry happy." She leaned into me and gently began kissing my neck, and that's when I decided to think about Dave in the morning. Right now I would let myself focus only on Barbie. I mean Jessica.

# Chapter 3

When I awoke around 6:30 a.m., Jessica was still asleep. Her room was pretty dark, so searching for my clothes was not an easy thing to do, especially because I had to look for them as quietly as I could. The last thing I wanted was for this chick to wake up before I could make a clean getaway.

I managed to find everything but one of my socks, which I decided wasn't important enough to risk my great escape for, so I walked out of the bedroom with one sock on and began searching for my shoes. I vaguely remembered taking them off in the living room.

While looking around for them I spotted some new CDs sitting on the coffee table. I picked a couple up to examine Jessica's music choices. Gwen Stefani, The Frey, John Mayer...not bad. I contemplated putting The Frey into my coat pocket but decided only the scum of the earth would sleep with a girl and then steal something from her place. At that moment I noticed a crucifix hanging on a nearby wall. I stared at it for a minute, the fear of God now in me for even slightly considering theft. Then I put on my shoes (which I spotted in the entryway) and headed out.

I was about to open the door when I realized I didn't have my wallet. Damn. Did I actually have to go back into the bedroom? Suddenly I remembered it was on one of the end tables next to Jessica's couch. I also realized I had used my last ten on the cab that took us here late last night. I needed cash or I was going to have to walk home, which if I remembered correctly was at least five miles away. Shit!

After picking up the wallet I headed back to the doorway and when I began to open the door, Jessica's purse caught my eye. It was sitting on the carpet next to the door. I froze. Only the scum of the earth would sleep with a girl and then steal money from her purse. Then again, only an idiot would walk around at 6:30 in the morning looking for a cash station. Without further hesitation, I quickly put my hand in her purse and pulled out the wallet. Two bills were in it, a five and a twenty. To take the twenty was criminal. The five would get me most of the way home at this hour. I looked up at the crucifix again.

"Sorry," I whispered to it, "Would it help if I went to church tomorrow?"

Jesus didn't answer me. He just hung there, staring at me accusingly.

"I promise...church, tomorrow morning..." I whispered at him. Then I grabbed the fin, shoved the wallet back into the purse, and opened the door.

"Jeff?" I heard Jessica call from the bedroom. I shut the door as quietly as I could, ran down the hallway, and took the stairs down to the lobby. Once outside I realized that there was a name for guys like me: assholes. I hailed a cab and headed home to go back to sleep.

The second time I woke up, it was 10:30 and I was in my own bed, thank God. I laid there thinking about the prior evening and let my mind drift back to the great sex I'd had just hours earlier. I liked Jessica. She was fun and pretty and sexy. But someone else began to seep into my brain, the someone with the round kissable cheeks and luscious lips. Anna.

As I thought about this nearly perfect woman, I couldn't help but wonder why she would be so desperate that she would act the way she had with Chris. I could not understand how a person so amazingly gorgeous and classy would have to ask her boyfriend to commit. Chris should be the one begging this knockout to be his. And why did Anna care so much about getting a ring? Wasn't it enough to be in a relationship with someone? In my opinion, girls who wanted to be married were insecure and dependent on men to fulfill them. For some reason, I pictured her sparkling eyes and I knew she wasn't like that.

But enough of Anna and her love life. I had a bigger issue to deal with; Dave. Now sober, I was absorbing what I had seen at *Marie's* and realizing just how bad the situation was. What was I going to do? The answer was a no-brainer. I had to tell my best friend what I saw. So I got up, took a quick shower, and headed to Einstein's Bagels, where I would pick up breakfast and then head to Dave's store.

The poor guy had to get up every morning (including weekends) and open his business by ten. Dave owned *Be A Sport*, which was a little store located on Wells Street in Old Town. He carried some athletic equipment, clothing, and knickknacks of Chicago sports teams but the main part of his business was sports memorabilia, i.e. autographed photos, balls, bats, jerseys, and other items.

At the time he was doing okay. In the five years since he had opened the shop, he was in no way breaking the bank, but he was able to live off his earnings. Dave really enjoyed owning his own business, plus he was a huge Chicago sports fan, so if his profits were paying the rent and he didn't have to go into an office and work for some jerk, the dude was happy.

Most Saturdays I would hit Einstein's around eleven and pick Dave up a bacon, egg, and cheese bagel. I myself preferred to order the toasted sesame bagel with the veggie cream cheese shmear. Then I would bring the bagels to his store and we would stand at his cash register, eating and discussing the prior Friday evening.

We would have a lot to talk about today, and the thought of it was making me queasy. How would he react to the news? I remembered how I reacted when it happened to me. I was pissed! And devastated.

Would Dave tear up? Would he get angry and violent and throw something? Would he immediately call Lori and go off? There was no telling what would happen. I was not looking forward to finding out.

When I walked into the shop, bagel bags in hand, Dave was helping a customer, some guy who was trying to decide between two framed autographed photos. One was Walter Payton, the other was The Fridge. He had a very concerned look on his face, almost as if he was making a life or death decision. If someone told me this guy just learned his brother needed a kidney and he was a donor match it wouldn't have surprised me. He seemed completely stressed out by the choice he needed to make. Dave motioned to me to hold on by putting his finger up. I guess he didn't want me butting into his sales presentation.

"Both are authentic and both come with a certificate to prove it," said the salesman/storeowner.

"This is tough," mulled the customer, "Both were great players…both with the greatest football team in the mid-eighties."

Dave interrupted, "Both did the Super Bowl Shuffle…"

The guy thought about Dave's input for a second and then did something surprisingly funny. He began to chant "The Super Bowl Shuffle," while clapping his hands and moving his feet.

"We are the Bears Shufflin' Crew
Shufflin' on down, doin' it for you.
We're so bad we know we're good.
Blowin' your mind like we knew we would."

The guy was getting really into it and I found myself getting into the groove. I put the bagels on the counter, walked over to them and began to clap and move my feet just like the guy. Dave did the same. I was amazed that the guy had this song down word for word. I thought I was the only one who knew "The Super Bowl Shuffle" by heart. He continued,

"You know we're just struttin' for fun.
Struttin' our stuff for everyone.
We're not here to start no trouble.
We're just here to do the Super Bowl Shuffle."

Then right on cue, Dave took over and began to chant the next verse.

"Well...they call me Sweetness
And I like to dance
Runnin' the ball is like makin' romance.
We've had the goal since training camp
To give Chicago a Super Bowl Champ."

I couldn't take it anymore. I wanted a turn. So I took one.

"You're lookin' at the Fridge,
I'm the rookie.
I may be large, but I'm no dumb cookie.
You've seen me hit, you've seen me run,
When I kick and pass, we'll have more fun.
I can dance, you will see
The others, they..."

I was rudely interrupted by another customer, an older guy who looked like one of those Saturday Night Live skit Ditka buddies who drank beer, watched games, and toasted to "Da Bears." Only this guy wasn't funny at all. He was a complete creep.

"Hey!" he shouted at us, "I need to return this." He held up a Bears jersey. "Do any of you work here?!" He seemed like he'd had a little too much coffee.

"I do," answered Dave. Then he turned to the Super Bowl Shuffle guy. "Sorry, dude. I'll be right back."

"No problem," said the guy.

Dave met the crabby guy at the register while I stayed with our friend to help him decide which autographed photo to buy. I could hear the conversation going on nearby and I felt sorry for Dave because it was obvious that the guy had worn the shirt already and Dave would have to take it back and eat the loss.

"Sir, do you have the tags for this?" Dave asked him in an attempt to credit him with a fair price.

"Listen, you little weasel, the shirt is too small and I ain't leaving here without my money."

Dave sounded defeated. "Fine," he said as he opened the register and handed the guy back full price for the shirt. With cash in hand, the guy grunted something that I couldn't understand and then walked out. Dave stood there helpless, so I left my guy and walked over there, thinking the bagel would cheer him up.

"Here," I said, handing him the bagel.

"Thanks," he said, "You know something? The small businessman always gets screwed."

I gave him a look of sympathy and then we began to eat our bagels in silence till our Super Bowl Shuffle guy walked up.

"Which one did you decide on?" Dave asked him.

"Neither," said the guy flatly, "I want to think about it."

Dave responded, "No problem," while trying to keep the sarcasm out of his voice. I couldn't believe it. I realized once again how tough it was to be in Dave's shoes.

After the guy left we continued munching on our bagels. "So did you hook up with that girl? Jessica?"

"Uh huh," I nodded while chewing.

"Fun?"

I nodded again and kept eating. I was inhaling my food because I found myself extremely nervous.

"You okay?" Dave asked with a nervous laugh. It's funny how a best friend can sense in an instant that something isn't right.

I stopped chewing and looked at Dave, who had a nervous smile on his face. With a deep breath I began, "Listen…" But just as I was about to drop the Lori bombshell I was interrupted by the sweetest voice.

"Excuse me…" I heard.

I looked up. Standing there was none other than beautiful Anna.

# Chapter 4

Anna was even prettier to me than the first time I saw her. On this day she looked more natural, less make-up, I think. And there was something about a chick in cut-off jean shorts that drove me nuts. She walked toward us. "I'm looking for a birthday gift for my boyfriend," she said, her lips looking beautiful even without lipstick, "Do you guys work here?"

Dave chewed as fast as he could and swallowed. "I do," he answered.

Anna explained to my buddy about how Chris was really into sports but that she had no clue where to begin when it came to buying him a present. As I listened and watched her, I realized there were only three words to describe this girl; hot, hot, and hot. I couldn't stop staring at her lips, except for when she giggled. That's when her eyes would sparkle and steal all the thunder and then I would be drawn to her big brown eyes and her long dark eyelashes.

After a few moments while Anna began looking around, Dave shot me a look, and when I saw he was trying not to crack up, I gave him a big grin. After all, this was hilarious. This girl had no clue that twelve hours ago we heard her in a huge brawl. Now she was out shopping for the guy? A thought briefly crossed my mind. Maybe Anna and Chris made up last night. Maybe Chris went over to her place after he left the bar and proposed. The thought of that scenario made me nauseous for some reason. Suddenly I felt like I could throw up. Was my veggie cream cheese shmear about to end up on some nearby Blackhawks jersey?

"How about a signed Walter Payton photo?" Dave asked her.

"Or the Fridge?" I asked.

"Umm...maybe..." replied Anna, still very unsure of herself.

"Come with me," said Dave as he walked Anna across the store.

I didn't want to miss anything, so I followed them like a little puppy dog. When they reached the table, Dave began to show Anna some options. She kept looking at me, perhaps wondering what I was doing here.

"How much did you want to spend?" Dave asked her.

"I don't know yet," she replied.

I couldn't take it anymore, so finally I spoke. "You say this is for your boyfriend?" I asked her.

She looked at me like I had three heads. "Yeah?"

"Is this a serious boyfriend?" I asked in somewhat of a mocking tone.

Anna picked up on the sarcasm. "Yeah, I guess."

I knew I sounded like a complete jerk, yet I continued. "A guy you see yourself marrying?" I was afraid to look at Dave because I was sure he wanted to kill me. After all, he did want her business.

"Maybe," Anna answered. She sounded completely annoyed by me until something seemed to click. It was as if a light bulb had just gone off in her head. "Wait a minute," she said while pointing at both Dave and I, "You guys were at the Burwood last night." Now she was semi-smiling, not the "happy to see you smile," more the "I'm glad I just figured out why you're being so condescending," type of grin.

"Yeah..." answered Dave, "that was us."

"I knew it!" she exclaimed, "So you must have heard..."

Dave and I nodded in unison.

"Oh God, I am so embarrassed. I usually don't act like that. It's just..."

"You don't have to explain," said my buddy, the wimp.

"You really don't, but do you mind if I ask you something?" I asked her.

"Sure."

"If you're so pissed off at the guy, why are you buying him a gift?"

I wasn't sure if Anna was going to answer my question or slap me. She chose to speak, but there was a sense of hopelessness in her answer.

"Well, I really do love him," she began, "I think we'll end up working things out. We just want different things right now."

So Chris didn't propose last night, I thought. This was a huge relief. Now I could finish my breakfast and not worry about puking.

"You want a ring, he wants to wait," Dave replied to her.

"Right," said Anna, "Eventually he'll come around."

I couldn't believe this. Eventually he'll come around?! Why does this perfect girl care if he "eventually comes around?" She could have any guy she wants. What was up with the lack of self-confidence? I couldn't take it anymore. I had to butt in. "Look, I don't mean to be a jerk, but…" I could see out of the corner of my eye, Dave was looking at me like, "Don't say it, dude." Still, I went on. "You're kind of going about this thing the entirely wrong way."

"What do you mean?" asked Anna, half wanting the advice and half wanting to tell me to mind my own business and shut the hell up.

"I mean, if you really want to get this guy to marry you, you need to change everything you're doing," I said matter-of-factly.

"And what makes you an expert on guys?" Anna asked sarcastically.

"I'm a guy," I said with confidence.

Now it was Dave's turn to be a smart ass. "And you're so in tune with marriage because you've been in so many relationships?"

I responded to the jab, "I don't get into relationships because all the girls act like…" I looked right into Anna's radiant eyes and finished my sentence. "You."

"Ignore him, please," said Dave, desperately trying to both console Anna and save a potential sale. "Look, here's an autographed photo of Sweetness," he said as he held up a black and white of Walter Payton.

I didn't care about Dave's sale or about Anna's feelings. For some odd reason, as awestruck as I was by her, I felt like being completely honest and open with this chick. Confidently, I said, "If you want me to show you how to get Chris to marry you, I'll be glad to."

"Hey, how do you know his name?" was her first response.

Dave answered, "We had a couple of beers with him after you left."

Now she saw a chance to get answers. "Oh my God! What did he say?"

I suddenly saw an opportunity for my buddy, so I put my arm around Anna and made her an offer she couldn't refuse. "Look," I began, cocky as hell, "Dave here is having a really bad morning sales wise. Tell you what…we will tell you exactly what Chris said, word for word, on one condition."

"What's that?" she asked.

"You have to buy something."

It took everything for Dave not to burst out laughing. As for Anna, she agreed whole-heartedly. Within a minute, was at the register with an autographed Kerry Wood baseball.

After ringing up the sale, Dave made a quick call to our buddy Mike, who lives in one of the apartments above the shop. He asked him to come down and cover the store for a few minutes while the three of us headed to Starbucks to discuss the business at hand. Sipping lattes, we sat at a table for four with the fourth chair being occupied by Anna's recent purchase.

"He just said he doesn't want to get married yet," Dave explained to our new friend, "He's not ready. I really don't think it has anything to do with you."

"Okay, what else?"

"He said he loves you, but he likes things the way they are right now," Dave answered.

I really wanted to add, "By the way, he does a great imitation of you…and why do you care so much about what the ring looks like?"

but I didn't. Instead, I sat there with a polite smile on my face, which is so uncharacteristic of my personality.

This girl conflicted me in so many ways. I hated her desperation but I loved her eyes. I loathed her neediness but I adored her cheeks. And I couldn't stand why she talked about Chris, a guy who clearly didn't appreciate her, like he was God's gift.

Part of me wished I could get trapped in an elevator with her so I could talk to her more, because I felt like something was clouding her judgment. I was sure that self-confidence and self-assurance were her true colors, hidden behind a shield, for some unknown reason.

"Is there anything else?" she asked, "I mean, did he say anything bad about me?"

"No!" answered Dave, "Nothing. I swear."

"So that's it?" she asked, "I just paid major bucks for a Terry Wood baseball and that's all you guys can tell me?"

"Kerry Wood," I corrected her while wondering how she couldn't know who Kerry Wood was.

"You know what I feel like?" she said, "I wish someone could give me a road map with specific directions on how to get to that place in Chris's heart where I could press the long-term commitment button."

"No offense," I responded, "But why should *you* have to press the button? Don't you think he should press it on his own?"

"You just don't understand."

I looked right into her eyes. "Actually, I do. Much more than you know."

True, I was a commitment-phobic womanizer, but I did firmly believe that no woman should worry about guys like me or any guy for that matter who didn't want the same things. "Move on," had always been my motto. There were so many hot babes (and so many good guys) out there. Why focus on someone who's not on the same page?

I wanted to say all this to Anna but I held back. I didn't know her well enough and it really was none of my business. At that moment she and I held our gaze for so long it made my heart skip a beat.

"I'm just so frustrated. If I knew what was really holding Chris back, maybe I could do something to change."

Neither Dave nor I could respond, although I felt like shouting out, "Why would you want to change yourself for some asshole?!" But I didn't, of course. I felt sorry for Anna. I knew what frustration was like. For the past eight years I had known what it was like to want something you just can't get. I knew what it was like to keep trying, to hang in there, to wait, and then to have nothing happen. I am referring to the professional rut I had been in since…well, forever. I was a sports writer, trying to get a steady, decent paying job. And at thirty years old, I was still struggling for work and for money.

Anna stood up and took her bag off the chair. "Thanks for trying, guys," she said with a sincere smile.

I looked at Dave, who looked as hopeless as he did during the fourth quarter of the 2006 Bears Colts Super Bowl. Then I watched Anna wave and walk away. Was this it? Was I never going to see this beauty again? I didn't want her to go. Think! Think!

"Anna," I called out to her. She turned back around.

"I think I have an idea," I declared.

She walked back to the table and stood there.

"The key is…specifics," I began.

"What do you mean?" she asked.

"Yeah, what do you mean?" Dave asked sarcastically.

"We need to find out specifically why Chris won't bite the bullet."

Now Dave caught on. It was as if he was reading my mind and he knew exactly where I was headed with this. This happens often with Dave and me. Again, when you've been best friends with someone since kindergarten, you tend to know how the other's mind works.

"Yes, yes, that's genius!" Dave declared.

Anna was intrigued. "What are you guys talking about?" She sat back down.

Now I was on a roll. I really did have a plan. I leaned into the table and lowered my voice. I felt like I was in a football huddle and I was relaying the winning touchdown play to my offensive teammates. "Okay, let's say Dave and I just happen to run into your boyfriend."

"Like, coincidentally," added Dave.

"That's what Chris will think," I clarified.

Dave continued. "Then we say 'hi,' start talking to him, and get it out of him."

"We'll find out exactly what the holdup is, and what it will take for him to commit," I finished.

"Oh my God! That *is* genius," said Anna happily.

"But I should warn you, we may find out some things you don't want to know," I cautioned, "If we're successful in revealing the truth, are you sure you're ready to hear it?"

"Yeah, like what if he says something to the effect of…he *never* wants to marry you?" asked Dave.

"Do you think you can handle that?" I asked her.

"Definitely," she said with assurance, "Look, as bad as the truth may be, I need to know it once and for all, right?"

"I would want to know," I stated boldly.

"Me too," Dave agreed.

"Okay, listen," Anna said, leaning into the huddle, "I know the perfect place where you'll run into Chris."

"Where?" asked Dave.

"Chris's body is very important to him," Anna responded with a giggle.

## Chapter 5

I couldn't believe how easy it was to sneak into Lakeshore Athletic club. If I'd have known it was so simple, I would have been working out there for years. Our buddy Mike belongs, so when we told him we needed to get in there to run into someone (Chris), Mike loaned us his membership card.

When I walked into the club, there were two people working the front desk, a cute little curly-haired brunette who was smiling and talking on the phone and an older guy who was eating a sandwich from Subway. I acted like I was in a slight rush, breezing past the two employees while holding Mike's card up so they could see it. Strategically I placed my thumb over the lefthand corner of the card, as this is where Mike's picture is located. The girl on the phone waved me on and the guy continued chewing while nodding his head. So I was in. It was that painless.

A couple of minutes later, I stood at the top of the stairs and pretended to be waiting for someone. I watched Dave walk in. He told the Subway guy he just moved to town and was interested in joining. The guy had him fill out a short form and a liability waiver and just like that my buddy was in too. Lucky for us the manager of new memberships was out sick, so Dave didn't have to do the tour and all that fun stuff.

Dave and I agreed to hook up in the locker room before heading into the workout area to seek out our prey, whom Anna told us worked out religiously on Monday, Wednesday, and Friday from five-thirty to seven. So here we stood, two imposters, solely at the club for the purpose of prying some much needed information out of Chris.

What was unbelievable to me was that I was doing this all for a girl I barely knew. I was attracted to Anna beyond belief, so why was I helping her get another guy to commit to her? I didn't understand it. What I did realize though, was that even if I could have Anna I would probably screw it up somehow, just like I did with every woman I dated. I had this habit of going out with a girl and then cutting myself off emotionally the second things began to get even remotely serious. Upon that realization, I would either break up with her or worse, just stop calling. I would rationalize my behavior by telling myself that the girl was better off and so was I because I needed to focus on my professional life. And then I would secretly admit to myself that I was scared. Deathly afraid for that matter, that if I did let anyone get too close, she would pull a Sheila on me.

So when it came to Anna, I realized I would probably end up treating her like all the other girls. The bottom line, I just didn't trust myself. I was like Anna's big brother, protecting her from me and making sure she ended up married (since she seemed to really want that). In retrospect, that was my rationale behind why I chose to help her.

"Okay, what do we do?" asked Dave as we walked around the club hoping to find Chris.

I was just about to concoct a strategy when I spotted our target. He was lying on his back, bench pressing what appeared to be about two hundred pounds. "Look…" I said to Dave, motioning to Chris.

"That's him!" exclaimed Dave, who seemed really nervous for some reason. I wasn't nervous. In fact, all this was extremely amusing to me.

"Listen, you take that machine over there," I delegated as I pointed to a neighboring tricep curl machine, "Then follow Chris to his next machine when you think he's just about finished. I'll come up to you guys after a couple minutes."

"Sounds like a plan," Dave agreed, "Don't screw it up."

"Relax, everything's cool," I said. Then I gave him a hard pat on the back and walked away.

I headed to a calf machine, and the second I sat down I heard a familiar voice call my name.

"Jeff?"

I looked up. Standing there was Amy. Amy… I couldn't remember her last name. What I could recall, though, is the nightmare that happened at her apartment a year earlier.

I met Amy at a party at Mike's place. I keep talking about Mike so I'll explain exactly who Mike is. Mike lives in one of the apartments above Dave's store, which is how we know him. He comes into the shop a lot and has often filled in when Dave needs to run a quick errand or sneak away for a few minutes, like he did a few days earlier for the meeting at Starbucks with Anna.

Mike is a good-looking dude and does extremely well with the ladies. So a year ago, when he told Dave and me that he was having a party, it was a no-brainer we would be attending. That night Dave was in a fight with Lori (no big shock) so he was a free man. As for myself, I was always a free man. Excited to meet hot girls, the two of us headed to Mike's.

The party met our expectations to the fullest. The selection of gorgeous babes was awesome and had it not been for Dave talking my ear off about his argument with Lori, it would have been a perfect evening.

"Did I do something wrong?" he asked me in an almost little boy-like voice, referring to the spat with his pain- in-the-ass girlfriend.

"No," I said unenthusiastically. Had I known at the time what a cheating scumbag Lori was, I'd have gone off right then and there and told my buddy to dump her. But I didn't. I was just sick to death of talking about this girl. I continued to sip my beer and look around the room at all the hotties.

"I mean, if you were a chick, wouldn't *you* like to get a diamond bracelet for your birthday?" Dave continued. Lori was obviously disappointed by her birthday gift. She didn't want a bracelet. She wanted a diamond engagement ring.

"I don't know," I said as I smiled at a very curvy girl with long black silky hair. She smiled back, of course.

"She's probably home pouting about it right now," he concluded, "You know what? Screw it. I'm not talking about it anymore. I'm going to forget about her tonight and just have a good time."

"Thank God," I responded, never taking my eyes off curvy girl, who began to walk toward me.

"Holy shit, do you know that girl?" Dave asked.

When the girl reached us, she smiled and said, "Hi! I'm Amy." Her waist was small, her hips were big and her chest was even bigger. Nice...

"I'm Jeff, this is Dave."

"Hi, Amy," Dave said excitedly. Dave was my best friend, but God he could be a nerd.

"So how do you know Mike?" Amy asked us.

"I own the store below this," answered Dave, pointing to the floor.

"What store?" she asked.

I was trying not to laugh.

"Be A Sport," Dave answered proudly, "We sell sports memorabilia." As Dave went on explaining his business, Amy tuned him out and gazed at me with her big smile. An hour later I found myself six blocks away at her apartment undressing her.

Two hours later, I was lying in her bed listening to her snore. The girl must have been really sleep deprived because she was out, big time. What to do? I wondered. I got up and got dressed and was actually considering going back to the party. When I left there with Amy, Dave was talking to some girl about the Lori situation, which I could not believe. He was actually telling a beautiful woman about his girlfriend's disappointment in his choice of birthday gifts and about how scared he was to get married. Instead of focusing on flirting with the beauty, Dave spoke to her as if she was his therapist. What a waste.

After I finished getting dressed, I gently closed the bedroom door. I tried to be as quiet as I could, but realized I didn't have to worry about it. I wasn't the slightest bit nervous about waking Amy. I don't think a major earthquake would have woken that chick up.

Once in the hallway I headed for the door but something made me glance back into the living room. I noticed the TV was on and the light coming from it was the only source of light in the room. The sound of it was almost muted. I took a couple steps closer and that's when I noticed a body lying on the couch. Something made me keep walking toward it. For some reason I wanted to see more. I reached the sofa. Lying on it was a beautiful girl in her nightgown. Some of her auburn curls were lying over her cheeks. She was fast asleep. What was with these women? Why were they so tired? It wasn't even midnight.

"Ahhh!!!!" screamed curly red as she sat up and put her arms over her chest to cover the see-through gown.

"Oh God, I'm so sorry," I tried to comfort her, "Please don't be scared. I'm a friend of Amy's."

She giggled a sigh of relief, still holding her pounding heart.

"You're Amy's roommate, I take it," I said, smiling. What a cutie, I thought.

"I'm Allison," she said shyly.

"I'm Jeff."

"Hmm...Jeff ..." she said in thought, "I don't think I've heard Amy talk about you."

"No," I replied, "I just met her tonight."

"Oh...I see Amy's playing hard to get again," she joked.

This girl was adorable. A total sweetie. Why wasn't *she* at the party? I wondered.

"Why weren't *you* at the party?" I asked her.

"I don't know. I'm sort of burned out on parties…and guys…and dating right now. I just felt like staying in tonight. I rented the first two seasons of 'The Office.' That to me is a better way to spend my time then going out and trying to meet people."

"I understand…I've been there before," I lied, "Mind if I sit down?"

"Go ahead. You can watch season two with me if you want."

"Sure, why not?" I answered. Hell, there was nowhere I had to be. I sat on the big chair next to the couch.

Allison and I watched "The Office" for the next hour and a half while Amy was sound asleep in her bed. As the episodes progressed we found ourselves watching less and less and talking more and more. Allison was interesting. She wasn't really pretty but she was cute. She wasn't really a flirt but she was witty and smart. And she wasn't extremely sexy but something was going on between us that made me want to kiss her.

"So are you going to call Amy after tonight?" Allison asked me.

"Truthfully?"

Allison nodded.

"No."

"Why not?"

"I'm not trying to be a jerk but…I'm not really looking for a girlfriend right now," I admitted honestly.

"Now see? Its guys like you who cause me to choose television…" she motioned to the TV, "over dating."

"Allison, I know what I am. I don't try to be something I'm not and I don't lie to girls. I never make promises to call or send roses and become a boyfriend."

"Well, there's something redeeming about that I guess."

"I'm glad you approve," I joked. Then I leaned over and kissed her gently on the lips. I wasn't sure if she was going to slap me, but I went for it anyway because I liked this girl. Surprisingly, she kissed me back and we continued to kiss for a little while. Nothing else, though. I didn't want to sleep with Allison. I wanted to take her to dinner. I was about to ask her if I could when I heard a gasp. We both looked up to see Amy standing in front of us. Other than a towel wrapped around her, she was completely naked.

Allison and I spoke at the same time.

"Oh my God! Amy, I'm so sorry!" Allison exclaimed.

"Oh shit!" I said. Then I stood up.

"What the hell is this?!" shouted Amy. She looked at Allison. "I can't believe you would do this to me!" Then she looked at me. "And you..."

Now I headed toward the door and out of the war zone while making an attempt to apologize to both of the girls. "I'm really sorry. I mean that to both of you."

"Get out of here, asshole!" shouted Amy.

Allison just sat there, not knowing what to say to me. She had this look of fear on her face which looked very similar to how Dave and I looked when we were eight years old and we were being screamed at by my mother for egging old Mr. Callahan's house on Devil's Night. I didn't want to be Allison right then.

I opened the front door to leave. "I feel horrible about this," I said in an attempt to sound like I had somewhat of a conscience. I walked out, and when I shut the door I heard some more screaming from Amy. I was glad to be out of there but I felt badly about abandoning Allison. I still wanted to try to go out with her. That's why when I passed the doorman in the lobby I told him the whole story. The guy was cool. He gave me Allison's last name and the name of the company she worked for. The next day, I called her at work and we ended up going out that night.

Allison and I were a couple for about two weeks when Amy found out about us. She had her suspicions about her roommate, so she did some checking up and looked at the recent calls on Allison's cell phone. She dialed the number, and when I answered she hung up. Amy was so angry that she gave Allison one week to get out of the apartment. And since it was Amy's name on the lease, Allison had to go.

The funniest thing about this whole story is that since Allison had nowhere to live, she ended up moving in with me, and of course things with us completely went down the tubes. Within a week we were broken up and Allison moved in with a friend of Lori's. Even though I had my issues with Lori, I had to give her credit for helping Allison get a place so quickly.

So here I sat on a calf machine, a foot away from a girl I slept with and left hurt and roommate-less. Help! "Amy...hi!" I tried to sound excited to see her even though I couldn't have been more uncomfortable because I knew she was holding a grudge.

"It's so disappointing to see you," she said with a fake smile, "I was hoping maybe you were dead." She wasn't just holding a grudge, she wanted me to die?!

I exclaimed nervously, "Still alive and healthy!"

"Too bad," she said, losing the smile. Then she simply walked away.

Seeing Amy brought back guilt and I felt badly about the whole thing, but I didn't understand why she couldn't just forget about it. I mean it happened a year ago. And Amy and Allison were never even good friends. Their relationship was strictly as roommates. In the end, Allison's company ended up transferring her to New York. She moved out of town and none of us ever heard from her again. So that was that. What was the big deal still? Why the death wish?

As I reminisced about A and A, I looked over at Dave who was now waiting for Chris's machine (or I should say Chris). I watched and overheard Chris tell my buddy he had one more set. Obviously Chris didn't recognize Dave yet.

"Take your time, dude," replied Dave, pretending not to recognize Chris immediately. A minute later, after Chris's intense last set of chest presses, he got up.

"It's all yours," he said to Dave.

"Thanks. Hey, you're Chris, right?" said the actor.

"Yeah," answered Chris. Suddenly a light bulb went off in his head. "Oh, I know you! Dave, right?"

"Yeah," Dave said excitedly. Then he stuck his hand out to shake Chris's.

"Do you belong here?" asked Chris, "I've never seen you here before."

"Oh yeah, I've been coming here for years. I'm surprised I've never seen you."

"Me too," agreed Chris.

At this moment I stepped up. "You ready, dude?" I said to Dave, purposely ignoring Chris.

"Jeff, do you remember Chris from the other night?" Dave asked me.

I turned to Chris and feigned surprise and recognition. "Oh yeah, I remember. What's up, dude?" I asked as I held my hand out to shake his. I realized right then that if sports writing didn't work out, I would make a terrific character actor.

"Hey, good to see you man," said Chris. He was a good guy and I suddenly felt a twinge of guilt.

"Do you belong here?" I asked him.

"Going on six years."

"That's amazing," I said, "We're here all the time. I've never seen you here." I looked at my buddy, "Have you Dave?"

"No," agreed the other fake scumbag, "I said the same thing. We're here what?...three...four times a week?"

I nodded in agreement. An awkward silence followed, broken by Chris. "Well, I'll see you guys around then," he smiled.

Oh shit! Was Chris done with us? As he turned to walk away I froze for a second, not knowing the next move. How could we get this guy to talk to us? Dave shot me a look of alarm, which was no surprise.

I love the guy to death and he is my best friend, but he's the last person I would choose to be with in a crisis situation such as a burning building. He cracks under pressure.

I have to mention that besides a great character actor, I would also make a good skydiver, because at that moment, I did not panic. Instead I overcame the difficulty of the situation and came through. "Hey dude," I called after Chris, "We were just about to have a beer at the bar. You interested?"

Chris hesitated for a second, during which both Dave and I were holding our breath. Then he smiled and said, "Sounds good."

I exhaled. When I looked at Dave, I could actually see beads of sweat running down his forehead.

# Chapter 6

Throughout the years, several women have voiced their opinions to me regarding the intelligence of men. One girl once told me point blank, "Guys aren't very smart."

The infamous Allison had said something about men that stuck with me. "They can be easily talked into things," she had said over a bottle of Cabernet one night, referring to her last boyfriend whom she'd convinced to take her on his two-week business trip to China.

Dave's mom had once said about her late husband, "Men can be tricked and manipulated as easy as fish take bait." She was referring to the time she had tricked Dave's dad into having a second child (who was Dave). She told us he was terrified of having another baby strictly for financial reasons. "I told him I was on the pill," she said with an almost wicked giggle, "but obviously I wasn't." She then turned to Dave and kissed his cheek. "When I told him I was pregnant and that it was a miracle because the pill is ninety-eight percent effective, your dad fell for it hook, line, and sinker!"

Sitting at the bar next to Chris, I suddenly realized how correct all those women really were about the stupidity of men. Chris was so gullible. He had no idea that my buddy and I set this whole thing up. Chris really thought it was an incredible coincidence that we bumped into him. Here he sat, sandwiched in between Dave and me, not realizing the interrogation that was taking place and certainly not having any idea what our motives were.

"I hate her dogs," grumbled our new friend as he took a sip of his second beer. This was Chris's third reason for not taking his relationship with Anna to the next level. He was on a roll. Everything we needed to know was coming out. It was comical. I had simply asked Chris straight out, why he did not want to marry Anna, and the floodgates opened up.

"Don't you like dogs?" Dave asked him.

"Sure I do, but six? Who has six dogs?" he bitched.

"Six dogs?" we both practically shouted in unison.

"Yup," Chris answered, "Six."

"I'm a total dog lover, but six," said Dave, "Wow."

"Seems pretty high-maintenance to me," I added. I wanted to say something else though, and that was that I believed there was something about Anna having six pets that was attractive, because dogs were a lot of work. So perhaps Anna was a selfless person. Maybe she was a giver. Most girls I knew were takers. Knowing Anna had six little creatures, all completely dependent on her, was refreshing.

I decided to get back to the business at hand. "Okay, what else?" I asked.

Chris's response was shocking. "Her hair."

"What about it?" asked Dave with a chuckle.

"It's got too many colors in it and it's too big, don't you think?" Chris asked us.

Dave answered quickly because he didn't want Chris to suspect anything. "Uh, we only saw her for a second."

I reiterated his lie. "Yeah, we just got a glimpse."

"Well, she needs to change her hair color," said Chris, "and style."

I couldn't believe it. I didn't peg Chris for being superficial. Plus, this was Anna he was talking about. And in my eyes there was *nothing* wrong with Anna's looks. In any case, I made a mental note to tell Anna she needed to visit her nearest beauty salon.

"Okay what else?" asked Dave, sounding somewhat impatient.

I sensed Chris was beginning to wonder about the twenty questions, so I remedied the situation. "We're just curious because Dave is in your same position," I lied. Suddenly, I felt a pang of nausea. Yes, Dave was in the same situation as Chris. But what Dave did not know was that his girlfriend was a lying, cheating, conniving woman who had enjoyed tonguing it with Mr. Mediterranean.

Dave added, "Yeah, I want to see if anything sounds similar to why I don't want to marry Lori."

Chris bought it and thought some more. "Well, actually, there is something else. Her parents, they are really annoying," he complained, "If I married Anna I would be seeing them all the time."

"What's wrong with them?" asked Dave.

"I don't know," Chris answered, "It's hard to explain." He thought for a moment and then went on, "They're just…too nice."

"What's wrong with that?" I asked, "Most girls' parents I've met are weirdoes or idiots or just complete assholes." I couldn't help but chuckle when I thought about what a liar I was. In actuality, I had not met the parents of a single girl I'd ever dated (other than Sheila).

"They're just very…annoyingly nice," Chris responded.

Neither Dave nor I responded and the three of us sat there for a moment in silence. Suddenly I sensed something else. When I looked at Chris, he seemed like he wanted to add something, but was holding back. It felt as if he was trying to get up the nerve to say what was on his mind.

"Is there something else?" I finally asked.

"Yes," he began, "Her dogs, her hair, her parents…they're not the biggest things."

"Then what is?" Dave asked.

It was then that Chris blurted out a shocking answer. "The sex."

I had just taken a sip of beer, which almost ended up all over the three of us because I spit it out, unable to hold back my laughter. Dave's jaw was on the ground. I know we seem like immature jerks but one, we were on our third beer and the buzz was kicking in; and two, it was just so funny to me that a complete stranger was about to get into detail about his sex life.

"It's not funny," Chris said defensively, "It's a big problem."

My wide-eyed buddy finally spoke. "How so?"

Chris took a big gulp of beer before continuing. "Anna and I...we don't have great sex. I mean, she holds back."

That was it? I needed more. "I need more. What do you mean she holds back?"

"She's just not really into it."

"How do you know it's not you?" I asked.

"Dude, I really don't think so."

"Then what do you think it is?" asked Dave.

"Does she fake it?" I asked. It was a serious question but it offended Chris.

"No!"

"He's sorry about that," Dave said on my behalf while kicking my leg under the table, which was difficult to do because he had to go behind Chris's chair to do it.

"Yeah, sorry," I said as a formality.

Chris tried to further explain and I could tell it was difficult for him. "Look...Anna has a great body...she's sexy...and sweet..."

Tell me something I don't know, I thought.

He went on, "But when I'm lying naked next to her in bed, it's like there's no warmth from her."

"I'm lost," I said.

"Yeah, dude," agreed Dave, "I'm not getting this at all."

"It's really hard to put it into words," he answered, "The funny thing is, this is the girl who is supposedly dying to be my wife and yet in bed, I just don't feel it. Maybe she doesn't really love me."

Upon Chris's bold statement, it hit me. I realized right then that he was correct in his thinking. Anna did not love Chris. And secretly I was psyched.

# Chapter 7

"Do you love him?" was Dave's first question to Anna after we said hello to her.

She seemed both startled and offended by his inquiry and answered, "What kind of a question is that?"

"That's *his* question," I clarified so Anna would know that it was Chris who was wondering and not us.

"Of course I love him," she answered defensively, "Chris knows that. I want to marry him, for God's sake!"

We were standing in a row, Dave, Anna, and me, at the counter of Dave's store. In Anna's hands were six leashes and on the six leashes were her six pets. They were a bit unruly but manageable, each one sniffing around as far as his or her particular strap would allow.

When Chris told us Anna had six dogs it was a bit surprising, but actually seeing her try to handle them was astonishing. It was overwhelming just to watch someone responsible for so many animals and I could not imagine what her home life was like. I sensed it couldn't be anything short of crazy; however, Anna did seem to be in control and I actually found myself feeling a sense of admiration for her choice of owning an obnoxious number of pets.

It was ten o'clock in the morning and instead of being at home writing an article that I suspected I could sell to the *Chicago Tribune* in two seconds, I was back at work for a girl named Anna. What the hell was I thinking?

An hour earlier, I had been sitting in the waiting room of Dr. Mary Rosen, a prominent dermatologist in the area. Did I have any type of skin problem? No. I was there to get a spontaneous interview with Lovie Smith, coach of the Chicago Bears. My buddy was dating Dr. Rosen, and tipped me off about the date, time, and place where the coach would be, so I showed up with no appointment, just a pad of paper and a pen. I knew Dr. Rosen really liked my buddy because it was easy to talk her into the plan, although she said if the truth came out she would claim she knew nothing about the set up. I respected that.

I arrived at 8:45, fifteen minutes before Lovie's scheduled appointment time, in hopes he would be early so we would have a chance to talk. As I sat there in the waiting room anticipating his arrival, I couldn't help but think about what a manipulator I had suddenly become. The night before, I had snuck into a health club to talk to Chris, and today I was pretending to be a patient to get a five-minute interview with a celebrity coach. Was I proud of what I was doing or was I disgusted with myself? Maybe a little bit of both.

Two minutes after I walked in, in walked Coach Lovie. I was so excited I wanted to burst. Even better, Dr. Rosen had agreed not to call her patient in until at least 9:10 to give me optimal time to ask questions and get a good interview. I quickly glanced at my watch. I had twenty-three minutes to get the ball in play, so to speak. I stood up and feigned surprise.

"Wow, what an honor," I said to Lovie as I held out my hand to shake his.

Lovie smiled and gave me a polite salutation. Before I had a chance to say anything else his cell phone rang and he answered it. Shouldn't I have expected this? He is Lovie Smith after all. I sat back down contemplating what I should say when he hung up. Fortunately, no one else was in the room to distract me. At least I had that going for me. When Lovie hung up, he would be all mine. That's what I thought anyway, until two seconds later when the door opened and in walked Cheryl Shane, sports reporter for WBBM radio. Shit! How did Cheryl find out about Lovie's appointment? It would later come out that Cheryl's cousin was one of Dr. Rosen's nurses. Just my luck.

"Hi Jeff," Cheryl said in her annoying, very non-sports-like voice.

"Hey," I said trying to sound as rude as I possibly could. I gave Cheryl a fake smile and she gave me the same condescending grin she always did, as if to say, "Sorry you still don't have a permanent writing job" and "My job couldn't be going better." Then we waited. Both of us. I checked my watch. Nineteen minutes left till Lovie would be called in.

Then as luck would have it, the most amazing thing happened. At the exact same time Lovie said "good-bye" to whomever he was talking, Cheryl's cell phone rang. Talk about good fortune! In an instant Cheryl walked out of the office. Apparently, the call was important. I wondered what could be more pressing than the task at hand and found out later through a friend that the call was from Cheryl's sister, who had just gotten into a car accident. The girl is fine, so I can thank God and thank Cheryl's sister because I ended up getting a nineteen minute one-on-one with Lovie Smith that led to some great material I felt I could get published in the paper of my choice.

But instead of turning my notes into cash, here I was at *Be A Sport* playing matchmaker to a girl holding six leashes and who made my heart stop every time she looked at me. Anna didn't know that, though, because as usual I was acting cool as a cucumber.

"Well, if you want to marry him," I told Anna bluntly, "you better start acting better in bed."

Dave almost fell over trying not to laugh.

As for Anna, her jaw was on the ground.

"He said…" Now I paused. I didn't know how to finish what I needed to say because suddenly I felt like a jerk.

"Go ahead, just say it," said Anna, "I'm a bad lover."

"No!" Dave quickly interjected, "That's not what he said. He just said he doesn't think you're that into it."

"You're not warm. Something like that," I added.

"That is so weird," said Anna, "Fine. I'll work on it. What else did he say?"

That was it? This girl was willing to let the sex thing go just like that? I realized right then how different men and women were wired. If I were Anna, I would have wanted to know every single detail about that part of the conversation. I would have also wanted to know what I could do to improve myself in the sack. Instead she brushed it off like it was a minor flaw in their relationship. Didn't Anna want a good sex life with the man she wanted as her life partner? I began to wonder how someone so amazing could deny herself something that important.

Anna was so caught up in finding out more scoop (other than the sex thing) that she didn't realize when a couple of the leashes slipped out of her hands.

"Uh…" said Dave as he motioned to two of Anna's dogs who were now roaming the store.

"Oh, they're fine," she said smiling, "They're all trained. They won't chew on anything."

"Your dogs have to go," I responded.

Anna had had enough of me. She was officially annoyed. "I just said they're trained." Was she gritting her teeth?

"I don't think you understand what I'm saying," I told her, "For the sake of matrimony, you have to get rid of your dogs."

In my life I had never seen eyes fill with tears quicker than Anna's did right then. "I can't get rid of my dogs!" she exclaimed.

"You must not want a ring that badly," I answered.

As Anna sadly contemplated her choice between Chris and her six little friends, the sucker next to me came to her rescue. "I have a great idea," exclaimed Dave. Then he looked at me. "Why don't *you* take the dogs? I mean…temporarily."

Now it was *my* jaw on the ground. The balls on this guy! I thought to myself, If Dave treated Lori the way he treated me, he wouldn't have the problems he did with her. He had no problem volunteering me for dog sitter, yet he couldn't get up the guts to tell Lori once and for all to back off on nagging him about marriage. If Dave was as unafraid of Lori as he was of his best friend, he would definitely wear the pants in that relationship. And one more thing, I guarantee Lori would not be the bird dog she was.

"No, thanks," I answered Dave, trying to stay calm. How could I stay calm, though, when big, beautiful, teary eyes were looking right at me?

"Just for a little while until I get engaged?" she asked me in her sweet voice, "Then I'll make something up and take them back." She whispered, "I promise."

Now who was the sucker? Anna's plea was tempting and I almost gave in till I brought myself back to reality and realized there was no way I was going to get conned into adopting six dogs, not even temporarily. "Look, I can't have six animals." Payback time. "Why don't *you* take them Dave?"

"Dude, you work out of your house. Plus…my building doesn't allow dogs."

"What do you mean? You have a dog."

"Well they don't allow six."

This dude was bugging me.

"What do you do?" Anna asked me.

"I'm a freelance sportswriter," I answered. I was always proud to tell people what I did for a living. The problem was my job didn't pay the bills. Literally, I was going broke. At thirty years old, I was watching all of my friends (with the exception of Dave) move up the corporate ladder. I felt like the dreamer in the bunch, the guy who wouldn't settle for some sales job just to make money. I was the guy who was willing to live cheap so he could do what he loved, which was writing about sports. And it never bothered me until recently.

Eight years after college, I was still living like I did the summer following graduation, surviving from paycheck to paycheck, residing in a studio apartment with the furniture I had taken from my parents' house, and peddling my sports stories to local papers and magazines. When would my big break come? I kept wondering. And when was it time to throw in the towel and get a real job?

"Do you read *Sports Illustrated?*" Dave asked Anna.

"No."

"Jeff did this awesome three part series on DePaul basketball and the Ray Meyer years," he told her.

"Like a year ago," I said in my best cynical voice.

"Still, that's unbelievably cool!" said my buddy. Dave really was my biggest supporter. He idolized me both professionally and socially. He was the brother I never had, repeatedly telling me never to give up on my writing career. And when it came to women he was my comrade in arms, always there to talk me up to the ladies in the bar. Not that I needed his help but if I liked a girl, Dave usually told her some positive thing about me or made up a story to make me that much more attractive to her. In this particular case he knew even before I knew, that I had the hots for Anna. And as always he was trying to make me look good in her eyes.

"*Sports Illustrated...*" said Anna, "That's impressive. Who is Ray Meyer?"

"You're kidding, right?" asked Dave.

"No," she replied, "Should I know that name?" Obviously Anna wasn't a sports fan.

"What do *you* do?" I asked her. I was very surprised at her answer.

"Actually, I'm a writer too. I'm senior editor for *Today's Chicago Woman.*

A fellow writer. Interesting. I didn't peg Anna for that career. I figured she was in sales or retail or something like that, given the fact that she was beautiful, gregarious, and very expressive. Not that I think writers are ugly and quiet, it's just that I saw Anna in a more extroverted career, if that makes any sense. She also dressed extremely well and I sensed she had an appreciation for fashion, which is why I wouldn't have been surprised if she told me she was a buyer for Neiman Marcus. But she wasn't. She was a writer like me. A writer who didn't pay attention to sports.

"That's another thing," declared Dave, "Chris said all you do is complain about your job."

"He's probably right about that," she said humbly, "I'm in a bit of a slump right now. The magazine revenues are down and I'm getting part of the blame. I need some fresh material."

As Anna went on and on about how badly the magazine was doing and how *Today's Chicago Woman* was a poor man's Cosmopolitan, I couldn't help but feel sorry for her. After all, I knew what it was like to be in a slump. I had been in one for more than a decade.

When Anna was finished bashing her job, I got back to the business at hand, which was getting Chris to the altar. "Look, sorry your magazine is in the shitter right now," I said, "but if you want to get engaged, quit complaining about it to your boyfriend."

"Fine," she pouted.

Just then one of her dogs began to hump my leg.

"Pepper, please!" she shouted, "You're ruining your chances for your new temporary home!" The look she gave me next was a hopeful expression that I could tell had been used on other men in the past. It was saying, "Please help me." Her eyes were begging me to rescue her. I wouldn't have been surprised if this chick practiced the look in the mirror in order to perfect it and reel in suckers like me.

"Do you want to hear the rest?" Dave asked, getting back to business.

"Is there more?!" asked Anna.

"Uh, yeah," Dave hesitated, "He hates your hair."

"What?!" exclaimed Anna, "He said that?! I love my hair!"

"Well, he doesn't so I would visit a stylist…like soon," I said.

"Seriously?" she asked.

Dave and I nodded in unison.

"Do *you guys* like my hair?" she asked us.

Dave was about to suck up in his usual manner but I interrupted. "It doesn't matter what we think, does it?"

"No," she said sadly, "It doesn't."

"For what it's worth, I think your hair is really nice," said Dave. There it was. The suck up.

Anna smiled for the first time in about ten minutes.

The dog who had been humping me a couple minutes earlier, Pepper, I think it was, and another dog began licking my leg. One had actually managed to stick its head under my jean leg and pull my sock down with its chin, exposing my calf. I had to admit they were sweet creatures. I picked up Pepper and began to pet him. Then I knelt down and pet the other one.

"They like you," said manipulator number one.

"It was meant to be," added manipulator number two.

"Shit," was all I could say as I continued to pet my new friends. I knew right then I was getting temporary custody of them. I looked up to find Anna standing there watching me with a patronizing smile on her face, as if to say in a typical chick's voice, "Oh, look how cute…"

I quickly put her in her place with one last jab. "I forgot one more important detail," I said, while continuing to pet the animals.

"What's that?" she asked, still smiling.

"Chris can't stand your parents."

Anna's grin turned to shock.

## Chapter 8

In my opinion, Topo Gigio is without a doubt the best Italian restaurant in the city. It's a quaint (but not too small) place on a fun street with lots going on. I always run into people I know there, plus I've actually seen both Jerry Seinfeld and Justin Timberlake at the place. But the best thing about Topo Gigio is its fantastic food from Northern Italy. I'd highly recommend the fettuccine alfredo. Topo also offers a great selection of wine and really amazing tiramisu. And I'm not even a dessert guy.

While sitting at the bar at the gym two nights earlier and uncovering Chris's reasons for not proposing to Anna, we found out what was on tap for the weekend for him. Chris planned to celebrate his birthday with his brother by having dinner at Topo Gigio on Friday night, which was two nights later.

I called the restaurant and confirmed Chris's reservation time, learning that Chris and his bro were eating at seven-thirty. We now had all the necessary information and our conspiracy was well underway. A minute later I called the restaurant back and made a seven-fifteen reservation for two people, which I can't even believe was available. Fate…

This was the plan. Anna would show up at Topo with a new guy and pretend to coincidentally run into Chris while on a date. She and Chris had not spoken since the big fight at The Burwood, so everything was fair game, right? Anna could pretend she was trying to move on with her life by seeing other people. The idea was, by seeing Anna with someone else Chris would re-evaluate his single status and realize he *had* to have Anna for his own. I was sure it would work. How did I know? Because I am a guy and I know how guys think. I know how we operate and how much it drives us nuts to see our chick with some other dude, especially a good-looking one.

It didn't take Dave and me long to figure out that our buddy Mike would be the date. He was the logical choice, the perfect pick. A good looking guy, a good dresser, pretty muscular (which we knew Chris would admire), and most importantly, completely willing to go along with the scheme.

"Let me get this straight," Mike said to me on the phone, "You want me to take this girl Anna to Topo Gigio and pretend we're on a date, to make her old boyfriend jealous?"

"Exactly right."

"What if I hit it off with her? I mean like genuinely."

"Mike, I know you're high on yourself and quite honestly, I get it," I complimented, "But this girl really wants to get this Chris guy. She wants to marry him, so hands off, okay?" I wanted to add, "Plus, the thought of you touching her makes me physically sick."

"Got it," Mike agreed.

"Thanks."

"Is she hot?"

I tried to answer as casually as I could. "Yeah, I guess so." If he only knew what I thought of her.

When Dave and I conference-called Anna to tell her about the plan, she was skeptical. "So I'm going on a date with this Mike guy…and I have to pretend I like him?" she asked.

"Yes. How are your acting skills?" Dave asked.

"I don't know, this is making me a little uncomfortable," she said.

"Do you want to get married or not?"

"Yes," she answered defensively.

"Then go with it."

"Fine."

"And your hair appointment?" I asked, "Is that happening before dinner?" Not only did Chris have to see Anna with someone else, he had to see her new hair. After all, whatever bugged Chris about Anna had to be taken care of to facilitate the marriage process.

"It's at 3:30, Elizabeth Arden."

"Perfect," said Dave in support.

At 7:10 that evening, I sat at the bar at Topo Gigio wearing a baseball cap and trying to look inconspicuous. My plan was to come to the restaurant incognito so that I could get a visual of Chris seeing Anna on a date. But I had to be careful that Chris didn't see me.

When I saw Anna enter the bar, I almost fell over. Her hair was now one color, very dark brown with just a few highlights. It was layered but very straight and silky and it hung down just below her shoulders. Along with her new hair, Anna had a new face. While at the salon, it was apparent that she decided to get her make-up done by a professional. She was truly stunning. Anna looked better than any supermodel I had ever seen. Truth be told, however, I knew in my gut that Anna would have been beautiful without any makeup at all.

She also had on a killer outfit for the occasion, a gold sleeveless top and a pair of Rockin' Republics, (I only know the brand name because a girl I went out with worked for the company) which made her butt look tiny and perky. On her feet she sported gold strappy sandals, which she later told me cost three hundred and twenty-five dollars. And that was the sale price. It was obvious Anna was ready. Ready to show Chris exactly what he was giving up by not proposing to her.

She waved and walked over to me. "Hi!" she said while giving me a hug that felt a bit awkward. I could tell she was extremely nervous.

"You look great!" I exclaimed.

The compliment seemed to surprise her. "Thanks," she smiled. Then she immediately got to the subject at hand. "I'm really rolling the dice with this, aren't I?"

"Yes, but I think you're going to win."

"What if Chris sees me and doesn't care? Or what if seeing me on a date with someone else makes Chris feel so betrayed that he never wants to speak to me again?"

"Trust me Anna, I know what I'm doing. Neither of those scenarios will happen. Chris is about to get the shock of his life. He's about to become obsessed with you." In my mind, Anna losing Chris over this wasn't even an issue. As far as I was concerned, this was a poker game and Anna was about to bluff in a big way. And I knew without question Chris would fold.

Moments later, Mike walked in. I waved him over and watched the expression on his face when he saw our Anna. He was in awe and it was making me sick that he was going to have fine wine and a delicious dinner with her while I would be hiding at the bar and watching the dining area like a guy watching a tennis match.

The envy I had of both Mike and Chris was killing me. I had to ask myself again why I was helping this girl. Chris was going to see her with Mike, see her new hair, freak out, and buy her a ring. Then Anna would be getting married. Bu-bye Anna. No chance for me. But why did I want a chance? Why was a guy whose last priority in life was marriage falling for a woman who desperately wanted to be a wife? It made no sense and the only thing that gave me even the slightest bit of comfort was that Chris would be the poor guy wearing the tux and sporting a gold band on his left hand in about six months from now. I would remain free and single and at liberty to do whatever the hell I wanted with whomever I wanted. The irony was, these thoughts were both relieving me and nauseating me at the same time.

"You must be Anna," said Mike, holding his hand out to shake hers, "I'm Mike."

"Hi," Anna said with a nervous smile.

A brief awkward silence followed, and then Anna excused herself and headed to the ladies room.

The second she was gone, Mike exclaimed, "Wow!"

"Pretty, huh?" was my response.

"Are you sure I can't hit on her? She may be happier with me than the schmuck who doesn't want to marry her."

"Just stick to the plan, please."

"Sure…"

"You got your cell?" I asked Mike.

"Do you really want me to record the conversation?" he asked.

"Only till the part with Chris is over. Then you can shut it off."

"Is Anna cool with being recorded?"

"Why do you think she's so nervous?" I asked with a chuckle.

Anna had objected initially to Mike recording the scene, but I had asked her, "How else am I going to be able to know what was said?"

She had answered, "I'll just tell you."

"If you really want me to do my job right, you need to let me record it."

Reluctantly, she gave in.

When Anna came back from the restroom, I said, "You guys should probably go get your table."

"Okay," she answered.

Then Mike did something that surprised me. He took Anna's hand as if he was her boyfriend. I guess the actor was commencing his role. As they headed to the hostess stand, Anna still seemed like a nervous wreck.

I felt like I had to do something to help her calm down so I called out, "Anna…"

They stopped and turned around. The look on her face reminded me of how I must have looked the first day my mom put me on the school bus to go to Kindergarten.

"Tonight is going to work out really well for you."

"Thanks, Jeff," she smiled.

The couple was seated immediately and not two minutes later a waiter came over and took their drink order. I watched them as best as I could but it was difficult because I had to remain discreet. I turned around every minute or so to get an update. A short time later, the waiter brought over a bottle of wine. While he was uncorking it, I saw Anna's face turn white. That's how I knew Chris had just arrived.

I looked at the entrance and saw Chris and his bro walking behind the hostess who would seat them at their table. I suddenly felt like I was watching a silent movie and I was about to see a key scene in it.

Back at Anna and Mike's table, I watched Anna point out Chris to Mike. They both looked really serious, so I sent a quick text to Mike: "Start acting more into her!" The guy never even checked his cell, but as if he had received it he took Anna's hand across the table. Anna was trying to smile but I could tell she was a basket case. Feeling hopeless, I proceeded to text her.

"This isn't real. Remember u r doing this for Chris. Keep smiling."

It was frustrating because she didn't look at her cell either. What was up with these people?! Whenever I heard my phone I always looked at it. It was exasperating.

Now I looked back at the two brothers. They were happily ordering drinks from their waiter. Obviously, Chris had not seen his ex-girlfriend yet. Luckily, their table was across the room from Anna's but unluckily, what if Chris never even saw Anna? It was a waiting game.

"Can I get another glass?" I asked the bartender. I figured it may be a while till anything happened. The plan was, Mike was going to come to the bar and give me his cell phone so I could listen to the recording right after anything significant went down. Until then, there was nothing to do but wait. Wait and drink.

A moment later I got a text. It was from Mike. "Quit texting us" was all it read. Understandable, I guess. They were busy. Still, it was frustrating to be watching everything and be unable to actually do anything.

Then, finally, just as I took a sip of my second cabernet, I looked back and saw Chris walking over to Anna's table. My heart was actually pounding. Here goes… I said to myself. I took a big gulp of wine and watched the dramatic scene.

I watched Chris spend a total of twenty seconds talking to Anna and Mike before he sadly walked back to his table. Poor Chris. He was heartbroken. As for me, I was pleased. Actually, ecstatic is a better word. I say that not because I am a cruel person who likes to see guys in pain, but because what had just taken place was great for Anna and believe it or not, it was also a good thing for Chris.

This was going to turn out to be the best thing that ever happened to the guy. I actually felt like walking up to him and saying, "Dude, don't even worry about it. It's cool. This chick wants to be your wife! Just do what comes naturally (like begging her to get back together) and you can have her! Forever!"

The only person who wasn't going to benefit from all this was the loser in the baseball cap sipping red wine at the bar. He was going to marry off a girl he was crazy about and go on with his same old life that consisted of little work, little money, and lots of women. And I was starting to realize that perhaps those things meant lots of emptiness and non-fulfillment.

A few minutes later Mike walked by the bar and motioned to me to follow him outside, where he would play me the video (which was sound only since he had placed the cell under the table). I put some money down on the bar and walked out the door. This whole espionage thing was kind of exciting for me. I thought about what a great private investigator I would make. I wondered how much those guys made.

Once outside, I told Mike how cool I thought it was that he was able to turn on the video camera so slyly while Chris was walking over to the table.

He let out a huge sigh of relief. "That whole scene…not pretty…"

"Okay, play it," I demanded.

Mike hit play and I heard, "Anna?"

"Chris…hi…" To my surprise Anna was a good faker. She sounded genuinely shocked to see Chris.

I heard next, "Hi, I'm Mike."

"This is Chris," Anna said, "My…"

Chris cut her off, "Boyfriend!"

"Uh, I think we're broken up," said Anna.

"Yeah, for like two minutes, and you're already seeing someone else?!"

"Dude it's just a date," said Mike.

Now I heard something which gave even me the chills. Chris said softly, "I can't believe you would do this to me." That was the end of the tape.

Mike hit stop and looked at me. "Did you see Anna tear up after he walked away?"

I nodded. "She'll be okay. What did she say after he left?"

"Well, she called herself a conspirator, a manipulator, and a con artist. She basically said she's sure Chris will never speak to her again and that she deserves it."

Upon hearing this, I smiled.

"Don't you even feel a little bit sorry for them?" asked Mike.

"Women are so clueless, Mike. This chick has no idea that she just nailed this guy."

"You think so?"

"I would be willing to bet that Chris will be calling her in the next twenty-four hours."

"Let's hope so. She's a really nice girl," Mike said."

"You better get back in there."

"Sure," Mike smiled, "I'm starving. Are you paying for this by the way?"

I handed Mike three $20 bills. "That's all I have. Literally."

Mike went back in the place to have a nice dinner on me (with my dream girl I might add), while I walked home since I had no money left for a cab.

# Chapter 9

After my long stroll home, I decided to sit down and write the Lovie Smith piece. It had been almost two days since the interview and ordinarily the article would have already been written and submitted to all my usual connections, but now that I had a new career as a husband catcher I had no time to do my day job.

I sat down on the couch and opened my laptop, ready to write. To my surprise, two hours later the screen was still blank. I found it almost impossible to focus on work because my mind was completely occupied in trying to visualize the rest of Anna's night with Mike and Chris. I couldn't stop thinking about all the different twists and turns the evening could take.

Would my plan actually work? Would Chris be so completely devastated about seeing his girlfriend out with someone else that he would commit to a lifelong relationship? Then I thought about a different way the night could have concluded. What if after seeing Chris's reaction in the restaurant, Anna caved and told him that her date with Mike was a set up? This was definitely a possibility. I didn't know Anna very well. Maybe she wasn't strong enough to be deceitful and calculating.

The worst case of all, though, would be if Anna and Mike made a connection. Mike was a major player and girls were always falling for that guy. What if Anna succumbed to his good looks and charm? It was making me physically sick to think about it. So here I sat, unable to work, watching the clock (and *Frazier* reruns) and waiting for the phone to ring. Was I the definition of a complete loser?

I didn't feel okay until Anna called and I knew she was home safe and sound and *alone*, and that she was still sticking to our plan. The first thing she did was thank me for dinner, which I thought was really sweet on her part.

"No problem. You can invite me to the wedding."

"I don't think there's going to be one, Jeff," Anna said sadly, "Chris will never forgive me. We're finished. I'm sure of it."

I responded to her by laughing heartily.

"What's so funny?" she asked.

"I'm laughing because you are completely wrong. Listen very closely to what I'm about to say."

"Okay."

"Chris is going to call you and want to get together and talk."

"Mike said the same thing," she said, "But you guys are crazy. Chris hates me. You should have seen the look on his face."

"I did and I still say he's going to call you."

"When?"

"I don't know…soon," I comforted her, "I'd say give it a few days. Anna, what you did tonight was, you played a card. A very important card. You made it clear that if Chris wasn't willing to give you what you need, there are lots of other guys who will."

Just as Anna began to object to my theory, her call waiting beeped. "Uh…hold on…that's my other line," she said. Anna clicked over and kept me on hold for a few seconds. When she clicked back over to me she exclaimed, "Oh my God! It's Chris!"

"Do you now believe in my ability to make you a married woman?"

"He wants to get together and talk tomorrow night. What should I say?"

"Say no. Say you're busy tomorrow night. Make him wait till Sunday. That stuff drives guys nuts."

"Okay…bye."

"Wait! One more thing," I said.

"Yeah?!"

"Tell him you're having dinner with your parents tomorrow night because they're moving to Arizona."

"Why would I say that? They're not moving."

"I know that," I answered, "But he doesn't like them. Let him think they'll be out of the picture."

"But they won't be."

"We'll worry about that later."

Anna realized how much I had helped her already, so she decided to go for the whole education program by Jeff. "Okay, if you say so." she said with a giggle.

Her chuckle made me smile and I wasn't sure if it was because she had a cute little laugh or because I was just happy someone admired me enough to actually listen to my advice.

After we hung up, I felt a sense of pride for what I had accomplished tonight. The tables were now completely turned for Anna and Chris. Thanks to me, she had him eating out of the palm of her hand and she was feeding him crumbs. I could not remember the last time I felt so confident in myself. I was helping someone get something she wanted so badly and I was good at it. When was the last time I was good at anything besides getting woman into bed? It was the most satisfying feeling I had had in years. Instead of being the enemy of a woman, I was being the friend. Instead of being selfish, I was spending my time focusing on someone else's life. And instead of feeling like a loser, I was feeling like a teacher, a mentor. And Anna was my protégé. My hot protégé.

I thought about Anna at this very moment. Had she hung up with Chris? Was she in her pajamas watching TV? Was she channel flipping? Or calling her girlfriends to tell them the good news? I knew one thing for sure. Anna would go to bed tonight a very happy girl. She would dream of her wedding and of being Chris's wife.

But something else was going on. It was very subtle but very real. I sensed there was a part of Anna who was not just thinking about her future husband. An unemployed sportswriter who had just helped someone he barely knew was beginning to drift into her mind more frequently than she felt appropriate. Don't ask me how I knew that, I just did. I had sensed early on that Anna was attracted to me but had ignored validating my intuition. Now I felt aware of it enough to realize a major spark was potentially igniting.

I suddenly felt a burst of energy, so I walked to the kitchen, got myself a bottled water and sat down in front of my laptop. Then I spent the next two and a half hours writing the Lovie Smith thing. I found myself writing with ease and with joy. The words were flowing and I knew to whom I owed the sudden surge of self confidence and pride that was coming through in my work. The credit had to go to Anna.

The belief I had in myself when it came to her was helping me write an incredible article, and when I finished it, I knew I had an extremely marketable piece in my hands. It wouldn't be hard to sell it for a nice price. True, I had done a lot for Anna so far and she had plenty to thank me for, but I realized now that in return, without knowing it, Anna had done wonderful things for me too.

## Chapter 10

Dave and I have a good friend from high school named Marty Abramson who now lives in L.A. Marty met a girl on a ski trip in Vail a year earlier, and shockingly, he was now engaged. When I heard the news, I called him and joked, "Hey dude, when's your funeral? I mean, your wedding."

"June," he replied, "and you better plan on being a groomsman, asshole."

"I have no problem being a groomsman, Marty," I joked, "Being a groom, on the other hand, may cause me to harm myself."

Marty asked Dave to be in the wedding too, and a couple months later our groomsmen duties had begun. Marty's sister was having a couples shower tonight at her house in the suburbs for her brother and his fiancé whose name was Sue, and as much as I was dreading it, it was imperative that I go. Marty was one of my best friends and I owed it to my buddy to celebrate with him, no matter how gay a couples shower was.

I wondered who actually came up with the idea of a couples shower. Probably some chick who was married at twenty and thought anyone who chose to stay single had some kind of serious brain dysfunction. The couple's shower just seemed so completely discriminatory against guys like me. Couldn't they just call it a shower or a party and let people decide if they want to attend with a date or fly solo? That to me made so much more sense. At any rate, I was dreading the evening and even worse, Dave was pressuring me to drive with him and

Lori, who by the way was completely looking forward to the couples shower since being a couple with Dave seemed to be her sole purpose in life right now (except for hooking up with other men).

Things really bottomed out when I found out that Marty and Sue's couples shower was a costume party. "Could this be any more of a nightmare?" I asked Dave when he told me.

"You have to dress up as a pair of something with your date," Dave explained.

"Well that may be a little tough for me since I'm going alone," I replied sarcastically.

In the end, Dave, the ultimate sucker, had agreed to wear a big ace of spades costume, chosen by his cheater girlfriend, who sported the queen of hearts. Together they were black-jack. Lori loved the idea. "I want to shoot myself," were Dave's exact words to me when he showed me the costume.

I decided to go as scissors, a costume suggested by the cool lady who owned a little costume store a few blocks away from my apartment.

"When people ask what you are, you can say...a *pair* of scissors," she giggled. It worked for me.

"What the hell are we doing?" Dave asked grumpily as the three of us got out of his car and headed up the driveway to Marty's sister's front door. I wasn't sure if he was speaking to me or Lori.

"Come on...it's going to be fun," Lori whined in a childish voice. She was having difficulty walking and holding the gift (which was from all of us) at the same time. Still, she managed to continue selling Dave on the shower. "Besides, look how cute you look," she continued.

"I look like a complete idiot," he grumbled.

I laughed. He did. But so did I. I was sporting a big painted cardboard loop on the side of each of my legs which were the bottom of the scissors. They connected at my waist to long blades that extended just over my head. The blades were spread apart, so I was taking up a lot of room wherever I went. Drawing attention to myself like this was so not my style, and if it had been anyone but Marty I would have told a person asking me to dress like this to go screw himself. But Marty was my friend so I had to suck it up.

Lori rang the bell. Almost instantly, the door opened and Marty's sister, dressed as a salt shaker, appeared in the doorway. She had a martini in her hand and was obviously buzzed.

"Dave! Jeffrey!" she shouted, "I haven't seen you guys in ages!" She then hugged us both.

"Hi, Holly," Dave and I said. I hadn't seen Marty's sister in at least ten years and let me tell you, the woman had certainly packed on the pounds. She was a sweetie, though. I just couldn't understand why girls who got married and had kids always seemed to remain overweight even after the kids were in preschool.

"Hi!" Holly smiled at Lori, extending a handshake, "I'm Holly Gordon. I'm guessing you're with Dave."

"Good guess, Holly," I joked, "I see your college degree was money well spent…by your parents I mean."

"Oh Jeffrey," she said with major sarcasm, "you don't need to go to college to figure out that she's not with you. Anyone who knows you would know you'd never show up at a couples shower with a date."

Holly had trumped me. I had to give it to her. Plus I knew her comment wasn't malicious. I chuckled and responded, "Call me Jeff, okay? No one's called me Jeffrey since I was five."

"Come on, *Jeff*," Dave emphasized, "Let's go get a drink."

"Yes, help yourselves," said Holly, "The bar is in the living room."

Lori set the present down on the floor next to a bunch of others and followed us down the hall. On our way, Holly's husband, a pepper shaker, stopped us. "Dave and Jeff, right?"

"Yeah. Stan?" I asked.

"Good memory," he said. We shook hands and then he and Dave shook hands. While Dave introduced Lori to Stan, I moved on. I chuckled to myself when I heard Stan ask Dave, "Is this your wife?" Poor Dave.

I met several other people before I reached the bar, each one introducing him or herself to me as I made my way there. "Hi, I'm Todd…" a golf club said to me. We shook hands.

"I'm Todd's wife, Betty," said a semi-attractive golf ball. She briefly looked me over. "I'm not quite understanding your costume. Where's your other half?"

"Actually, I don't have another half. I'm a whole person. I mean…"

"I don't get it," she said.

Jesus, did I have to spell it out for this chick? "I'm not married," I practically screamed, "I'm here alone."

"Oh…" said Betty, the golf ball brain. I quickly moved on. The bar was now in sight, thank God.

"Hi…I'm Pamela Anderson!" said a very non-Pamela Anderson look-a-like. She definitely had the hair and the fake lips but unless you added about fifty pounds to the real Pamela Anderson, this woman looked nothing like the Baywatch babe. "Just kidding! I'm Ruth," she giggled.

"No shit," I thought. "I'd have never known!" I flirted back to Ruth, sending her into hysterics.

"I'm Ruth's husband, Glen," said Tommy Lee.

"Jeff…" I smiled at them. I kept moving, wondering if they knew that Pamela and Tommy Lee weren't married anymore, and that she'd already gotten married and divorced again. Maybe twice.

"Hi, I'm John," said a guy dressed as a doctor, "You think I look like Patrick Dempsey? My wife made me dress up like McDreamy."

"I could see it," I responded.

"You *totally* look like him," Lori piped in with a smile. I didn't realize the happy couple had caught up to me.

"I'm John's wife, Julie," said a woman who was trying to look like Ellen Pompeo. I had to admit she did look a bit like her, which is probably why she chose to make her husband dress up like McDreamy. So self-serving, I thought.

"Jeff…" I smiled to them.

"What are you?" Julie asked me, "Scissors and what?"

"Actually it's just me. I'm single. I'm here alone."

They all just gazed at me momentarily. It was as if meeting a single person was so foreign to them they needed a minute to absorb it. Life in the burbs, I guess.

In an attempt to break the ice I continued, "I'm a *pair* of scissors." I didn't get the laugh I expected. For some reason, my shtick seemed a little more witty at the costume store. "Excuse me…" I said, "I'm going to the bar. Anyone need anything?" I didn't wait for a response and I didn't look at anyone else till I reached my destination.

"What can I get you?" asked the guy playing bartender. He was dressed as a martini and for some reason I found his costume hilarious. From his calves to his waist he wore a skinny clear plastic tube that was the stem of the glass. The wide part of the martini glass began at his waist and widened almost to the top of his neck. Arm holes gave him free hands but other than that this was the ultimate pain in the ass costume. Worse than mine, I had to say. The plastic was so wide at the top I wasn't sure if he could fit through a standard doorway in it.

"A beer, anything not light," I answered.

"You got it," said martini, "I'm Karl."

"I'm Jeff," I said as I took the beer from him. Karl was the first guy I felt any connection with so far. He seemed normal. Not so pussy whipped like all the other suckers here. I was about to find out why.

"See that olive over there?" he asked me. He was pointing across the room to a tall, skinny, and very sexy woman with short blonde hair. She was talking to Holly and she looked like she was having a great time.

"I'm guessing she's with you," I said.

"She's my wife."

I wasn't sure where Karl was going with this. "Oh, she's really pretty," I said solely because I didn't know what else to say. Something weird seemed to be going on.

Next Karl dropped the big one. "We're getting divorced," he said in a low voice.

"What?!" I asked, "Really?!" I wanted to add, "And you're telling me this because…" Why Karl was sharing his news with a total stranger was baffling.

"Yeah, no one knows yet."

"Oh…well I'm sorry," I said. Then I chugged my drink big time.

"Dude, don't think I'm nuts…" said Karl, "I just had to tell someone and since you're the only guy here I don't know I thought I would spill. I have to say…it feels pretty good to get it out."

"Well, are you looking forward to being a free man again?" I asked Karl, "Just so you know, I'm single and it works for me."

"Hell yes," he answered, "I'm already banging this one chick and let me tell you, I'm having a lot of fun."

Now Karl had just gone from being cool in my eyes to being an asshole. I looked back over at the olive, who was now standing alone nervously sipping her red wine. I didn't know the story and I didn't know anything about these people but what I did know was that this poor olive didn't deserve her husband to cheat on her. I was reliving the Dave situation (and the Sheila situation, of course) all over again, but this was worse because Karl was married.

I may not have been Mr. Committal and I certainly didn't deserve any awards for being an outstanding boyfriend, but one thing I would never do to a woman I was dating was cheat, and it wasn't just because of my traumatic high school experience. Guys like Karl were the reason I wasn't married yet. I didn't want to be a cheater and a liar, and I hadn't met anyone to whom I wanted to stay faithful. Why Anna popped into my head at this very moment scared the crap out of me. She may have been the one woman who was the exception. But now she was headed toward getting engaged, so I forced myself to get her out of my head.

I had to escape from Karl, so I brushed the loser off immediately. "Hey, that's great," I said, hitting his arm for fake support, "Good luck! Hope it works out for ya." Then I went to find my buddy Marty so I could say hello, meet his fiancé, give him some sentimental congratulatory remarks, and get the hell out of this party.

In the kitchen I found everyone I needed. Marty, Sue, Dave, and Lori were standing around laughing and talking. "Hey, loser!" I joked to Marty.

All of them (with the exception of Lori) looked up and smiled at me. I hugged Marty and met Sue, who seemed like a sweetie. Two minutes later, the engaged couple got called away to take some photos.

"Let's get a drink," said Dave.

The three of us headed back to the bar and to the jerk who was serving the drinks. Dave said to me under his breath, "Every single person here is married. Can you imagine the shit I'm going to catch from Lori tonight?"

Right then and there I wanted to tell my buddy about Lori and the guy from the other night, but Marty's party certainly was not the place. Plus, I was hoping Dave would realize here tonight, seeing all these married suburbanites, that matrimony was a serious undertaking and that one actually has to be in love to be successful at it. Wishful thinking gave me the idea that maybe Dave would soon break up with Lori and I wouldn't have to tell him what I saw at *Marie's* until the distant future.

We reached the bar and the next thing that happened made me sick to my stomach. "Be right back," Dave said to me, "I've got to go to the bathroom." He then dashed away, telling Lori he would be right back. Had my buddy not had to use the facilities he would have seen what I saw, which was Lori's reaction to seeing Karl. I knew instantly that she had slept with him because her mouth was wide open.

"Hi!" she said to Karl.

"Hi," he answered flatly. Karl instantly realized that I was connected somehow with Lori. He also knew he just fucked up royally by telling me he was "banging someone."

Now things would be complicated. Would Karl tell Lori about our conversation? Maybe he would take a chance and hope I thought he was talking about someone else. It was nice to see him squirm. "How do you guys know each other?" I asked.

"Uh, from the gym?" Karl answered.

"Yeah…from the gym," Lori supported. Then she asked, "Did you meet Jeff?"

"Yeah, I did."

Lori emphasized, "He's *best friends* with Dave…my boyfriend."

"Oh…" Karl cringed.

I smiled at him as if to say, "I'm on to you, fucker."

"So what are you doing here?" Karl asked Lori. Watching Lori and Karl make small talk was nauseating and I decided the most logical thing to do till Dave got back was to pound the beer Karl had given me. I had to be somewhat polite, because like the night at *Marie's*, I didn't know what I wanted to do with this information yet and I didn't want Lori to corner me and beg me not to tell Dave anything. I had to try to act normal so if that meant drinking heavily, that's what I would do.

Up walked Dave with a huge smile on his face. "Can I get a beer, dude?" he asked Karl.

"Uh…sure…"

Karl served my buddy and Lori introduced them. Then something occurred to me. Maybe Lori wasn't cheating with Karl. Maybe I was wrong. Maybe Karl was talking about some other girl he was sleeping with. Again, this was wishful thinking. I would guess I was about eighty-eight percent sure that Lori was involved with the martini, and watching Dave speak civilly to a guy who was in all probability "banging" his girlfriend was disgusting to me.

"Hey," I interrupted, "Do you guys want to get out of here?"

Lori gave me a dirty look and said nothing.

Dave, on the other hand, had a huge smile on his face. "Let's tell Marty Lori's not feeling well."

"I love that idea!"

"No!" she said adamantly, "I'm not being the fall guy."

Dave nestled up to his girlfriend and put his hand on her stomach. "Is your tummy bothering you again, sweetie?"

Lori took his hand off in disgust.

"Let's get you home," he said.

I added, "What a shame…I was having so much fun."

Dave and I burst out laughing. Lori looked like she wanted to kill us.

The highlight of my evening turned out to be in the car on our way back to the city. I got a text from Anna, saying that she would be bringing her dogs over to my place at 3:00 the next day. It was frightening to me that seeing her name pop up on my phone and reading her message elated me to the extent where I was extremely cheerful, almost jolly for the entire car ride.

Lori was still sulking about having to leave couples heaven so she didn't notice the sudden change in my demeanor. Nothing got past my best friend, on the other hand.

He looked in the rearview mirror and asked, "What are you so happy about?"

"What makes you think I'm happy, asshole?" I replied with a chuckle, my fingers merrily texting back the girl who stopped my heart to tell her 3:00 was fine.

Dave looked at me again. "Who are you texting?"

"No one."

He smiled at me and nodded his head in approval, and I knew he knew who the text recipient was.

I hit "send" and looked up. "What?!" I asked defensively.

# Chapter 11

At 3:00 the next day, I was sitting on my couch watching ESPN while editing the Lovie Smith piece one more time and waiting for Anna's arrival. My windows were open, so I actually heard her and her entourage coming down the street around 3:09. Six dogs barking all at the same time were making a lot of noise, and when I looked out the window I couldn't help but laugh. Anna was holding six leashes of six very unruly dogs. She was also carrying two big bags of her friends' belongings, making her journey over to my place quite difficult.

"Keep it down!" I shouted out the window, trying to be funny.

Anna looked up and smiled when she saw me. She looked relieved that she was finally here.

I ran down the stairs to meet her and help her up to my place. When I took the bags out of her hands, I noticed she was sweating and out of breath. She still looked hot, though.

Once at my door, the dogs went wild and forced themselves into my apartment, dragging Anna in with them. We both cracked up.

"I really appreciate this, Jeff," she said, still chuckling a little bit.

"Sure, no problem," I said in a casual tone that I hoped wasn't coming off as apathetic, because in reality I was psyched that Anna was standing here in my apartment with me. She let go of the leashes and my new roommates immediately began aggressively sniffing around the place.

"I brought all their food and some of their toys and stuff," she explained, "I'll have to show you what each one eats."

"Uh…yeah, okay. Maybe later. Want a beer?" I asked.

"Sure."

I walked into the kitchen and sensed Anna was probably checking out my place. That's why I had spent the whole morning cleaning it. My apartment at this very moment had not been this clean since the day I moved in. I truly didn't want Anna to think I lived like a pig.

"So," I yelled from the kitchen, "Are you excited about the big date tonight with Chris?"

"Nervous," she replied.

"Don't be. You've got him wrapped around your finger," I yelled, "And wait until he notices the dogs are gone!"

Anna did not respond and I wondered why. A minute later, when I walked into the room with our beers, I found out. She was sitting in front of my open laptop reading the Lovie Smith article.

"Uh, what are you doing?" I asked her.

I startled her so much she practically jumped up off the couch. "I'm sorry…I…"

"Is it a reflex for a chick to start snooping around a split second after the guy is out of sight?"

"I'm really sorry," she repeated, "I was just curious."

"Don't worry about it," I said in defeat. Then I motioned to the laptop. "Be my guest."

She sat back down and continued reading my article.

While I waited for her to finish, I looked around the room to assess the canines. They had settled down a bit. Four of them were lying on the floor resting and the other two were still walking around sniffing but in a much calmer manner.

After a few minutes, I asked the editor of *Today's Chicago Woman* (bearing in mind she knew nothing about sports), "What do you think? Do you know who Lovie Smith is?"

Without looking up, she answered, "Of course I know who Lovie Smith is!" I wondered why my question offended her. It was a valid one. After all, she had no clue who Ray Meyer, one of the all-time best college basketball coaches was. As she continued to read I stood there anxiously awaiting her critique, wondering why I cared so much about what she thought. Who was *she* to comment on anything in the sports arena?

After another minute she looked up at me. "The intro is way too long." Her eyes then went back to the screen and she kept reading. A minute later she looked up again, "The wording is harsh, almost offensive."

I couldn't believe it. She hated it. "So, you think it sucks?"

Now Anna looked up at me, her pretty eyes sparkling. "I didn't say that. Don't be so sensitive." Then she put her head back down and kept reading, and I continued to nervously wait for the editor to finish my article so she could rip it to shreds some more.

When she was done, she didn't say anything right away. She simply closed my laptop. One of her dogs jumped up on her and nestled itself in her lap. She began to pet him.

"So?!" I asked. This was frustrating.

"Here's what I think," she began, "I think this piece has something special…something unique…a different voice…one I've never really heard before."

"Is that good?" I asked as I sat down next to her.

"It's edgy…fresh…" She took a swig of beer. "That article kept my interest. It was entertaining. The words and the dialogue were fun. And I don't even like sports."

Wow. She liked it. Shocking. All of a sudden, one of Anna's little furry friends jumped into my lap. I began to pet him or her. "Well, I wish you were the editor of *Sports Illustrated* instead of *Today's Chicago Woman*."

Just then, the dog who was on Anna's lap jumped off of her and onto the floor. During flight, however, the animal knocked over Anna's beer. "Pita!" she scolded. "Oh God, I'm sorry!" Anna said to me as she got up and headed to the kitchen in search of paper towels. "I'm so sorry, Jeff!" she shouted again from the kitchen.

"It's fine," I shouted back, "Don't worry about it. Pita? That's his name?"

Anna came out of the kitchen with a roll of paper towels that I had never seen before. Leave it to a woman to rapidly find cleaning supplies. "Yes, Pita," she said as she began to get on her knees to clean the beer off the rug.

"Move…" I said to her with a smile as I knelt down beside her and took the paper towel roll out of her hand, "I got this." Then I began dabbing the spill.

"Thanks," said Anna as she stood up. Then she proceeded to point to each dog and tell me his or her name. "And that's Pretty Boy, Poo-Poo Platter…Poo-Poo for short, Pepper, P.J. and over there…that's Passion."

"Passion…I like that," I flirted. Why the hell was I flirting?

"I named her Passion because she has very powerful emotions. Kind of like me."

Anna? Passionate? This was surprising to me, given the fact that her boyfriend said otherwise. All I could think about were Chris's comments. "Anna holds back. She's just not that into sex. When I'm lying naked next to her in bed, there is no warmth there."

As if she was reading my mind, she continued, "That's why I don't understand what Chris meant about me not being into sex."

I looked up at her. "Maybe you're just not that into it with him."

Now came the most stressful moment of awkward silence I can remember in years. Did Anna realize I was right? Was she going to come clean? I even thought for a second she might kneel down and start kissing me. I was very wrong.

"I am," she said adamantly. Anna was unwavering, but I was not convinced. Sex between Anna and Chris was not rocking Anna's world. Still, there was nothing I could say. It wasn't my place. It was none of my business. My job was to get her a ring. That's why I quickly shifted gears.

I stood up, put the wet paper towels on the coffee table and sat on the couch. "So, let's talk about tonight."

"Okay," she answered, taking a seat next to me. Anna was sitting awfully close to me and it felt kind of strange. Here was a girl in my apartment, inches away from my body on the couch and I wasn't trying to nail her. I was being her friend, which was a weird concept. Focus... focus... I kept thinking.

"Chris is coming over before dinner, right?" I asked her.

"Right. He has to come to my place so he can see that the dogs are gone."

"And why are the dogs gone?" I asked her. Really, I was coaching her.

Anna had obviously rehearsed her answer. "Because I realized I wasn't home enough during the day to handle all my pets and it wasn't fair to them." She rolled her eyes.

The coach was satisfied. "Okay, good."

Anna had a scared look on her face and I immediately knew what she was thinking so I responded, "Don't worry. After you get engaged, we'll figure out a way for you to convince Chris to take the dogs back." That statement put a smile on her face.

"So...he learns the dogs are history...you go to dinner... have some drinks...talk..."

"Right..."

"Then, he's going to ask you to get back together with him."

"How do you know that?"

I smiled smugly, "Please, don't doubt my ability to read guys."

"Okay, so when he asks me to get back together..."

"You say, 'I need some time to think about it.'" I went on, "And whatever you do, do not," I said dramatically, "I repeat, do not...sleep with him. I mean it."

"Why? Because I'm bad in bed?" she asked sadly.

I smiled at her. "First of all, I'm sure you're not bad in bed." I realized my voice was shaking when I said this and I hoped she didn't notice.

"Well, Chris kind of said that in a way."

"No he didn't, Anna," I explained with sincerity, "But that's beside the point. The reason you can't sleep with him is because making him wait will only make him want you more."

Anna sat there pensively for a moment and I knew she was thinking about the advice I was giving her. What she said next was unexpected. "I want to ask you something."

"Okay."

"Have you ever had a girlfriend? I mean, a serious one?"

"Why are you asking?"

"Because I'm willing to bet no."

I smiled sadly and answered, "Actually, you're wrong. I've had one serious girlfriend."

"Who was she?"

I grinned nervously and asked, "Why do you want to know?"

"I just do," she said with a smile that for some reason comforted me a lot.

"Her name was Sheila…Sheila Brooks. I dated her for a year in high school. She cheated on me like the first week of college."

"How did you find out?"

"I walked in on her with some other guy."

Anna seemed both amused and sad for me at the same time. "Really?"

"Yeah."

"What did you do?"

I said with a laugh, "I punched the guy, and then he punched me."

"Are you serious?" asked Anna with a giggle.

"Yup. I left there with a black eye and a promise to myself that I'd never trust another female again." I hesitated and then finished, "Ever."

"How long ago was that?"

"I was eighteen, so…twelve years ago?"

Anna didn't say anything. She just nodded.

"What?"

"Jeff…" she said, "Don't you think it's time to let that go and give love another shot?"

"I don't know…maybe."

"Not all girls are like Sheila."

"I know. I've got issues," was my lame attempt to end this conversation.

"I mean, don't you miss that feeling of being gaga over someone and just feeling sick…but in a good way…every time they walk into a room?"

I looked at this woman sitting so close to me on my own couch and thought to myself how funny it was that she would say this, simply because Anna had just described how I felt about her. With each day that passed, I was having a harder and harder time denying it.

"Is that how you feel about Chris?" I asked.

"Sure," she said casually. She wasn't fooling me for a second. I may have been a guy who needed to let go of a traumatizing event, but Anna was a girl who was fooling herself. She was trying to convince herself she was in love just as much as I was trying to sell myself on the fact that not all women were heart-breaking cheaters.

Right then Anna leaned over and gently kissed my cheek. "Thank you so much for all your help, Jeff," she said sweetly, "The dogs…and the advice…the set up…I appreciate it much more than you know."

Feeling Anna's beautiful lips on my cheek was better than any French kiss I had ever had in my life. It actually caused my entire body to get goose bumps. I didn't get to enjoy the kiss or the goose bumps for very long, though, because two seconds later both Anna and I looked over at Pretty Boy, who was taking a big poop on my rug. Anna looked at me like she was five years old. "Sorry," she simply said.

# Chapter 12

Early the next morning, I decided to take my six new roommates for a walk to Wiggly Field. Not *Wrigly Field*, home of the Chicago Cubs, *Wiggly Field*, a doggie park located about a quarter mile from my apartment.

At Wiggly, dogs are free to roam around, much like Cub fans do in the bleachers. At Wiggly, dogs tend to sniff whomever they choose, much like Cubs fans do to chicks in the bleachers. And at Wiggly, dogs love to play, hump, chase bones, and drink and eat whatever they want, exactly like Cubs fans do in the bleachers. The two parks are very similar, only the dogs have a lot more class and tend not to drink as much as Cubs fans.

Anyhow, here I was on this crisp clear morning trying to hold my Grande coffee from Starbucks in one hand and six leashes in the other. "Come on buddy," I hurried P.J, who had taken three poops on the walk over. Must be nice to be so regular, I thought. "Passion…let's go…" I grumbled to her because she had to stop and sniff every tree and plant we passed. "Pepper…or are you Poo-poo Platter?" I asked the dog who was chewing on my pant leg every time I stopped. I kept getting those two confused. I was also concerned that if anyone overheard me call a dog "Poo-poo Platter" and thought I had named him, that person would think I was the biggest fag on earth. Fortunately, no one was around.

I continued on till I finally reached Wiggly. Sixteen minutes it took me to walk a quarter mile. But who cared? Why was I in such a rush?

There was nowhere I had to be. I had no job to go to today. I had no writing assignment, no deadline to meet. I had a few messages into some editors regarding the Lovie Smith piece, but I was still waiting for calls back. That's why I brought my cell phone with me.

As soon as we got to the park, I set my coffee down on a bench and unhooked all of the leashes, letting the pets do their thing. Then I glanced at my cell to see if I had messages. Nothing yet. As I sat on the bench drinking my coffee, I began to wonder how Anna's evening had gone. She didn't call me after her date with Chris so I figured one of three things happened. A. She and Chris made up and she slept with him. Because she ignored my advice, she was too ashamed to call me. B. The date did not go well and Anna chose to cry herself to sleep rather than call me and blast me for bad advice. Or C, which was my sick fantasy, Anna got home and realized she was not in love with Chris anymore. She didn't want to call me because she felt badly about wasting my time and pawning her dogs off on me. She went to bed thinking about where she was going to take me to lunch to show her appreciation for all my help.

"Is that your dog over there?" I heard a girl's voice ask me. I looked up. Standing in front of me was a cute little brunette with a short hair cut. She reminded me of Demi Moore in the movie *Ghost*. I looked over to where she was pointing. Passion was humping some dog.

"Oh yeah…" I said feeling obligated to get up and stop her. If she were *my* dog I wouldn't have done anything, but I figured I may want to get Demi's phone number and I wanted to seem like I cared. "Thanks," I said. Then I placed my coffee back down on the bench and headed over to the horny nymph. When I reached Passion, she was so into it I had to pick her up and carry her over to the other side of the park. I looked around for the victim's owner but no one was claiming him or her.

As I headed back to my bench with Passion in my arms, I could see Demi smiling at me. She definitely wanted to party with me. I knew the look. All of a sudden I heard my cell ringing in my jacket. Demi would have to wait a minute for me to get over there. This could be a call about the Lovie article. I put Passion down and answered the phone.

"Hello?"

"Dude, what's up?" It was Dave.

"Nothing. You?"

"Had a big fight with Lori last night. Get this. Her niece...who is only twenty-five...is engaged. I'm sure you can imagine what hearing that news did to Lori."

"Oh," was all I could say.

"That's all you have to say?"

"Dave, what do you want from me?" I asked, very frustrated and dying to hit him over the head with a heavy object to knock some sense into him. "Want me to tell you to marry her? If that's the case, go ask someone else for advice." While scolding Dave, I continued to watch Demi. It was cute how she was playing with her dog. I wondered what she did for a living that enabled her to be at a park this time of day. Waitress maybe.

"I know," Dave whined, "But she's upset. I tried calling her a bunch of times last night, and she didn't even pick up."

I thought to myself, of course she didn't pick up. She was with the martini...or maybe the guy from *Marie's*. My poor buddy. He was so naïve. He reminded me so much of myself at eighteen, a college freshman thinking my girlfriend was sad and missing me as much as I was missing her. Truth be told, Sheila was very much not upset about the distance between us, just as Lori was not M.I.A. because she was upset about Dave. Both chicks were cheaters. And liars. When was I going to tell my best friend what I knew? Soon, I told myself. But how do you tell your best friend his girlfriend is a heartless tramp?

"I don't know what to tell you, dude," was my cowardly way out of the conversation.

Fortunately, Dave changed the subject. "Listen, Anna just called me. She's coming over here…to the store. She told me to call you and tell you to meet us here in half an hour."

I was surprised. Why would Anna call Dave? Why wouldn't she just call *me*? I felt like a love-struck chick. "What's up?" I asked him.

"I think the dude dumped her," said Dave.

At that moment I looked across the park and watched Poo-poo Platter knock my Starbucks cup off the bench. The lid popped off and a coffee puddle quickly appeared on the ground. I reacted by responding to Dave, "Thank God. Now I can get rid of these dogs!"

"Don't be a jerk," said Dave. Sure…he wasn't the one who was out three bucks and a well-needed cup of Joe.

Just then Demi waved good-bye and left the park. She had given up on me. So much for getting her number. "I'll be over there in a few," I said to Dave. I hung up, gathered all my kids, and managed to get them on their leashes and out of the park in less than ten minutes. It then took another fifteen to get them over to Dave's store. When I reached his door I felt like I had just climbed Everest.

I walked into *Be a Sport* and found Dave standing with a customer who was admiring three chairs from the old Bears stadium. "How much?" I heard the guy ask.

"$350 for all of them," answered Dave.

"Are you kidding me?!" exclaimed the guy, "How about $150?"

Dave was about to respond and from what I had seen in the past I knew he would consider the guy's price, which I thought was completely ridiculous. Three seats from the original Bears stadium were well worth $350. Dave had probably paid $150 himself for the chairs. Why should he have to break even on the deal? Why should he have to give in? Just like Lori. Why should he have to give in and marry her? The bottom line, my buddy needed more self-confidence in many aspects of his life. I was beginning to realize that even if *Be a Sport* had the potential to be a big money maker, Dave was too nice of a guy to run it profitably.

I wanted to run over to him and his customer and stop the tragedy that was about to occur regarding the Bears chairs. I couldn't, however, for two reasons. One, I had to respect my buddy. After all, he was the owner, not me. I was just a freelance writer guy with an unsold Lovie Smith article sitting on my laptop at home. And two, my six canine buddies were itching to get off their leashes; and busting into Dave's conversation with a lot of barking, sniffing, and licking probably wouldn't be very professional.

"The best I can do is $250," Dave responded. He immediately looked over at me with this helpless wimpy face because he knew I wouldn't approve.

The guy sat on one of the seats. "Ummm, $200," he said matter-of-factly. Dave looked back over at me.

"Don't be a pussy," I mouthed to him.

He looked away. "Done," he said softly to the guy. Within twenty seconds the customer pulled out two $100 bills from his pants pocket, handed them to Dave, picked up the merchandise, and headed for the door. "Don't you want a receipt?" Dave called after him.

"No, thanks," said the guy as he headed out.

I let go of the leashes and let the pets roam the store so I could hold the door open for the person who had practically stole Dave's Bears chairs.

"Have a nice day!" I shouted with as much sarcasm as I could muster.

"Don't say anything, asshole," Dave said with a smile.

"Pussy."

"Where's my bagel?" Dave asked me.

"Go buy one yourself with your $200," I said smugly.

"Go screw yourself," he laughed. Then he changed the subject while he walked over to a rack of Bulls jerseys and began to organize them according to size. "I finally talked to Lori," he said.

"Oh, yeah?" I didn't want to go here with him so I immediately switched gears. "Did Starbucks raise their prices?"

"I guess she spent the night at her parents' house last night. That's why she didn't pick up when I called."

"Oh?" I responded casually. It was obvious Dave wasn't convinced.

"Yeah," he assured himself, "She's done that before."

"Cool."

Now there was an awkward silence before Dave spoke again. "Dude, if you want to say something, just say it."

How could I not be straight with my best friend? "Okay," I began, "Did you ever think Lori may be lying? I mean, maybe she's seeing someone else."

Dave stopped organizing the shirts and looked up at me in disbelief. "Are you crazy?! Dude…I swear to God, there is no way." He still did not sound confident.

"If that's what you think…" I said to my naïve friend, "You would know. I'm sorry I said anything." I decided right then that immediately after Anna left, I was going to tell Dave what I knew.

A second later, Dave and I heard something horrible. It was the sound of a girl sobbing. The girl was Anna, and the crying grew louder and louder as she approached us, covering her face with a tissue. So Dave's instincts were correct. Our little plan had failed and Chris had dumped our protégé. I was completely shocked. How could I have been wrong? I felt awful. I also felt guilt beyond belief. Seeing Anna cry was literally killing me.

Dave elbowed me really hard in the ribs and whispered, "Do something."

I responded to his elbow by asking Anna, "Are you okay?"

"I'll be fine," she said through tears.

"Think of it this way," I semi-joked, "You can take your dogs back now."

I could feel Dave shooting me a death look.

Slowly Anna lifted her head up and away from the tissue. Then she stopped crying and said, "No, I can't."

I didn't get it. If Chris were out of the picture, why wasn't she dying to take her pets home? Before I could even begin to guess, I got my answer. Anna's sad face instantly broke into a huge grin as she held up her left hand. On her ring finger was a giant solitaire diamond. "I'm engaged!" she screamed with laughter, "Can you believe it?"

"No!" said my wide-eyed buddy.

As for myself, I was speechless. I think my mouth was hanging open.

"I wanted to surprise you!" she said to me, still elated. Her hand remained in the air this entire time and all I could do was gaze at the rock.

"Wow…" Dave managed, "We're…really happy for you."

All eyes were on me. "Are you going to say something?" Anna finally asked me.

"Congratulations?" I asked, forcing a smile on my face.

"Thank you," she said politely. She didn't seem too happy about my reaction. Why was this so awkward, I wondered. "Listen, I can't stay," she continued, "I have a 2:00 appointment with the caterer at the Ritz. That's where the wedding is going to be, I think. I still can't believe this!"

"Wait a minute," Dave responded, "You've been engaged for less than twelve hours and you already have an appointment with a caterer?" Suddenly Anna was reminding Dave of his own bride wannabe.

"I know it's quick," she answered, "but I'm excited." Then she spoke with sincerity. "Hey, I just want you guys to know…I realize this all happened because of you. And I appreciate what you did for me." She looked me right in the eyes. "I'll never forget it."

All I could manage was, "Well, we were glad to help."

She turned to go and that's when I realized something. The entire time she was in the store she had not even looked at her dogs. Not even once. They were jumping on her and licking her legs and sniffing her and it was like she didn't even notice them. How quickly a big diamond could affect someone's priorities, I thought.

"Oh," she swung her head back around, "I haven't worked out the dog thing yet but another couple of days at the most. I promise. Is that okay?"

"Sure," I said.

"Hey," Dave shouted, "What about your parents?"

Finally she acknowledged her roommates by patting a couple of their heads. "I'll find a way to tell him they're not moving. I'm not too worried about it." Then she bent down and kissed Pepper, scratched Poo-poo Platter under the chin, and was gone in an instant. When the door swung shut, two guys were standing there feeling like we had just gotten struck by lightning.

"What the hell did we do?" Dave asked me, "Our little program actually worked." As Dave began rehashing everything we told Anna to do to get Chris to propose, I stood there unable to move or to speak. All I could think about was the diamond ring that now sat on the finger of a girl I really, really liked.

# Chapter 13

"How would you like to make a shitload of money and have some fun while you're doing it?" Dave asked me as he shoved a huge piece of eel into his mouth. The two of us were sitting at our favorite sushi bar, stuffing our faces with different kinds of rolls and sashimi.

I had just eaten a big piece of salmon, so when I answered, no one but my best friend since grade school could have understood what I was saying. "Sure. If you haven't noticed, I need money. What's up?"

I was sensing Dave had something very strange up his sleeve. He had a little smirk on his face and he looked like a five year old who just stuck his gum under the couch pillow. He explained, "Do you realize? We got a guy we barely know to get engaged to a girl he didn't even want to be engaged to? How unbelievably genius is that?"

"Right, genius," I replied sarcastically, "So tell me how we're going to make money."

Dave confidently said, "We're going into the marriage business." I knew he was nervous to hear my reply because right after his bold statement he took a huge gulp of sake.

My first reaction was confusion. Come to think of it, I thought he was joking. "I don't get it."

"We are going to help other girls get their boyfriends to propose to them, just like we helped Anna."

Now I looked at my buddy like he was completely insane. "Let me get this straight. You want to go into business to trick guys into giving their girlfriends engagement rings?"

"That's one way of looking at it."

"How else should I be looking at it?"

"We would be helping desperate woman get something they really want. We would be turning frustrated ladies into blushing brides." He shoved another piece of eel into his mouth.

I motioned to the waiter to bring more sake before I further responded to Dave's ludicrous idea. "Let me explain something. I spent hours manipulating this Chris guy…and telling Anna how to act with him…when I could have been working and making money. Not to mention, I've got six dogs living with me right now. The cash I've spent in dog food, toys, and grooming items I've bought for these pets has put me in even more debt than I'm already in." Sarcastically, I finished, "I don't think I can handle any more jobs."

"We could make a fortune."

"Forget it," I told him, "It's the stupidest idea I've ever heard."

"It's not stupid," said a familiar voice from behind me, "I would have paid thousands of dollars for the help you guys gave me."

My heart stopped. How long had Anna been standing behind us, I wondered.

Dave immediately turned around, stood up and hugged her. "Hey, cutie," he smiled.

Hey, cutie? What was that all about? Dave was acting like we'd known Anna for years. He was so relaxed, so calm. He was treating her like an old friend from high school. As for moi, I was more nervous than I was the day I found out Michael Jordan was coming back to the NBA (the second time). I turned around, stood up, and waited for my turn to hug the new bride-to-be. God, she looked amazing. She was wearing this black halter top that revealed her gorgeous toned shoulders. Her skin was tanned and it glittered. I wondered for a second what it would be like to put my lips on that skin. Then I snapped back into reality and hugged her like a brother would hug his sister. "Hi," I smiled.

"Hi, Jeff," she said just before kissing my cheek. My heart was pounding and I sort of wanted to slap myself for acting so whipped. Anna sat down on the other side of me and before I knew it she was ordering sake.

Dave elbowed me like an eighth grader. "Trust me. We're going to get rich," he said in a low voice.

I had to nip this in the bud. "Anna, listen..." I said as I turned to face her. She smelled amazing. "I am really happy for you," I lied, "and I'm glad we could help you. The truth is..." For some reason, at that moment I noticed the same glitter that was on her shoulders was on her eyelids. Sexy... I thought as I went on, "I really don't have time for this."

Before Anna could respond, Dave stuck his head into the conversation. "Sure you do. You need the money. You said it yourself."

I could have killed the guy at this point.

"Dave," I said trying to remain calm but wanting to choke him with my bare hands, "Can we keep my finances out of this, please?"

Anna began her sales pitch. "Jeff, I know at least three women who are in the same situation I was in a few days ago. I also know for a fact that they would be willing to pay big money for the chance to be engaged. And trust me, these are all career girls. They can afford us."

Dave finished chewing his spider roll and said, "I figure we charge $2000 for each engagement."

"With word of mouth alone," added Anna, "we could make $50,000 doing this."

"Did the two of you rehearse this presentation?" I asked them. "Because newsflash...it sounds ridiculous."

"Come on, Jeff," said Dave.

"No. Completely out of the question."

"What a bummer," said Dave to himself as he chugged some sake.

I ignored him. "Want to order something, Anna?" I asked.

She didn't answer me immediately. She just sat there quietly. Was she sulking? I hadn't pegged her for the petulant type.

"Listen," she said, turning her entire body to face me. I wasn't sure what was coming next but I had a suspicion that Anna was up to something.

"Yeah..."

"My magazine might be interested in your Lovie Smith article."

"What?" Now she definitely had my attention if that's what she was aiming for.

"My magazine...I think we might be interested..."

I interrupted her, "I heard you. Your magazine, *Today's Chicago Woman*, is interested in an article about the coach of the Chicago Bears?"

"Yes," she said pensively, "It would have to be geared more toward our audience...but yes...I think we could do something with it."

"Is this a bribe?" I asked the gorgeous editor seated next to me.

Her answer was very businesslike, but she was smiling. "It's more like a deal," she began, "I'm thinking...take on a couple of clients with Dave and me...and I'll try to buy your article. I mean, it's not entirely my decision, but I'll get it in front of my bosses."

"Why is this so important to you?" I asked Anna.

Her sparkling eyes lit up when she spoke. "Jeff, what you guys did for me was unbelievable. You've changed my life. And if I can help other women in my situation...that would make me really happy because I know how they feel. I know their frustration and their pain. I know that feeling of wanting to get to the next step...and the disappointment of waiting and waiting...and the arguments...it's really difficult." The concerned look on her face now turned to a huge grin. "And now, everything is perfect."

I assessed the smile. It really did seem genuine, although I was pretty certain Anna hadn't thought her whole life through. Or maybe that was wishful thinking on my part. Nonetheless, I liked the fact that Anna was trying to help her friends. It spelled thoughtfulness to me.

The asshole on my other side chimed in, "And who knows? If your article gets published and you get good coverage it could lead to some great opportunities!"

Had both people sitting with me completely lost their minds? Were they crazy? "Look," I explained, "For one thing, people who read *Today's Chicago Woman* don't care about Lovie Smith."

"How do you know that?" asked Anna.

"I just know."

"I'm the editor," Anna argued, "Why don't you just let me do my job?"

"Fine," I said, my next objection already making its way into my head. I kept it to myself, as not to offend Anna, but what I wanted to say is that the thought of tricking guys into marriage would make me feel like the slime of the slime. I'd be the manipulator of other guys, guys like me! I wasn't sure I was interested in being an impostor whose business was based on lies and trickery. Even though my morals weren't the best, I didn't know if I could handle such a devious role.

Then I looked at Dave. He looked so happy. I think it was the first time in a long time he wasn't completely focused on Lori. Next I looked at Anna. Aside from looking hotter than ever, she appeared very confident that her idea was solid. I could tell Anna's drive and determination to do this were based solely on good intentions, not revenge or ill purpose.

I thought about it for a couple more seconds. Tricking poor bastards into matrimony was pretty sleazy. On the other hand, giving my best friend some happiness in life, and at the same time selling one of my articles to the only publisher currently interested, were both good things.

So I extended my hand out to Anna's and said with as much enthusiasm as I could muster, "Let's do it."

Dave screamed, "Yes!" as loud as he does when the Cubs get a hit. While smiling at each other, Anna and I held our handshake much longer than most business people do.

# Chapter 14

*Be a Sport* is a pretty decent sized store for the amount of rent Dave pays. I would say he's got about twelve hundred square feet, which includes a bathroom and a small private office in back. Dave thought his office would be the perfect venue for us to conduct our new little business, but when he opened the door to this tiny little room I wasn't so sure.

I had not seen the inside of Dave's office since he opened *Be a Sport* five years earlier. The cute, clean empty little room I had seen at that time had turned into something that looked like a hurricane hit it. How does a store owner accumulate so much shit in such a short time, I wondered. Stacks of paper were everywhere; not only on Dave's desk, but also all over the dirty beige imitation Burberry carpet. Opened boxes lined the walls, old Starbucks cups of coffee were all over the desk, and empty bags of O'Kee Dokey popcorn were scattered in different parts of the room. The most disturbing thing I noticed, though, was the overflowing garbage can in the corner. The trash literally stacked up against the wall well over two feet above the round can.

"Why is it that men can't take out the trash?" asked Anna upon the sight of it. "That is the most disgusting thing I've ever seen."

"Aww, come on…" Dave responded, picking up some old Snickers bar wrappers off the floor, "With a little work…"

"And some industrial strength cleaning…" I added.

"It's got potential," finished Dave.

"Yes, it does," Anna agreed cheerfully. She rolled up her sleeves. "Let's get to work." She then headed to the desk and began picking up the old coffee cups. Looking at Dave she said, "Big huge garbage bags would be really helpful."

"Leave it to a woman to take charge and start giving everyone orders," I said with a laugh.

"Uh, I think I have some in the john," said Dave, who seemed humorously submissive to me right now, "Be right back." And in an instant he was off to fetch the much needed trash bags. Anna continued to pick up garbage around the room. She began placing trash in one of the empty boxes against the wall. I realized right then that for this girl to jump right in and start cleaning this absolutely filthy room, she was passionate to get our little venture off the ground.

"Are you going to help?" she asked me, as I stood there assessing how much time it was going to take to make our new office an acceptable place to do business.

"Uh, yeah…" I said, "Let me go find the vacuum cleaner."

An hour later, Dave's pigsty was shaping up into a very nice looking office space.

"I know a great carpet cleaner who will take a small job like this," said Anna who was wiping Dave's desk with some Pledge for the third time, "Can I call him? It will cost like a hundred bucks or something."

"Sure," we answered in unison.

Then she said, "I have some pictures we can hang on the walls. I'll bring them by next time."

"Why bother?" Dave responded cheerfully, "I've got lots of pictures we could hang."

"No offense," said Anna, "But our clientele are women; women in love who want to be brides. While they sit here and tell us their problems, they can't be looking up at a picture of Ryne Sandburg playing third base."

I tried not to burst out laughing. This chick really did not know her sports. For some odd reason, I found it extremely cute.

Dave couldn't resist correcting her. "Ryne Sandburg played second base," he said to her in a condescending tone.

"Oh…" said Anna.

"We need some furniture," I declared.

Dave exclaimed, "What about Mike's sister?"

Anna giggled, "What about her?"

"She's moving in with her boyfriend, some investment banker."

"Older guy," I added.

Dave went on, "He owns this mansion in the Gold Coast…fully furnished…so she is selling all her stuff."

"She's probably got a couple of couches and a chair or two, don't you think?" I asked my new business partners.

Anna was the first of the two to respond, "I'll have to see it first," she said, "It's got to look nice, plus it should be comfortable."

"Are you a control freak?" I blurted out.

"Well let's see," she began. She held up her left hand making sure her brand new engagement ring was in full view. "Notice the obvious," she giggled as she pointed to the ring, "I just had two guys I barely know find out from my boyfriend why he didn't want to get engaged to me. Then I fixed everything he didn't like, acted like I had a new boyfriend…" She let out a cute little laugh, "Yeah, I would say I'm a control freak."

I couldn't help but chuckle. I gave Mike's number to Anna; told her to call and get his sister's number and go take a look at the stuff. "Don't pay more than a couple hundred bucks for everything," I warned.

"Now who's being controlling?" she asked. Was she flirting with me? Yes! She was! And I loved it. But I had to pinch myself and remember that this girl was taken. So I pinched. Hard.

Dave interrupted my self-inflicted pain. "Hey, I thought of a great name for our business!"

I ignored him. "What is it?" asked Anna.

Dave stated with a proud smile, "Hook, Line and Sink Him."

At the exact same time I said "That is so stupid," Anna exclaimed, "I love that name!"

"I know...isn't it great?" answered my friend who I was now beginning to classify as a metrosexual.

"So, tell us about your friend," I said to Anna.

"Our first official client's name is Liz Sullivan." Then she dug into her purse, pulled out a photo, and handed it to me.

The picture was of two teenagers in prom dresses, one of whom was Anna, and the other, I assumed, was Liz Sullivan. Liz was cute but Anna was really cute. Looking at the photos, I guessed that while Anna probably wasn't the homecoming queen or the most popular girl in high school, she was without a doubt a well liked, smart girl with a good reputation. Anna was probably one of those women who would attend her twenty-year high school reunion and all the guys' jaws would drop when they saw her walk into the room. They would be in awe of how well this woman had aged and they'd all regret that they never asked her out in high school.

"Liz has been my best friend since ninth grade," Anna continued. "We vowed to be maids of honor in each other's weddings."

I handed the photo to Dave. "Wow, total cuties!" he said.

Anna continued, "Liz will be mine when I marry Chris. As for her, she is in need of a groom first."

"What's the story?" asked Dave.

Anna told us about how Liz was a high-powered real estate attorney whose client list was very impressive. "Liz is actually one of the lawyers representing Donald Trump in a couple of his new Chicago properties."

"Wow!" exclaimed Dave.

"So what's the deal with her guy?" I asked, "Why does Liz need us?"

Anna replied, "Liz needs us to get Sam, her boyfriend of four years, to pop the question." Then she told us the Liz/Sam story from start to finish. Four years earlier Liz had been introduced to Sam by a co-worker who was married to one of Sam's co-workers. Sam, by the way, was a technical sales representative for Oracle at the time and was making half a million a year. I tried not to gasp when Anna told us that part of the story.

"Just before the two met," said Anna, "Liz had ended a two-year relationship with a United Airlines flight attendant."

"Wait a minute," Dave interrupted, "Liz dated a flight attendant? A *male* flight attendant?" He was holding back his urge to crack up.

"Grow up, Dave," Anna replied.

"Why did they break up?" I asked, hiding my own urge to chuckle.

"Because he finally realized he was gay," Dave laughed.

I looked at Anna before I even considered laughing at Dave's joke and she shot me a look that scared the hell out of me. I decided to forego the chuckle and told her to continue.

"The main deal breaker was that the guy did not want kids, which was something Liz couldn't handle."

"Okay, so let's hear about Sam," I said.

"A week later, a woman Liz worked with suggested she meet her husband's good friend Sam. Understandably, Liz was hesitant to get back into the dating scene so soon, and…"

"Okay, so she decides to go out with him. Then what?"

Anna seemed offended that I was rushing her through the story. She looked at me and said, "I'm sorry…are we in a hurry or something?"

"No, it's just that I want to hear the story before I turn forty," I said with a chuckle.

This sent Dave into hysterics. I could always count on my best friend to support my humor.

Anna did not think I was funny. "Well, if you want to help Liz, you need to know all the details."

"Fine," I said, "Continue."

"So they went out for dinner and really hit it off."

"So their first date was a blind date?" asked Dave.

"Yes."

I was so bored at this point I wanted to shoot myself. What kind of business was I getting into? I didn't care about all this crap. I just wanted to be a sportswriter.

"So then what?" asked Dave. He was actually into this. I could not believe it. Actually, I could. Dave was the kind of guy girls opened up to. He was every woman's best friend. For some reason, they all liked to tell their guy problems to sweet Dave. And Dave would always listen and try to give them advice. Maybe this was the perfect business for the guy.

I couldn't even count the number of girls who went to Dave over the years for counseling regarding me! Dave had talked to so many women so many times about me, he could have easily begun charging them and he probably would have made a fortune. Although come to think of it, he never actually helped any women get me to commit. Still, maybe assisting women in getting rings was what Dave was meant to do.

"Well," Anna gushed, "Liz told me Sam was an amazing kisser. The best ever…"

"Wow," said Dave, who was actually starry-eyed by this.

"So here's where things get a little weird," Anna explained, "At the end of the night, Sam gave Liz his business card instead of asking for hers."

I was finally intrigued. "Why?" I asked.

"He told her he didn't want to be her rebound guy."

"From the flight attendant guy…" Dave added.

"Right. So get this. He told her that if she still wanted to go out with him, she should call him in six weeks. He even set a date for her; Halloween."

Now I was smiling. Sam seemed like an interesting guy all of a sudden.

"So what happened next?" asked Dave.

"I remember it so well," Anna began, "Liz could barely function that fall. She became completely focused and obsessed with getting through the six weeks so she could kiss Sam again…that was if he was still available. She actually bought a wall calendar and a bright red magic marker and put an "x" through each day, as if that would make time pass more quickly."

"And when Halloween came?" I asked.

Anna said with a smile, "On October thirty-first at 9 a.m., Liz made the call."

"And the rest is history," said Dave.

"Yes. Liz was able to exhale for the first time in forty-two days. Sam was very happy to hear from her and immediately wanted to see her. Liz told me she knew right then she was going to marry him. But now, four years later…still no ring."

"Bad sign," I said.

"What's a bad sign?" Anna asked me.

"Well, here's a guy who just met this girl he really likes…"

"Right…" said Dave. He knew where I was going with this and he agreed.

"Yet he tells *her* to call *him*."

Dave held up his index finger, "*And,* he tells her to wait six weeks."

"I don't get it. What's wrong with that? He was respecting her break-up. He wanted to start their relationship off on a good note," Anna defended.

"You really *don't* get it," I answered, "Here is a guy who risked losing this girl."

"If you really love someone from day one," added Dave, "You don't take that chance." He turned to me. "Am I right?"

"Dead on," is all I said.

"I really don't see it that way," said Anna, "I mean, they've been together for four years."

"And they may be together for another four," I said, "But this guy...I just don't know."

Dave sadly nodded his head in agreement.

Anna had a look on her face like her dog Pita, after I yelled at the pooch for peeing on my new sheets. Still, she wasn't giving up. "I don't care," Anna declared with authority, "I'm here to do a job. Liz is prepared to give us $2000 if we can get Sam to propose to her. I think we can. My question for you two is...are you up for the challenge?"

"I always like a challenge," Dave responded.

Anna looked at me with sincerity, "Look, I have to tell you. Liz is my best friend. I want her to be happy. I think Sam will make her happy. And I think she will make Sam happy. And I truly believe in the end, once he is engaged and married to her, Sam will wish he had done all this much much sooner."

I looked into Anna's sparkling brown eyes and smiled. I did not agree with what we were doing, yet I was going to do it anyway. As she smiled back at me, I thought about what it would be like to kiss her. As Liz thought with Sam, would Anna think I was an awesome kisser? If Anna and I kissed, would she then think Chris was a bad kisser? Maybe Chris *was* a bad kisser. After all, he thought Anna was a bad lover. Maybe Anna was a bad lover with Chris because Chris was a bad kisser. Without having proof, I knew one thing for sure. Anna was not a bad lover. She was a great lover. And she was a great kisser. Don't ask me how I knew this. I just did.

"So?" Anna nudged me, "Are you in?"

I snapped out of my daydream. My business partners were waiting for my approval. Both of them looked like kids who just asked their parents if they could go out for ice cream.

"When is Liz coming in?" I asked.

# Chapter 15

At 9 a.m. the next day, our first official client, Ms. Liz Sullivan, walked into the office of *Hook, Line and Sink Him*. Liz sat in one of the folding chairs that Anna had set up earlier, part of our temporary furniture, just till we were able to get Mike's sister's stuff into our hands. Seated across from Liz in the other folding chairs were three idiots who for some odd reason thought we might be able to help this girl get hitched.

Anna was looking spectacular as usual, dressed very businesslike in a black suit with a gray silk tank underneath. I had asked her earlier if she wore the formal attire just for our new client, but she assured me this was not the case. Apparently, she had a big meeting scheduled with her senior editors and some investors that afternoon. The only reason I believed her was that her cell phone kept ringing while we were trying to talk with Liz and I could tell it was her staff calling her with last minute questions in preparation.

When I first saw Liz, I was surprised by how attractive she was. I guess when you hear the story of a woman desperate enough to attempt tricking her guy into marrying her, you don't expect much. Liz was really cute though, just like her high school picture. She was very tall and slim, muscular, but not too body builder-ish. Her hair was straight, silky blonde, and cut in a long bob. She had dark brown eyes and high cheekbones. Except for the brown eyes, Liz reminded me of Krystle from Dynasty.

I thought about Liz and Anna's friendship. These girls had been best friends since ninth grade. In my opinion, there is something about a childhood friend that is different than a college friend or any other kind of friend in the world for that matter. I know this because of Dave and me.

Childhood friends have history, which is huge. No matter what you are doing, what is going on in your life, or how busy you are, if your friend calls you up and needs something, you do it. It's as simple as that. If he needs money, no problem. If he needs to talk, you drop everything and ask him where he wants to meet. If one of his parents die, you fly to the funeral. If his girlfriend is cheating on him and you know it but he doesn't…well, that's one thing I didn't know how to handle, and it was definitely keeping me up nights.

The point is, just like Dave and me, Anna and Liz had a true bond. Therefore, Anna would do anything to help the girl. Anna's heart was really in this. The $2000 fee seemed a bit odd to me. After all, who would charge their best friend for their help? Anna made it very clear, though, that Liz understood the assistance she was getting was not only from her best friend but also from two other guys whom she never met before, two other guys who needed the two grand pretty badly. Also, money was not an issue for Liz. She was loaded, so she didn't care and she insisted on paying our price.

"Why don't you begin by telling the guys what happened the other night," Anna suggested to Liz.

"Um, okay," Liz replied. She seemed extremely nervous.

"It's okay," Anna assured her best friend, "Jeff and Dave are really cool. They're here to help you and they're very good about keeping it purely confidential, right guys?"

"One hundred percent correct," Dave answered.

I then said, "Yeah, definitely."

Liz began, "Sam called me a few nights ago and asked me out to dinner for the following night."

"He never does that," Anna added.

"Right," Liz agreed, "So I knew something was up."

"I thought so, too," Anna added.

"So I spent the whole day getting ready for the date."

Anna once again added her two cents. "Manicure... pedicure...waxing...new outfit..."

I had to put a stop to this. "Anna," I asked politely, "Would you let Liz tell the story, please?"

"Sure..." she said nonchalantly but I knew she was offended.

"That night when Sam came to pick me up he brought me a dozen roses. That's why I was sure he was going to propose."

"Wouldn't you think so?" asked Anna. Then she looked at me and with a smirk said, "Sorry."

I smiled. God, she was cute.

"We ate at Spiaggia and he ordered champagne and everything."

"I would have thought it too," Dave interjected.

"Then he told me he had to ask me something."

Dave seemed like he was on the edge of his seat. Was he playing the part of the good listener? Or was he genuinely intrigued, I wondered.

Liz finished, "He popped the question all right. He popped the wrong question, 'Will you move in with me!'"

"Ouch," Dave said.

I asked, "So what happened next?"

"I got upset and ran to the bathroom. I was hysterically crying and felt hopelessness beyond belief." Now Liz was tearing up and before I knew it she was crying. Hard.

Anna hugged and consoled her while Dave and I just looked at each other, not knowing what to say or do.

After a couple of minutes, Liz was able to control her sobbing enough to finish what she wanted to say. "Then, all of a sudden it hit me. Why not do what Anna did? Why not get in touch with the two guys who were responsible for Anna's large diamond engagement ring?"

"Well," I interrupted, "We're not really responsible for the actual size..."

"Or shape," Dave said.

"Of the ring," I finished.

Liz went on, "I just felt sure you guys could help me, and instantly a huge burden was lifted from off my shoulders. I was completely calm and collected. It was amazing! I was suddenly a new person with a great sense of empowerment."

"Glad we could help," Dave said.

I looked at him like he was nuts. Then I asked Liz, "So how'd you leave things with Sam?"

"I actually went back to the table and told him I overreacted and that I would think about his 'proposal.'"

"So you didn't break up with him?" I asked her.

"No."

"May I ask you," Dave asked, "What do you think is holding Sam back from marrying you?"

"I wish I knew," replied Liz, sniffling.

I decided I had heard enough and was ready to talk business. "Well, Liz, if you want to work with us, we can find out for you what is really going on."

"Like you did for Anna?"

"Exactly like what they did for me," Anna answered on my behalf.

"Our first step, as you know, is to talk to your boyfriend," said Dave, "without him knowing you've hired us, of course."

"I think Liz is aware of that Dave," I said with a tad of sarcasm.

"The point is, sweetie," Anna said as she put her hand on Liz's knee, "We'll find out exactly why Sam wants to live with you versus get engaged to you."

"But then it's up to you to make the adjustments," I added.

Liz slowly nodded her head and smiled genuinely for the first time since she'd entered our office.

Now Dave added what sounded like a canned sales pitch. "After that, you will follow our three-step program, which we will explain when it gets closer."

What three-step program? When did he come up with this shit? I wondered. I ended up finishing the canned sales pitch with the cheesy close. "We charge $500 up front and $2000 if you get engaged within six months. Is this something you feel you would like to try?" Any salesman would have been proud of the direct way I came right out and asked for the order.

Liz stood up, pulled her shoulders back proudly, and announced, "You bet!"

The next conversation was about where and what time Sam typically ate lunch. A few hours later, I found myself at a busy pizza place in the Loop, waiting for the victim to walk in for a couple slices.

"She said he usually comes in around noon," I told Dave, who was on the other end of my cell phone, "It's quarter after. Where is he?" I was leaning against the condiment counter watching all the hurried businesspeople wait in line to order their food, while talking to my buddy, who had just called to tell me that Lori was on him again about getting married, surprise, surprise.

"He'll be there. Keep your pants on," Dave scolded, "Call me when it's done."

"Cool," I said before snapping my phone shut. The plan was to call Dave back as soon as I befriended Sam and got some much needed information out of him. What scumbag would be doing this, I wondered as I continued to watch for the poor guy, picture in hand.

While I lingered, I people watched. There must have been 15 pizza lovers waiting in line for their lunches. All seemed rushed, nervous, and under serious pressure to fill their tummies and get back to the office. I wondered what was so important that they couldn't just relax for an hour and enjoy a meal. Of course, this was coming from a guy who had all the time in the world since hardly anyone wanted to buy anything I wrote and no one wanted to hire me full time. Who was I to judge these hardworking earners? I continued to go down the self-destructive path of criticizing myself for not having a real job until something (or I should say someone) caught my eye.

A very pretty girl was walking toward me with a tray of pizza crust and a half-full Diet Coke. She was obviously done with her lunch and was headed to the garbage can, which I suddenly realized was right next to me.

"Excuse me," she said to me with a smile.

I quickly moved out of the way. "Oh, sorry."

The girl emptied the tray a lot slower than she should have, giving me the signal that she was receptive to my starting a conversation.

"How was the pizza?" I asked.

She looked up. "It was delicious," she said before breaking out into a huge grin, "How was yours? Or, do you work here?"

I couldn't believe it. Or maybe I could. Here I was dressed in a tee shirt and jeans while everyone else was in suits, dresses, or business casual attire. I was also loitering at the condiment counter. So suddenly it occurred to me that I did appear to be an employee of the place. "No," I answered, "I'm just waiting for a friend." With my arms now at my side, I made a fist, scrunching (and hiding) Sam's picture.

"Oh my God, I'm so sorry!" exclaimed the girl, "I hope I didn't offend you." She actually didn't. At least if I was working at the pizza place I would have a job. Little did she know I was worse off than someone who might be working the condiment counter here.

"Absolutely not," I smiled, "What's your name?"

"I'm Jodi," she answered, holding out her hand to shake mine. Thank God Sam's picture was in my left hand.

As I shook Jodi's small manicured hand, we made direct eye contact for a couple of seconds. I liked this girl. She was very petite but she had the confidence and poise of a giraffe. She held her head high and her posture was perfect. Jodi's light blonde hair was pulled back tightly and held up by some clippie thing. I had a quick image of what it might be like to rip the clippie out of her hair, grab her and kiss her, and feel her long silky hair come down onto my arms. It might be nice to see someone so put together, so prim and proper, let loose. "I'm Jeff."

Jodi and I talked for a minute or so, but I was aware the entire time that Sam could walk in. That's why I cut to the chase with her pretty quickly. "Listen Jodi, you probably have to get back to work. Would you like to get together some time and talk more?"

"Sure," she said excitedly, "Let me give you my card." As Jodi reached into her purse, I spotted Sam. Perfect timing. Jodi handed me the card and I saw Sam get in line and raise his head to look at the big menu on the wall in front of him.

I quickly glanced at the card and saw that Jodi worked for Morgan Stanley. "You're a stockbroker?" I asked.

"Financial Advisor," she flirted. I noticed a girl had come up behind Sam in line and I realized I had to get in there quickly. I needed to stay close to Sam and order right after him so we could eat together.

"Right," I smiled, "I'll call you."

"Okay, Jeff," she answered. She seemed puzzled by the rushed exit but pleased at the same time that she just met someone. Jodi left the place without looking back, thank God. I shoved her card into my jeans pocket and took my place in line.

Sam had already ordered and was waiting for his food and the girl in front of me in line began to order. I now got to experience that irritating feeling you get when you're in a hurry and people ahead of you are taking their sweet old time deciding what they want. "Do I want mushroom or just cheese?" the girl asked the guy behind the counter, "Hmm…"

I was ready to punch this girl. If she only knew what kind of pressure I was under.

"I'll go with the mushroom," she finally said.

"What would you like to drink?" asked the guy behind the counter.

"Umm…"

I was dying. A girl with a decision-making problem was going to blow this whole deal for me. Now I saw Sam get his food. The clock was ticking.

"I'll have a coke," she finally said.

I watched Sam walk to the condiment counter where I had been standing a few moments earlier. He was nice looking but heavier than someone I would picture Liz to be with. Liz was so slender. You could tell Sam liked to eat and not work out. Nevertheless, Sam had that look about him. The appearance of wealth. He actually looked like a rich person, completely opposite of me.

I finally got to order my food and when it came I quickly headed over to Sam's table. He was seated at a two-top, the seat across from him thankfully vacant. There were only a few empty seats in the place so when I asked Sam if I could sit with him, he wasn't at all suspicious.

"Sure, no problem," he said before looking back down at his newspaper and taking another bite of pizza.

I put my tray down and sat. "Anything interesting going on?" I asked.

Sam looked up at me for a split second. "Not really," he said. Then he returned to the paper. While perusing some articles, he continued, "Another bombing in Iraq…a three alarm fire in Bucktown at a Laundromat…the Lincoln Park rapist is still on the loose…" Then something caught his eye. He exclaimed, "Oh…and a new study shows the more you do Sudoku, the better your brain will function long-term."

How do I work this in? I thought to myself. How do I get on the subject of Liz?

Sam put the paper down. "I think my brain functions pretty well as it is, and I rarely do Sudoku."

I took a deep breath and made the segue as best as I could. "Speaking of brain function, mine isn't doing particularly very well right now." I took a sip of my Diet Coke and continued, "My girlfriend just moved out of our apartment this morning." Would Sam take the bait and begin to open up about his situation?

"Oh, sorry to hear that," was all he said. Now there was silence and I began to get panicky since there were only a couple of bites left of his lunch.

"Yeah," I continued, "She moved out because she wanted to get married and I didn't."

"Oh," was all he said. Then Sam did something I could not believe. He began to get up to leave. I guess he wasn't going to finish his pizza, nor was he going to share his situation with me. As he rose I gave it one last shot.

"What's the difference between living with someone and getting married? I don't see the big deal with waiting to say 'I do.'"

Within a second, I knew I just won. Sam sat back down. "Actually, I'm in that exact situation…"

"No way," I faked, "What's the deal?"

## Chapter 16

1. *Liz's boobs are too small.*
2. *Liz is a remote control freak.*
3. *Liz can't cook.*
4. *Liz never initiates sex.*

This was Sam's list of reasons why he wanted to live with Liz before committing to a lifelong deal. Upon hearing Sam say that if Liz were to change some or all of the things on the list, he might consider proposing, a question instantly popped into my head. Does living with someone actually make them change? Sam was dreaming. None of my business, though. My business, literally, was to relay some much-needed information to my client to help her get Sam to take their relationship a step further.

According to the list, Liz was going to need a boob job and cooking lessons. She would also have to be more giving, both at the television and in bed. Fortunately, these were all things Liz could actually control. Unfortunately though, Liz's new habits (and new breasts) would probably not be enough to make Sam go out and buy her an engagement ring. As in Anna's case, my theory was that Sam would have to feel like he was losing his girlfriend. That's how me and my business partners (and our buddy Mike of course) could step in to help.

I called Liz from my cell phone as I was walking out of the pizza place and told her I just spent half an hour with Sam.

"Oh my God! What did he say?" she asked excitedly.

I did not want to tell Liz about the list quite yet because I didn't know her very well and I was afraid she would freak out and start crying, or worse, go off on me by screaming and yelling that she liked her boobs just the way they were and that she makes a killer tilapia Florentine.

"Are you free later?" I asked her, "I'd like to talk about this at the office. Can you come by tonight around seven?"

"I'll be there!" she exclaimed.

I hung up with Liz and then texted Dave to tell him about the meeting. Then I called Anna to make sure she could be there, too.

"Jeff?" is how she answered her phone. I was startled (and secretly very psyched) that Anna either had my number in her cell phone address book or even better, she recognized my number when it came up.

I tried to sound casual. "Yeah. Hi Anna."

"How did it go?" she asked, "Did you see him?"

"I did."

"And?"

"Dave and I and Liz are all meeting back at the office at seven. Can you make it?"

"Sure."

"Okay, I'll see you then," I said, flagging down a cab.

I was just about to snap my cell shut when I heard Anna ask, "Hey, where are you right now? Are you still downtown?"

"Yeah, why?"

"I was wondering if you would meet me somewhere."

"Like right now?"

"Oh, do you have to be somewhere?" she asked.

"No, I'm free. What's up?"

"Would you come to 642 Michigan Avenue, second floor?"

"Um…okay. I'll be there in five."

"Great. See you then," she said, just before hanging up.

After a short cab ride, I found myself in front of the requested address, which was the store *The Ultimate Bride*. I wasn't very surprised. After all Anna was an elated bride-to-be. She was doing what she was expected to do; bride stuff. I paid my cabbie and walked into the very fancy bridal shop.

The second I entered the place, I was attacked by a heavy-set older woman wearing lots of make-up and a humungous smile. "Hello, sir! May I help you?" she gleamed.

I liked this woman instantly because of her positive energy and good mood. I guess if you work in a bridal shop you have to act happy all the time, because everyone who goes in there is getting married and is ecstatic. Therefore, the help has to keep up, right?

I smiled. "I'm meeting a friend here."

At that moment, I heard "Jeff!" I looked up and saw a sight that made my heart stop. Here stood Anna, the most beautiful bride I had ever seen. She was wearing a white dress of course, strapless silk with a little bit of beading and some sparkly things at the waistline. It was very full but it didn't look like she should be standing on top of a wedding cake or anything. It had sophistication about it. On her head, she wore a white veil that hung down to her waist. I couldn't help but think that if Chris had seen her in this dress before, he may have actually proposed on his own, as opposed to having been tricked into it.

"Are you alright, honey?" the cute saleslady asked me. I realized right then that I must have been standing there with my mouth hanging wide open. And come to think of it, I did feel a little dizzy.

"Yeah," I answered, "fine." I spoke to Anna. "You look amazing."

This comment brought a huge smile to her face, and when she looked at me I felt like we were best friends. "Really?" she asked, "Be honest. It's a lot of money."

I nodded my head and smiled, "You should get it."

I thought my affirmation would make Anna happy, but all of a sudden she looked disappointed. Why did my comment make her sad?

She was finally getting married. Isn't this what she wanted? I realized right then that Anna was having doubts about Chris. We stood there in silence for a moment till the saleslady continued doing her job.

"If you buy it today, you get ten percent off," she said eagerly.

Anna continued to look at me. Was she seeking my advice?

I finally offered some. "Don't worry about the ten percent. If you're not sure, you should shop around." Now I thought the saleslady was going to punch me.

"No, I'll get it," she said confidently. Her assurance didn't fool me, though. I knew she was uncertain about this decision.

"Splendid!" cried the saleslady, who was in her glory.

Anna went into the dressing room to change back into her clothes and the lady followed her as she explained how the measurement process was going to work. I heard a lot of "uh huh's" from Anna while I walked around the shop, looking at all the veils and jeweled headpieces displayed on several different counters. So many to choose from. I realized at that moment what an enormous deal the whole wedding dress thing is to a woman. How had I never realized this before? Easy. I don't have a sister. Plus, at the time, I had probably attended half a dozen weddings in my life, weddings of my sucker college buddies whose girlfriends didn't need my help in getting them to settle down and get hitched.

"Looking for a tiara?" Anna joked, her head suddenly over my shoulder. I didn't realize that my face was practically inches away from the glass case I was peering into. Immediately, I looked up.

"I can't believe there are so many different styles."

"Well, let me give you a little bit of insight. A girl starts planning her wedding around six years old, so there's definitely a market for wedding attire." She smiled and reflected, "I used to stand in front of my bathroom mirror with a white towel draped over the back of my head and pretend I was a bride coming down the aisle." Now tears formed in her eyes. "Is that stupid?"

I was smiling but I didn't respond right away. I just stared at Anna, trying to imagine her as a little girl, dreaming about her wedding day.

"Is it?" she asked again.

I slowly nodded "yes" and said with a big grin, "No."

Then Anna did something so mind-boggling that even the saleslady couldn't believe, judging by her look of utter shock. Anna took my face in her hands and gently kissed me on the lips. "You're a sweet guy, Jeff," she smiled, "Sheila has no idea how badly she messed up."

"Do you know you're the first girl I've ever told that story to?"

"You mean about Sheila?"

I nodded.

"Really? Why me?"

"I have no idea."

"Yes, you do."

I looked at this beautiful woman standing next to me, who I now thought was just as attractive on the inside. "I feel safe with you, comfortable. I trust you."

"I'm really glad," she said with a smile.

At this moment my insides were screaming and I wanted to grab Anna and run out of the store with her. I wanted to take her away somewhere, like to a desert island, and never come back.

The sales lady interrupted my fantasy. "What credit card will you be using for the deposit dear?" she asked Anna, who was still smiling at me.

Anna turned to the lady. Her happy face turned somber. Sadly, she answered, "Visa."

# Chapter 17

"Which way are you headed?" I asked Anna.

We had just come out of the bridal place and I was noticing that the bride-to-be did not seem particularly cheerful. She didn't appear miserable, yet her mood did not resemble a girl who had just purchased her wedding dress. I almost felt like Anna was numb about what she had just done and her indifference was making me uncomfortable.

"I have to go back to the office," she answered, "I have a 2:30 meeting. How about you?"

"I'm headed to the Glenbrook South High School swim meet. I freelance for the Pioneer Press from time to time."

"Do you like it?"

"It's okay," I said as I put my hand up to hail a cab for Anna. It helps pay the bills."

"Well," she smiled, "When Sam and Liz get engaged you'll have some more income."

I looked Anna right in the eyes. "That sounds great and everything, but just so you know, I'm a writer. This business…tricking guys…it's temporary. You know that, right?"

"Listen, Jeff…" she said, her beautiful eyes looking right back into mine, "Have you ever considered just taking life one day at a time and letting things play out the way they're supposed to?"

"This coming from the girl who let two commitment phobic guys facilitate her engagement."

"Okay, you got me," she said with a smile, "I have no response to that."

"Anna, I know what I'm supposed to be. A journalist… a sportswriter. It's in my bones. And even though I have no clue as to how I'm going to break into the business and actually make a decent living, writing is what I love." I wanted to add, "besides you," but I didn't, of course. "This marriage business…it's just a distraction."

"Oh my God!" she exclaimed, "I can't believe I haven't told you this yet."

"What?"

A taxi pulled up to the curb and I opened the door for my business partner while waiting for her to spill. A huge smile was on her face when she announced, "Our senior editor really liked your article. We'll probably use it in next month's issue, if you're okay with that."

"Seriously?" I asked. "How could you have forgotten to tell me this?!"

"I didn't. I'm telling you now. I think he's thinking 15 cents a word. Is that acceptable?"

I wanted to scream, "*Yes!!!*" but like anything in life, the key is not to be too eager. I responded casually, "That sounds pretty good, I guess."

I sensed Anna was on to me, judging by her formal tone. "I'll relay that to my boss."

"See you tonight?" I was trying not to show her that I had so much adrenaline I wanted to start doing jumping jacks in the middle of Michigan Avenue.

"Sure." Anna then got into the cab and shut its door. Instantly her window came down and she shouted, "Congratulations!"

I smiled and waved. Then I watched her taxi head south for a moment before hailing another cab for myself. I needed to go in the opposite direction. I had to be at Glenbrook South high school by 3:30, so my plan was to cab back to my place, get my car, and head to the suburb of Glenview, which was a possible one hour trip with traffic.

I wasn't too worried about being late, though, given the news I had just heard from Anna. I had a strange feeling that today's meet would be one of the last high school sporting events I would ever cover. After all, *Today's Chicago Woman* is a pretty decent-sized magazine, and I knew I would get a ton of exposure once the article was published. I felt great, confident for the first time in a long time.

I was just as excited as I was when I found out my Ray Meyer series was going to be in *Sports Illustrated*. That was about a year earlier. At the time, I thought I had finally gotten my big break. As it turned out, I was wrong, and unable to get anything printed in any reputable publication since. "Maybe now," I thought as I sat in the back of the cab, "Maybe this is the break I need to jumpstart my career."

Of course, *Today's Chicago Woman* wasn't exactly a sports-oriented magazine. Had they ever published any sports-related pieces? They had to have covered Anna Kourikova, maybe Annika Sorenstam, right? I realized right then that I was probably going to have to make some major changes to my article so women like Anna and her readers would be more interested in it. Oh well... that was the price. And speaking of price, for 15 cents a word I could certainly do some editing for my new favorite magazine.

My cell phone rang. Dave. "What's up?" I answered.

"Get this one...Lori booked The Late Night Band for July tenth."

"What's July tenth?"

"According to her, our wedding!"

"Are you effing kidding me?!" I exclaimed. I was outraged that Lori actually set a wedding date for them and hired a band, all while she was cheating with at least two guys. "Please tell me you went off on her," I said.

"Well, I said I would think about it."

Now my outrage turned to disgust. I was completely appalled that my buddy was such a pussy. Why did Dave continue to put up with the way Lori treated him? She had no respect for him. And he knew that, yet he continued to stay in the relationship. Now I knew I had to step in and help. After all, if the situation were reversed (I'm stretching here because that would never be the case) and if I was the one who was being rushed into a wedding by my girlfriend, I would hope Dave would give me a much needed kick in the ass.

"Hello? Are you still there?" Dave asked.

"Yeah, listen, Dave, I have to talk to you about something."

"I know, Jeff. You think I'm a complete pussy-whipped idiot."

"Dude…I friggin' love you. You're my best friend. I don't think you're an idiot. Pussy-whipped…yeah. I just think…" I could not bring myself to tell him about Lori. How could I tell him over the phone? I had to wait till I saw him to break the news that his girlfriend was a ho.

"What?" he urged, "Just say it."

"Tonight…after the meeting with Liz…let's talk more about it."

"Cool."

I hung up with Dave and felt like puking. Two minutes earlier, I had felt like a determined, self-assured aspiring writer. After talking to Dave, I now felt like a nervous, guilt-ridden messenger, not only because of Liz, but also because now I had to break some bad news to Dave as well. How would he take it? Would he be angry with me because I didn't tell him right away? That part I didn't care so much about.

What was mainly worrying me was that Dave would be crushed and heartbroken. He would somehow turn it around and rationalize that the reason Lori cheated was because of him. Dave would take fault for his tramp's actions. I knew him so well. He would blame himself and say that if he would have proposed, she never would have cheated. I could only imagine what would happen after that. Dave might even be desperate enough to go out and buy her a ring. As much as it was going to suck, I had to tell Dave what I knew and I had to do it tonight.

Once in my car and on the highway, I found myself stuck in major traffic. I had lots of time to practice exactly what I would say to

Dave. "Dave, remember a few weeks ago, when I left you at the Burwood and went to *Marie's* with Jessica?" I rehearsed, "Well, I saw Lori there. She was kissing some tall dark guy who looked European." It would probably be better to leave out the details of how good looking the guy was. "Dave, remember a few weeks ago, when I left you at the Burwood and went to *Marie's* with Jessica?" I said again, "Well, I saw Lori there and she was kissing some guy." I played around with other ways to tell him. "Dave…Lori was making out with some guy. I saw her." "Dave…your girlfriend is cheating on you with at least two guys."

It seemed that any way I sliced it, it was going to taste the same to my buddy. Nonetheless, I was now ready to spill; and quite honestly, I was feeling a bit relieved already. It was as if someone just took a giant gorilla from the Lincoln Park zoo right off my back. Knowing that after tonight I wasn't going to be keeping a major secret from my best friend any longer was rejuvenating.

But I still had Liz to deal with. Tonight, my new job would require me to tell this poor girl everything her boyfriend wanted her to change. Liz would then compromise her lifestyle, values, and true self to win the love of the man she wanted to call her husband. In the meantime, three manipulators would devise a scheme where Liz would run into Sam while on a date with our buddy Mike. The guy would be crushed, and if he was anything like Chris he would propose to Liz within days. The thought of these events was making me sick. Then again, doing all this was advancing my writing career. Was that such a bad thing?

At 7:05 that evening, I entered the back office of *Be a Sport*. My entourage was sitting there when I walked in. All three of them, Dave, Anna and Liz looked like little kids at a birthday party waiting for the clown to begin his act. I, of course, was the clown, and the show would entail a word for word recap of my lunch with Sam.

After some brief chitchat Dave jumped right in and asked for the scoop. "So, we're all dying to know…what did he say?"

The list... the list... I was going to have to tell Liz about it sooner or later so I blurted out, "Your boobs are too small, you hog the remote, you can't cook, and you never initiate sex." The clown was anything but funny. He was a jackass.

The three of them sat there in shock. The room was completely silent. A moment later, Liz began to sob. I looked over at Anna, who was giving me a really mean look. Then I looked at Dave, who was trying to comfort Liz. Suddenly I felt like the biggest jerk on earth.

I rushed over to Liz, kneeled down beside her chair, and put my arm around her. "Look, I'm really sorry. I didn't mean to make you feel badly. This is just bothering me. When Sam told me all this...it's just too much information for me."

Liz answered me through tears, "Sam hates me!"

"No...no...he doesn't hate you!" I comforted, "He also said a lot of really good things about you!"

"Really?" she was semi-hyperventilating, "Like what?"

Now they were all looking at me, awaiting my next words in hopes they would calm our client down.

"Like...he said you're pretty...and you're really smart...you're good at your job..."

"See?!" Anna smiled at her.

"He said that?" Liz asked.

I nodded my head "yes" and continued, "And he said you're really fun...you guys both like the same kinds of music."

"That's great!" said Dave in a cheerleader kind of voice.

"Liz, again, I apologize if I hurt your feelings. I want to address Sam's issues with you."

Liz was receptive to my suggestion. "Okay," she agreed. I guess I was redeeming myself pretty effectively.

"And then we'll talk about what you're going to do to get him eating out of the palm of your hand," said Dave.

Anna added, "Yeah, Liz. You know we're going to send you on a date with our friend Mike."

Liz nodded while wiping her cheeks with a Kleenex.

We spent the next half hour going down the list and tackling each thing. In the end, it was decided unanimously that Liz would immediately sign up for cooking classes at *The Chopping Block*, a neighborhood cooking school with a great reputation. She was also planning to schedule an appointment asap with Dr. Carmine Bongio for a consultation for breast implants. We all agreed that Liz did not have to decide right away if she wanted to go ahead with surgery, but it was a good idea to get a professional opinion and to get educated on costs, risks, and, of course, benefits.

Now came the conversation I was dreading most; sex. "So..." I began slowly, "What to do about..."

"Let's not go here, okay?" Anna chimed in. She sounded annoyed that I would bring up the subject.

"Actually, we have to go here if Liz wants to get married," I responded with sarcasm.

"Well, maybe we could let Liz figure this one out on her own," Dave suggested.

I fired back before anyone could say anything else on the subject, "No, we can't let Liz figure this one out on her own. She obviously needs some help in this area."

"I think I know how to have sex," Liz defended.

"I'm sure you do," Dave said nervously. What was he so worried about? Was he afraid Liz was going to get up and leave? I knew Liz might get angry discussing her lack of interest in sex, but she certainly wasn't walking away at this point. She had too much invested. Besides, a great testimonial was seated right next to her. Anna was living proof that if Liz was open to executing our advice and following our program, she too would soon be planning her wedding.

I took Liz's hand. As I began to speak, I could feel Anna's deep concentration in an effort to listen to what was about to come out of my mouth. "Look, Liz…let's back up a little bit. One of our big rules is, you aren't going to be sleeping with Sam for awhile. If you follow our plan, you're going to break up with him."

"And even when he tries to get back together, you're not going to sleep with him till he proposes," Dave added.

Anna smiled at her, "It worked for me."

I panicked. Wait a minute. Had Anna slept with Chris?! My heart stopped and I suddenly felt nauseous. But why? Wasn't it natural for a woman to sleep with her fiancé? I wanted to ask Anna how it was. I was dying to know if she was now having good sex with the guy who said she "wasn't warm" in the sack. As if she read my mind, she offered an explanation. When she spoke, she addressed all three of us, but I knew she was talking mostly to me.

"After Chris gave me the ring, we had the best sex we've ever had!" Now she looked directly at me. "I made sure I was warmer."

"Are you being sarcastic?" I asked.

"A little bit," she smiled, "But there's a lot of truth to it. I really tried to act more into the sex, thanks to the much needed-information I got from you guys."

"That's great!" exclaimed Dave.

"Yeah, good job," I said, unenthused. I sat there thinking for a second. How sad that Anna had to "try to act more into the sex." Even worse, with a guy she was planning on spending the rest of her life with! I wanted to shake her and say, "What are you thinking?!" Instead, I looked at Liz and exclaimed, "So, let's talk about the break up. We'll address your sex life later."

Needless to say, Liz left the meeting a very satisfied customer. She and Anna ended up going out for dinner. As for the boys, we had things to talk about. Now that I was done delivering Liz's news, I had to give Dave his. And unlike the Liz situation, there wasn't a simple solution involving manipulation and con artist games to solve his problem.

"I love what we're doing," Dave said to me after the girls left.

"I knew you would," I told Dave, "You're a good person and you like helping people."

Dave smiled and now neither of us spoke. In our entire lives, I could never remember an awkward moment with us until now.

Finally, I said, "Listen." I stood up and paced the office. Dave was looking down at the ground but I could feel him watching me out of the corner of his eye.

"Dave, I have to tell you something."

"Hey, Jeff?" Dave interrupted, "What if I told you I didn't want to talk about it?"

Did Dave know?! I suddenly sensed he had some idea that I was about to give him some information he clearly was not ready to hear.

He went on, "Look, I've thought about this a lot. I realize that Lori is not the perfect girlfriend. She's a pain in the ass and she's got issues. But I really love her and I'm not ready to end it with her. For me, there's still a chance. So whatever you have to say about her…just keep it to yourself for now. I'll let you know when to tell me."

"But Dave, this is a pretty big deal."

Dave sadly shook his head and said, "Please…not now. Trust me, Jeff. I'm not going to get engaged without talking to you first. But I don't want to hear anything right now. Let me try to work things through with my girlfriend."

"Fair enough," I answered, "I'll keep my mouth shut. For now anyway."

When I left Dave's place, I could not have felt more depressed. He had basically just told me that he knew Lori was cheating on him. Even worse, he did not want to address it. He was going to continue sitting by and allowing Lori to get away with her behavior. I couldn't believe it. But since this was Dave, I could.

Dave, the friend, the sweetie, the guy girls kissed on the cheek and called "adorable," the sucker who let them all take advantage of him. I realized right then that a man who was half Dave and half me would be the perfect guy, half-womanizer, half committal (with the right woman). Dave and I were on two different ends of the spectrum. And over the years, I had learned a lot from him about what kind of person I aimed to be. Hadn't he learned anything from me?

The bottom line was, this was his life and he had the right to do things his own way and in his own time. I was sure that in the past Dave must have questioned why I did certain things, but he always respected me enough to let me deal with my problems in my own way. He supported the fact that I chose to be a struggling writer. In fact, he had always encouraged me to keep trying. Also, Dave had never, not even once, questioned and or criticized me for the way I handled any relationship with a woman. Sure, he teased me about it, but he never judged me. He respected the fact that I was the fish who refused to be caught, and that my past had left me with a scar that might never fade completely. He understood me. And he accepted me for who I am.

Dave was a true friend. He was the brother, the family I never had. Today, I had tried to do what friends do; protect. And Dave had refused my help. But I felt okay about it now because at least he was aware of the fact that I tried to warn him about Lori. And as long as Dave knew I would always be in his corner, I felt okay. When he was ready to face his problem, I would be there for him. And I wouldn't judge him. I would listen and comfort. I would do my job of being his best friend.

# Chapter 18

Liz broke up with Sam the next afternoon. I met her in front of Barney's at 12:30 to tell her exactly what to say to him. By 12:45, she was speaking to Sam on her cell, repeating my exact words.

"Sam…I told you…I just need some time to myself." Liz was seated on a bench outside the Oak Street store and I was next to her for support. She sounded so calm, almost happy, and I understood why. It was because Liz wasn't really ending anything. In her mind, this call was actually moving the relationship forward. And she certainly wasn't sad about that.

I nudged her and mouthed, "Act more upset."

She nodded and continued, "I am truly devastated by having to do this, but it seems like the right thing." Then she did a little fake crying, which I thought was highly effective. Then Liz didn't speak for a few moments and I could tell Sam was begging her to reconsider.

"No, this isn't because you asked me to move in with you," she responded to what Sam must have said, "Actually, I'm glad that happened. It forced me to look at things from the big picture and I know now…you're right, Sam. We're not ready to be engaged. In fact, it made me realize I'm not sure you're the one. I love you, I just need some time to myself to figure things out."

"Yes!" I mouthed to Liz while clenching my fists and putting my arms up in the air as if the Bulls had scored a three-pointer (which was almost a nonexistent occurrence these days). I wanted to hug this girl. She was doing an amazing job.

Liz just smiled at me and continued to listen to Sam.

I heard through the phone, "Please…don't do this."

Liz answered, "Sorry, Sam. I'm doing it. I've got to go." When she hung up, she had a worried look on her face. It was the same look Anna had on her face when she was walking toward her table at Topo Gigio with Mike.

"Good job!" Coach Jeff said to Liz.

"What the hell am I doing?" she panicked.

"You have to trust me. Things are going to work out."

Liz stood up. "I hope you're right. I'm risking a lot here."

I stood and said, "No offense, but I don't see it that way. The path you were on with Sam was not headed in the direction you wanted…unless you want to be his roommate for life."

"No…I don't want that," she responded as she stood up and walked a few feet to the windows of Barneys.

"Liz, I guarantee this will work out for you," I said. I briefly wondered why I was guaranteeing anything.

Liz smiled and then said something so shocking it almost caused me to stop breathing. "Hey, what about you and Anna? What's happening there?" She said it so casually that it was frightening.

"Um, what do you mean?" I managed to say with a nervous laugh.

"I don't know," she said nonchalantly, "Just seems like there's something going on between you two."

"Liz…Anna's engaged. Did you forget?"

Then she simply said, "I know," like it was no big deal. We could have been having a conversation about the weather and I could have said something like, "You know…it's supposed to rain today." And Liz could have said "I know" in that exact same tone. It was baffling. But it was exciting. Anna's best friend had caught on to the little spark that was flickering between the new business partners.

"So, what do you think of Chris?" I asked her.

Liz giggled, "Well…he's hot. You know, dark skin…good body, but honestly, I'm surprised that Anna chose him."

"Why?"

"I guess I always pictured her with someone who is completely gaga over her...someone who loves her for who she is. I mean, she's pretty high-maintenance...with those dogs and everything..." Liz let out a laugh and said, "Yuck!"

"You're not a fan of her dogs? Or I should say...*my* dogs, since they're shacking up with me these days."

"I didn't peg you for such a sucker Jeff," she joked.

"Trust me, I know. I didn't either. So you don't think Chris is gaga?"

"I think Chris is as gaga over Anna as he could be with any girl. But he's not the type to be gaga over anyone. He's just not built that way."

Suddenly, I had this desperate urge to grab Liz and confess that I was gaga over her best friend. I wanted to tell her that I liked Anna just the way she was and that she didn't have to change her hair or get rid of her dogs or stop complaining about her job. I wanted to tell Liz I would take the original version of Anna. I didn't, though. The pussy chickened out.

Liz continued, "Look, Anna's my best friend. I just want her to be happy. And truthfully, I'm not sure she will be with Chris. I feel horrible about it, but that's my honest opinion. I hope I'm wrong."

What was I supposed to say? I hope you're wrong, too? I didn't want to respond that way because secretly I hoped Liz wasn't wrong. I wanted her to be right. I wanted Anna not to be happy with Chris. Because I wanted Anna. And although I was a little disgusted with myself for thinking this way, I couldn't help it. I wished I could take some kind of pill to snap back into the old Jeff mode and rid myself of these new and unfamiliar symptoms I was having, tinges of pain in my heart at the thought of Anna, headaches from overload of thinking about her too much, and lack of self-confidence because I felt like a love-struck idiot every time I saw her. Anna was making me lose control; and that hadn't happened to smooth, slick, womanizing Jeff in a long time, perhaps ever. And it was bugging me.

"Hey...speak of the devil!" Liz exclaimed.

I turned around. As usual, I felt like a nervous, awkward thirteen year old when I saw Anna walking toward us.

"Hey, guys!" she said happily, "How did it go?"

"As good as it could, I guess," Liz responded, referring to her break up.

Anna put her arm around her best friend. "It will be okay." Then she looked at me. "Right, Jeff?"

"Right, Anna," I said with a smile.

"So what time is your appointment?" she asked Liz.

"It's at 1:30."

"What's at 1:30?" I asked.

Liz answered, "Dr. Bongio...plastic surgeon."

"Breast implant specialist," added Anna.

"Do you guys need my help?" I joked, "I'd be happy to tag along and give you my professional opinion."

Both girls giggled and then declined my offer to join them for the consultation. I kissed both girls good-bye, and when I was smooching Anna on her milky round cheek, I could feel Liz watching carefully. It was almost as if she was assessing whether Anna and I could work in a relationship. I realized that the conversation Liz and I had a few moments earlier was significant, both of us dancing around a really big issue; the very obvious mutual attraction between a commitment-phobic womanizer and a girl wearing a huge rock on her left ring finger. What was so cool about Liz, though, was that I didn't have to worry. I felt confident the two of us had a secret and a bond and we both knew with certainty neither of us would reveal it to our mutual friend.

I watched the two walk down the block and then I went home to take out my pooches. As for Anna and Liz, they headed to the posh office of the department head of plastics at Northwestern Hospital, double board certified Dr. Carmine Bongio, II.

Anna would tell me later that the great Dr. Bongio looked more like one of Tony Soprano's guys than a world-renowned plastic surgeon. The fifty-four year old Italian, with his slick-backed hair and his rough-around-the-edges style, hardly seemed like the prototype for the prestigious position he held at the hospital. Nonetheless, his reputation was enough for Liz, so she decided to ignore her catty thoughts about his demeanor and take advantage of his brilliance in boob enlargement.

She sat on the exam table with her shirt off while the doctor took measurements and then wrote down notes on a small pad of paper. Anna sat in a chair across the little room with her head down, reading the text I had just sent. "How's the consultation going?" I texted her.

"I feel weird being in here," she texted back, "But Liz begged me."

"Your new breast size would be a fairly large 34 C," said Dr. Bongio in his heavy Italian accent.

"Wow," was Liz's response, "That seems pretty big. Doesn't it, Anna?"

"I don't know," said Anna, wondering what had all of a sudden made her the expert on appropriate boob sizes.

While Dr. Bongio showed Liz the exact places where the incisions would be, Anna watched with great curiosity; that is, until she received another text from me. She giggled when she read it. "Well, since you're already in the exam room, maybe you should take your shirt off and see what the doctor has to say about you. Just kidding!"

She texted back, "No, thanks. I can live without huge boobs. I'm happy the way I am."

"I think you look great the way you are," I responded.

"I wish Chris thought so," she texted next.

"What do you mean?" was my next message.

"Well, he likes my chest but not my hair, my dogs, my parents, or my demeanor in bed."

I was at a loss for words. Literally. What was I supposed to text back? "You're right? The guy's a superficial asshole and I think you should dump him and start dating me?" Not appropriate. I went with, "For what it's worth, I really like your hair and your dogs. Your parents and your sexual ability are unknown to me but I have a feeling they are both good."

A couple minutes later I got the text that would give me a perma-smile for the rest of the day. It read, "Do you happen to have Sheila's phone number? I want to call her and tell her what an idiot she was for cheating on you!"

"Ur sweet," was all I wrote.

That was the end of our text exchanges, because at that moment Dr. Italian stallion said good-bye and exited the exam room. Liz, still sitting on the table, exclaimed, "Oh my God! I really liked that guy. I think he could make me look amazing!"

Anna looked at her best friend sadly.

"What's wrong?" asked Liz.

"Nothing."

"Anna...I really think I'm going to do this. What do you think?"

"It depends on who you're doing it for. Do you want bigger boobs, Liz?"

"I don't know...maybe..."

"I mean, here you are in a consultation with a plastic surgeon, when I know you would never have come here if you didn't know what Sam said about you. Don't you think there's something majorly wrong with all of this?"

"It's no different than what you're doing. You changed your hair, which looks amazing by the way, but still, you never would have changed it. Your parents are supposedly moving to Arizona...and your dogs are living with Jeff...which is a major subject in need of discussion in and of itself."

"What do you mean?"

"Anna, I've known you since you were fourteen. You know what I mean."

Anna wasn't going there. Not even close. Instead, she went back to the business at hand. "Look, you're right. I'm just as guilty as you. Maybe worse. But the point is, why are we making changes for these guys? Shouldn't they want us the way we are?"

At that moment, Liz looked at Anna and realized her friend had big tears in her eyes. "Anna…are you crying? Oh my God!" She jumped off the table, put her shirt on, walked over to Anna's chair, and knelt down beside it. "Anna, I want to marry Sam so badly you have no idea. And the thing is…I'm willing to do anything I can to have that happen. Am I sure that going to this extreme is the right thing? No. But in the end, if Sam ends up being my husband, then it was worth it. He's all I really want."

Wide eyed, Anna looked up at the woman who was as close as a sister to her. "I'm not sure I feel the same," she said sadly.

Liz gave her a big hug. "I know."

## Chapter 19

"Sam has a friend visiting from out of town and they're supposed to go out to dinner Friday night," Liz told me over the phone the next day, "That may be a good night for me to run into him."

Liz was exactly right. It was perfect. The big question, however, was where Sam would choose to take his buddy. We had no clue, which was why on Friday night, I had to go undercover and sit in my car in front of Sam's building till he and the guy came out. I waited for almost an hour till I saw the guys walk out the front door and hail a cab. Then I followed them to their dinner destination, which turned out to be *Carmine's*, a fantastic Italian place located just off Rush Street in a little area Chicagoans call "Viagra Triangle," because it's one of three neighboring hot spots that attracts a crowd mostly in their forties and fifties.

The second I saw Sam and his buddy enter the restaurant, I called Liz and Mike, who were both on stand-by, waiting to find out where they should quickly show up. I told both of them I was parked across the street and that they should get into my car to meet each other before walking into *Carmine's*.

Mike was the first to arrive. Climbing into the back seat of a 1992 Honda Accord, he said, "Dude, a hundred bucks, plus you're paying for dinner, right?"

Boy, Mike had certainly gotten greedy in his short time as our employee. I answered, "One hundred and yes, I'm paying for dinner, but no expensive bottles of vino, got it?"

"So, what's up with this chick? What's her story? She hot?"

"Very cute," I replied. "But nothing like your first date," I wanted to add.

At that moment, Liz knocked on the window. Mike opened the door and scooted over to the other side to make room for her.

"Hi, Jeff!" she said excitedly.

I turned around. "Hey, Liz."

Liz then extended a handshake to Mike. "Hi. I'm Liz."

"Mike..." he said as he shook.

"Liz, you look really nice," I said sincerely.

She did. Anna had told me that she had bought a new outfit at Barneys, and it was really working for her. The funny thing about it was that the top made her boobs look really big. Maybe all Liz needed was some hot new clothes to highlight what was already there. Of course, Dave and I call dressing to enhance and or enlarge any parts of the body "false advertising." But as far as Sam was concerned, maybe seeing his girlfriend looking this hot would cause him to reconsider the boob job part of his wish list. Not that it was an issue anymore, as Liz was now seriously considering having the surgery.

"Thanks, Jeff," she smiled, "This is a big night."

"Are you nervous?" Mike asked.

"Yes. Very. This is risky."

"Trust me, Liz..." I comforted her, "Everything's going to turn out great."

"It will," Mike reassured, "Look at Anna."

Yeah...look at Anna, I thought, Engaged to her dream man and resigned to having bad sex for the rest of her life.

Out loud I asked, "Ready?"

"Showtime!" Mike exclaimed.

Then he got out and walked around my car to open Liz's side.

"Wish me luck, Jeff!" Liz said just before getting out.

"You don't need it, but good luck anyway," I smiled.

"Later, dude," said Mike while Liz got out.

"No wine!" I joked, "Diet coke!"

Mike gave me a courtesy laugh and slammed the door. Then I watched him put his arm around Liz and walk toward the entrance of *Carmine's*.

"Look out, Sam!" I laughed to myself.

Once I saw they were in the door, I looked at the clock in my car. It was 7:30 already. I now had half an hour to get home, shower, hail a cab, and get to my date's apartment, which was at least fifteen minutes away from mine. That gave me exactly three minutes in the shower and one or two to get dressed and out the door.

Yes, I had my own plans tonight. I was going out with Jodi, the girl I met while waiting for Sam at the pizza place. I was taking her to *Kevin*, a quaint little French restaurant I had heard about from Mike. We would then probably head to a club and go dancing or something, depending on how well the date was going.

Dave had called me earlier in the day to ask me if Jodi and I wanted to meet up with him and Lori after dinner. I guessed they were getting along tonight, probably because Lori was on her best behavior, considering Dave had told her he would think about hiring the band for their wedding. But I knew he would eventually back out of those plans, and if he didn't, I was fully prepared to tell him everything I knew about the cheating even if I had to tie him up and force him to listen to me.

"We'll see," I told Dave about hooking up with him, "Who knows how the evening will go." I wanted Dave to think I was hesitant to introduce him to Jodi since it was a first date and all; but truthfully, I could not stomach seeing Lori. I wasn't sure if I could actually be nice to the girl.

I pulled into my garage, parked the car, and hurried upstairs to begin getting ready for Jodi. My allotted three minutes turned into six, but after rushing to hail a cab and begging the driver to haul ass, I managed to get to Jodi's building at 8:03. Now I could exhale and have a good time with my little stockbroker, I mean…financial advisor.

When Jodi opened the door, I was pleasantly surprised by what I saw. She was completely transformed from the businesslike person I'd seen a few days earlier. Jodi was dressed in a tight pair of dark jeans and a strapless black silk top. On her feet, she wore high-heeled black sandals. In this outfit, Jodi looked even more petite than she had in her suit. Her jeans had to be a size zero. Perhaps the biggest change in Jodi's appearance, though, was her hair. Instead of the tightly wrapped bun she sported the first time I met her, Jodi's hair was down to her elbows. It was slightly held back by a very thin sparkling headband. To sum it up, Jodi looked hot hot hot.

"Hi, Jeff…" she said.

"Jodi…hi…" I said, trying not to act too eager.

"Come in…" She led me inside her apartment and into the living room. "Sit down. I'll be ready in two minutes."

I sat on her couch and she disappeared into the bedroom. The second my date was gone, I stood up and began to walk around the room and look at the art displayed on the walls. I have always believed you can learn a lot about a person by what he or she chooses to hang in his or her home.

The first thing I noticed was a large black and white photo of the 1986 Chicago Bears, with signatures all over it. I walked over to get a closer look. So Jodi was a Bears fan. Very cool. I had been in countless chicks' apartments. Never had I seen anything hung on their walls resembling an interest in sports, let alone a piece of sports memorabilia as expensive and valuable as what I was admiring at this moment.

"My brother bought me that for Christmas last year," Jodi said, walking up behind me.

"It's really cool." I wondered if her bro got it at *Be a Sport.*

"I'm a huge Bears fan."

"I see that," I smiled, turning around to face Jodi who was now wearing some kind of a wrap scarf thing over her top. "Ready?"

"Sure," she smiled, "Where are we going?"

I told Jodi about the restaurant as we walked out of her place and hailed a cab. Sitting next to her in the back of the taxi I got a whiff of her perfume. Jodi smelled amazing. In summary, the girl sitting next to me was a very attractive sports fan whose perfume was turning me on big time.

But as much as I loved the way Jodi smelled, my mind would not let me forget or even discount my Anna. It was Anna's smell and Anna's cute little cheeks and Anna's complete and utter lack of sports knowledge that kept my mind on her twenty-four/seven these days. I now craved every part of her. And that information was my little secret, although I sensed Dave was on to me. And after my little conversation the other day with Liz, she obviously was too.

It wasn't till I mentally kicked myself in the ass and reminded myself that Anna was now the owner of a five thousand dollar wedding gown that I was able to let her go, if only for the night, and focus on Jodi. My date and I were going to party tonight and I refused to let Anna ruin my fun. As I continued to try to charm the girl sitting next to me, I silently told my heart to take a night off from Anna. I urged it to forget about her for the next few hours. I assured it that in the morning I would allow Anna back in there to occupy her spot.

Dinner turned out great. Mike's recommendation, as usual, was superb. It amused me to think of Mike having dinner with Liz in Viagra triangle. He was probably wishing he was here at this hot spot.

During our meal, Jodi and I talked a lot about sports and the Bears. She told me she was a sports fan because she grew up with three brothers. Jodi was very impressed when I told her I was a sportswriter. It was nice being able to talk sports with a chick, definitely something foreign but nonetheless very enjoyable. We also talked about Jodi's job. I got the impression she made a lot of cash, based on her comments that she had three assistants and that she was considering accepting a management position with the company.

"So, what were you doing at the pizza place?" Jodi finally asked me just after we ordered dessert.

"Oh," I scrambled, trying to come up with some kind of story.

"Jeff, I didn't mean to pry. You don't have to tell me."

"No…no…" I attempted to recover, "You're not prying. I was meeting a friend there for lunch."

"It's okay if you were meeting a girl. You can say it."

"Jodi…I can assure you…I was not meeting a girl at the pizza place. I was meeting my friend Sam."

"Okay," she smiled. I had just taken a sip of hot coffee when Jodi continued, "Who is Sam?" At that point I almost choked, accidentally spitting a little bit of coffee out.

"Sam? Sam is a friend I've known for awhile." Desperate to change the subject, I continued, "Anyhow, Jodi, why don't you have a boyfriend?" I really didn't care to know about Jodi's love life but I had a strong desire to shift the conversation to her and not think or talk about my new profession to hook line and sink guys into marriage.

"Actually, I had a boyfriend till about a week ago."

"Oh…" I was genuinely surprised.

She hesitated and then began, "We broke up because…"

I waited a moment and figured Jodi didn't want to talk about her situation. "It's okay, don't tell me."

"No," she said, "I want to tell you."

"Okay."

Just then our fried banana with three dipping sauces arrived. Jodi picked up her fork, cut off a piece of the amazing looking concoction, dipped it in a dark chocolate sauce, and put it in her mouth. She chewed slowly and closed her eyes. "Yum," she smiled.

I followed suit and dug in.

Then Jodi dropped a bombshell. "My boyfriend wants to get married and I don't."

I couldn't believe it. Was Jodi the only girl on earth who didn't want to be a wife?

"Well, let me ask you this," I said while trying to chew, "Is it that you don't want to get married…or do you not want to marry *him*?"

"I'm not sure."

"Not sure if he's the one?"

Jodi took another bite of banana before answering. She thought about what she wanted to say while she chewed. "Right. He definitely could be the one, I just don't know," she smiled, "Do I sound crazy?"

"No. But I have another question. What's wrong with the guy? I mean, what's holding you back?"

As I said these words, something felt a little bit weird. It was strange because I felt like I was back in work mode. I was about to have the same conversation with Jodi as I had had with Sam. And Chris for that matter. Confusion was setting in. Was I working or was I on a date? Was I going to find out from Jodi why she didn't want to get married to her boyfriend and then go back and tell him all the reasons so he could change himself to win Jodi's love? Of course not, but I continued asking questions because I was truly interested. I was sitting at dinner with the only woman on earth whose boyfriend was pressuring *her* into getting engaged. And that was fascinating to me, whether I was in the marriage business or not.

The waiter came by to ask if we wanted the check, and I suddenly felt the need to order another drink, so I did. Maybe Jodi would think I was strange for ordering a cocktail after dessert, but I got the feeling that she needed some more alcohol in order to open up to me. So the two of us spent another hour at the restaurant, while Jodi told me some things she would like her ex-boyfriend to change.

"I really do love him," she said, her words now beginning to slur, "And I really didn't want to break up. But he insisted that if we didn't get engaged, it was over."

The story was so familiar it was scary. If her boyfriend were my client, I would have told him he was doing the right thing. All he needed was the information I just received from Jodi, plus a date with a female Mike to make her jealous, and he would get his girl to marry him. I was sure of it. But tonight wasn't business. Tonight I was on a date. As I watched Jodi take the last sip of her martini and put the empty glass down, I asked, "Want to get out of here?"

Minutes later, we found ourselves staggering into Jodi's apartment and laughing hysterically while singing every song from the Jimmy Buffet "Songs You Know by Heart" CD. When I saw Jodi's couch, I practically dove onto it. I was tired. And drunk. I sat back and closed my eyes for a moment. When I opened them, Jodi's face was about an inch from mine. She was leaning over me and she was about to kiss me. I liked this girl. She was sexy and smart and funny.

"Hi," I whispered.

Jodi responded with a long warm kiss, and I pulled her onto my lap. We continued kissing for a few moments and I had a suspicion that clothes would soon begin to come off. Then a moment later something (or I should say someone) popped into my head. I thought of Anna. Jodi was close to perfect, and the way things were going, I would probably be having sex with her in the next few minutes. But Anna was Anna, and for some reason I decided right then and there that I didn't want to have sex with anyone else. I backed away.

"What's wrong?" Jodi asked.

"Jodi, I really like you. I just…I think I should go."

"Oh my God…did I do something?"

I felt horrible for hurting this girl I liked so much. "No! It's just…"

"It's my boyfriend, isn't it?" she asked, "You don't want to get involved with me because you think I'm getting back together."

I decided to lie. After all, this would certainly please Jodi, right? Why did she have to know the truth? "You're right." Honestly, I did have a gut feeling that Jodi would get back with her boyfriend, so maybe my decision to leave wasn't such a bad thing after all.

Jodi kissed my cheek. "You're so sweet, Jeff," she smiled, "Do you think we could be friends for now?"

I held her hands. "I would really like that."

I kissed Jodi good-bye on the cheek and left. As I slowly strolled down the block I thought about three things. One, I had just passed up what could have been amazing sex. Two, I had forgotten how much I loved Jimmy Buffet. And three, I was in serious trouble. How was I going to get Anna out of my head?

# Chapter 20

The next couple of weeks were extremely productive as I spent my time doing all my different jobs. First, I had to complete several rewrites of the Lovie Smith piece before the final draft was to be published in *Today's Chicago Woman.* Second, I had landed a few small jobs for the Pioneer Press covering different high school sporting events and a minor league baseball team in downstate Illinois.

Then there was Liz. I was communicating with her daily to gauge the progression of her work with Sam. She would call me every morning with an update and I would coach her onto the next step. Apparently her dinner with Mike worked like a charm. Sam had been flipping out ever since, trying to win his girlfriend back. The big question remained, how far would he go? In other words would Sam go out and buy Liz a big rock to show his strong desire to stay together? My bet was yes.

Two days after the big dinner, Liz told me Sam wanted to come over and talk. "Big shock there," was my sarcastic but good-natured response to Liz. I advised my client not only to accept, but to make dinner for him.

"But Sam hates my cooking," Liz panicked, "And I haven't even started the classes yet!"

"I know…I know…" I said trying to calm her down, "Mike's sister is going to come over and cook the meal for you. She'll leave right before Sam gets there." According to Mike, his sister was a fantastic cook and now that she had moved in with the rich guy and quit her job, she had tons of time on her hands. "Now Liz," I mocked, "After dinner, if you guys decide to watch TV…"

"I know…" she giggled, "I will relinquish control of the remote."

"And?"

"And I will not sleep with him."

"Good girl."

"Thanks, Jeff," she said before hanging up, "I'll keep you posted."

And that she did. Every morning, right around the time I was getting back from my morning walk with the dogs Liz would call. It became my routine. At 5:30 a.m, Pita would jump up on my bed and let me know she had to pee. I then had two and a half minutes to get the dog out the door before she had an accident. And even though it was barely dawn, I figured as long as I was headed out, why not take all the dogs for a walk?

Just these pooches alone were an entire job, each one more high maintenance than the next. Pretty Boy loved to snack and was constantly nagging me for food. I was out buying more doggie treats at least every other day. P.J. and Pepper were constantly fighting with each other so I spent a lot of time breaking them up. Pita loved television but was very specific about the shows. It was a huge bummer to realize she hated sports, but no surprise because I'm sure there was absolutely no sports watching going on at her real home. Poo-poo Platter didn't require much attention but she cried a lot. I think she was missing her mommy. And I have to confess, I was too. As for Passion, she loved to be scratched and massaged pretty much all day long (no surprise there). So needless to say, dog-sitting could have easily filled my day had it been my only job. But it wasn't.

Aside from writing and reporting, coaching Liz, and dog sitting, I had additional work, thanks to Dave. The day after Liz went on her fake date with Sam, Dave set up a website for our business, and invested a little money in some internet advertising. He also posted a flyer on the advertising boards in four local coffee houses. The flyer read, "Are you frustrated with your boyfriend? Do you want to be engaged? Do you wonder why he hasn't popped the question? 'Hook, Line and Sink Him' can help. We can find out what's holding your guy back and get you the rock you've been waiting for. 'Hook, Line and Sink Him' will transform you from a bitter girlfriend to a blushing bride. Give us a call at (312) 281-0073."

Now, if I had seen the flyer, there is no way I would have allowed Dave to post it. It made us sound like psychos. *Hook, Line and Sink Him*? What kind of a name was that? Actually, truth be told, I did think the name was kind of cute and not just because Anna liked it. But the bottom line was, my buddy had gone off the deep end with this whole marriage business. He was out of control, but I couldn't stop him because he had Anna backing him a hundred percent. And there was something else. Part of me didn't want to stop him, because *Hook, Line and Sink Him* was making Dave happy. It was diverting his attention away from Lori. How nice it was to see my buddy enjoying something in life. Who was I to take that away from him?

"Hook, Line and Sink Him" received quite a few phone calls shortly after the flyers went up. Most were just inquiries, people who were curious to know more about us. Dave fielded the calls and made sure not to get into specifics unless he thought the call was a serious lead and could generate business.

A woman named Frieda Goldenrod was our first non-referral-based customer. Frieda was a very short, semi- heavyset woman in her mid fifties who was by far the cutest person I had met in a long time. When Frieda spoke, she was loud and expressive. The woman was very dramatic and used her hands a lot to emphasize her points, the main one being that for the life of her, she could not understand why her boyfriend of three years, a Mr. Simon Stein, would not marry her.

As Frieda sat on our new couch, which Dave and I had finally moved into the office, she began telling the three of us about her life. Frieda explained that she had been divorced for years and that she had two grown children, a daughter who was married with a baby, and a son who was a law student in New York City.

Frieda referred to her ex-husband as "the dancing bear." She had given him the nickname years ago after attending a Bears game and noticing the mascot (which is a dancing bear) on the field.

"No one really pays attention to the dancing bear," she joked to us, "That's kind of how I view my ex." She also told us she had a vanity license plate on her silver Acura TSX which read, "Was His."

"So tell us about Simon," I urged.

After a dramatic sigh, she began, "I met Simon on the Jewish dating service, J-date, three years ago, which was about a year after his wife died of ovarian cancer."

"And how was it at the beginning?" Anna asked her.

Frieda answered, "Fabulous. Actually, after our second date, we both agreed to take our profiles off of J-date. We knew instantly we were soul mates."

"So you got serious pretty quickly?" Dave asked.

"Yes," said Frieda. "We discussed moving in together numerous times but in the end we decided to wait till we got married. We figured, why ruin a good thing?"

Upon hearing this, I said, "I'm sorry, I'm not quite understanding the problem here. You're happy...you're having fun...you're talking about living together...things seem good."

Frieda fired back at me with sarcasm. "I'm sorry...am I in the right place? Isn't this *Hook, Line and Sink Him*'s office? Don't you know why I'm here? I want to get married!"

"Ignore him," Dave said to Frieda, "He doesn't sample the merchandise."

"What does that mean?" she asked.

"It means that even though he helps other people get married, he doesn't want to get married."

Anna stepped in and defended, "He doesn't want to get married right now. That doesn't mean forever."

"Thank you," I said to her with a smile.

"Can we get back to me?" asked Frieda.

"Yes," answered Dave, "Does Simon know you want to get married?"

Frieda put her hands up over head dramatically, "Of course he does! That's why I'm here! Do I have to spell it out for you? I want a ring! I want to be Mrs. Stein! For some reason, Simon doesn't feel the same way. Can you help me?"

"Do you have any idea what may be holding Simon back?" Anna asked her.

"Well…he says…" Frieda rolled her eyes, "He feels guilty about his wife."

All three of us must have had really sad looks on our faces at that moment because Frieda exploded after seeing our reactions. "That's a bunch of crap!" she shouted, "He's using it as an excuse."

"How do you know?" asked Dave.

"How do I know?" she said, the volume still cranked, "Because I know this man. And I know there is something else. I just can't put my finger on it."

"Well that's where I think we can help you, Frieda," Dave said.

Anna chimed in, "Our first step would be to talk to Simon…"

"Without him knowing you've hired us, of course," Dave added.

"We would find out the truth, if in fact it isn't because of his wife…" said Anna.

"Trust me honey, it's not."

"Okay…" Anna smiled.

"Then it's up to you to make the adjustments," said Dave.

Through their whole shtick I sat there silent. I was getting a kick out of the fact that my friends had our sales pitch down pat.

My buddy continued, "After that, we guide you in our three-step program, which we will explain when it gets closer."

Frieda asked some specific questions about how exactly we would get to know Simon and we told her how we worked. What we didn't say was how devious and manipulative we knew how to be. I wanted to tell our client that we were grade A con artists who knew how to scheme and plot things and maneuver innocent guys. Instead, I chose to inform Frieda of the costs.

"We charge $500 up front and $2000 if you get engaged within a year. What do you think?"

Frieda was ecstatic. "Where do I sign?"

I wanted to tell her she was nuts to agree to this. I wanted to tell her to run the hell out of here as fast as she could. I couldn't, though, because my editor was seated next to me and I was just days away from being published. Don't blow it now, I told myself.

Ten minutes later, Frieda walked out the door and I sat there with her check in my hand, wondering why the lady trusted us. There was no contract, no paperwork, nothing. Just our word. And for some reason, Frieda did not question it.

"The power of wanting something so badly makes people do things they wouldn't ordinarily do," Dave said pensively, as he stared into space.

Anna nodded as if to say she wholeheartedly agreed with this deep thought.

"Isn't that line from the movie 'Wall Street'?" I asked.

Dave thought about the question as we all sat there in silence. Then, as if on cue, all three of us burst out laughing.

"Yes! I think it is," Dave laughed.

And while we all continued giggling for a few moments Anna gave me a wink that stopped my heart.

## Chapter 21

"Come on, guys!" I yelled to the dogs, "A little peace and quiet, please!"

It was already 4:00, and I was writing on deadline for the Pioneer Press, finishing up an article on Brian Burns, Glenbrook South High School's star basketball player. The piece was about Brian's personal life, specifically how he was coping with his brother's sudden death.

Brian was a great kid and stories like his were what kept me motivated to become a successful sports reporter and writer. So needless to say, I was trying to make Brian's piece the best I could. This was a difficult task, though, since I had six dogs barking, sniffing, howling, knocking things over, and basically bugging the crap out of me while I tried work. I was sitting on my couch, laptop on the coffee table, and guess who was napping on my lap? Passion. I have to confess, however, I enjoyed this since I was becoming as attached to Anna's dog as I was to Anna.

Finally, I began to overcome the distraction of the dogs, and productivity kicked in. However, minutes later, another interruption. The phone rang. Ordinarily, I never pick up the phone while writing, but since it was sitting right there next to my computer and since the ringing had made Pita and Poo-poo start barking again, I did.

"Hey," I answered the phone.

"Guess who got engaged?" Dave asked me.

"You're kidding, right?"

"Nope. Sam proposed last night."

"Wow, this shit really works, doesn't it?"

Dave seemed thrilled by the news he was giving me. "Now, don't you feel good that you are one hundred percent responsible for Liz's happiness?"

I sat back and continued to massage Passion, who was still in my lap anxiously awaiting my touch.

"Listen to what I am about to say," I told Dave, "I am in this for myself. The bottom line is, I did this to get my article into Anna's magazine. And as soon as that happens, I'm done."

"Come on, don't you even get a little bit of satisfaction? Think about it…this is the second person whose life we just changed. And we haven't even helped Frieda yet!"

I thought about cute little Frieda. Who were we to play with her fate? If she and Simon were meant to get married, wouldn't that be in the hands of the big man upstairs?

Just then my buzzer rang. "Hang on Dave. Someone's at my door." Passion wasn't too happy when I got up and placed her on the couch. I walked over to the intercom and pressed the button. "Hello?"

"Hi, Jeff! It's Anna. I'm downstairs."

"Oh," I said, surprised. I would never admit this to anyone, but my heart began to pound. "I'll buzz you in." Then I hit the buzzer. "Dave?" I said into the phone.

"Yeah, yeah, I heard," he joked, "Go eat an Altoid."

"Shut up," I laughed. Then I hung up the phone and actually took his advice. Why was I nervous? Actually, I was borderline panicky. Who was I turning into? I did a quick check in the mirror, ran my fingers back through my hair, and took a deep breath. Then I heard my visitor knock on the door. Of course, the dogs went wild, barking and dashing to the door, tripping over each other. I didn't think it was possible for them to get even more rowdy, till I opened the door. All together, they jumped on Anna, practically knocking her over. Anna just laughed, knelt down, and began to hug and pet them.

"They missed their mommy," I said with a chuckle.

"Aw, well mommy missed them," she answered. I thought her reaction to the animals was adorable, that is until she began kissing a couple of them on the lips. Right then, adorable turned to disgusting.

"Come in," I said.

"Thanks." Anna managed to get up and make her way into my place. She was now carrying Passion in one hand and Pita in the other. The rest of her pets were still sniffing and kissing her.

"Sit down. Can I get you something?"

"Actually I brought *you* something," she answered as she sat on the couch and put the disappointed dogs down on the floor. Anna then went into the huge handbag she was still carrying on her shoulder and pulled out a bottle of wine and a magazine. She held up the bottle and said, "This is for us to celebrate." Then she handed me the magazine and finished, "And this is what we're celebrating."

I took the magazine and looked at the cover in disbelief. I shouldn't have been surprised because I knew the issue of *Today's Chicago Woman* with my article was hitting newsstands the next day. Still, there was something very exciting and unbelievable about holding this tangible proof in my hands. "Wow," I said trying to stay calm, "I can't believe it."

"Believe it, Jeff," Anna said proudly, "Because when this hits the public, lots of things are going to start happening for you. And me…since I found you. Your article may be the official end of my slump."

"Well I'm glad I could help your career," I joked.

Anna began telling me how her bosses were very impressed with her for going out on a limb with me. As I listened to this girl who captivated me so deeply, I wondered, was there anything she didn't have? Why was she settling for Chris and bad sex?

"I'll go open this," Anna said as she rose, "You find your article." She went into the kitchen while I sat there leafing through the pages of *Today's Chicago Woman*, seeking my article. I couldn't believe what my life had turned into. I was Jeff, a complete and total guy's guy. I was also a major womanizer. If someone would have told me I would be turning the pages of *Today's Chicago Woman,* looking for an article I had written, I would have said they were nuts. Furthermore, if someone would have said I would be running a business called *Hook, Line and Sink Him* to help girls trick guys like me into getting engaged I would probably have killed myself. I now understood the phrases, "Life doesn't always turn out the way you expect," "Don't take life too seriously," and "If you want to make God laugh, make a plan."

"By the way," Anna shouted from the kitchen, "I'm sure you heard the news."

I knew immediately that she was talking about Liz and Sam. "Yeah…I did."

Anna came out of the kitchen with a glass of wine in each hand. "Pretty great, huh?" she asked as she put them on the coffee table.

"Yeah…" I said trying to sound positive instead of sarcastic. I continued paging through the magazine.

Anna sat down on the couch next to me. "You don't seem that thrilled."

I looked up at her. "No, I am," I lied. Then I continued looking for my article. Two seconds later, I found it and held it up to show Anna.

"Very exciting!" she smiled, "Cheers!" She held up her glass. I followed suit with a smile. Anna and I toasted and sipped our wine. Then I perused the pages on which my writing was printed. I have to admit it was extremely cool and I was ready to burst with excitement.

Anna just sat there watching me and sipping her drink for a couple of minutes. When I finally looked up at her, I was surprised to see her wine glass almost empty. Why was Anna pounding her wine? Was she nervous about something?

"Anna," I began, "I want to tell you something."

"Okay." She took another huge gulp.

"I just want you to know how much I appreciate this. I mean…giving me such a great opportunity. This could turn out to be a huge break for me and I just want you to know that I realize that."

Anna smiled, "Well, I was happy to do it. Look what you did for me, both with Chris and with work."

I nodded in agreement, although I wasn't so sure I did her any favors by helping her with Chris.

"How about some more wine?" she asked. My glass was still full but Anna obviously was on a roll. She stood up and headed back into the kitchen. On her way there, she changed the subject. "By the way, Liz gave me a $2000 check this morning." Just before she entered the kitchen, she turned around and looked at me. "I think you and Dave should split it." Then she was out of sight.

"What? No! We'll split it three ways," I shouted.

Anna headed back to me with the wine bottle in her hand. She poured herself a glass and put the bottle on the coffee table. "No, Jeff. You guys deserve it. I didn't do anything. You're the one who met with Sam and coached Liz. You guys split it."

I was speechless.

"Hey, guess what else?" she asked.

"What now?" I joked.

"We have a new client, thanks to Liz. Her name is Jamie Lee. Liz works with her. She's coming in tomorrow morning."

Now I was the one who began to chug. I think I drank my entire glass of wine in two gulps.

Anna giggled as she watched me imbibe. "Does that news bother you?" she asked through her chuckle.

"I have to be honest with you. It does."

"May I ask why?"

My answer to Anna lead to a conversation about the ethics (or in my opinion the lack thereof) of our business. Anna thought what we were doing was a good thing. She called it a "mitzvah," a good deed in the Jewish religion. I called it borderline despicable. Bad behavior. Surprisingly, though, I found myself respecting Anna's opinion. And she did the same.

Anna was like no woman I had ever met. She was a knockout, a beauty, yet she also had a brain. She was smart (except when it came to sports) and she was opinionated but not judgmental. This was a first for me. I had never wanted to have serious conversations with a girl (not even Sheila) *and* hang out with her *and* joke around with her *and* go to bed with her. Wanting the whole package in a woman was new to me. Was this what love was?

Anna and I moved on to other subjects. We talked all through the evening, about everything. We shared our backgrounds, our goals, our political views, and we told each other stories about our past relationships. We even took the dogs for a walk together. Three hours and one bottle of wine later, Anna and I were still chatting nonstop.

"Should I break open another bottle?" I asked her, "I have a really expensive red that someone gave me for Christmas last year."

"Sure," she said enthusiastically.

I went into the kitchen and Anna went into the bathroom. As I opened the bottle of Syrah, I suddenly felt like I was on a date. A really good date. Anna must have felt the same, because when I walked back into the living room with our wine, I noticed she had reapplied her lipstick while in the john. I knew girls and I knew that if a chick put on lipstick this late into the evening, she was interested.

I handed Anna her glass and she politely thanked me.

"Look at them," she smiled, motioning to the six animals fast asleep all over the room, "They feel so comfortable here."

I wondered if perhaps Anna was referring to herself when she made that comment. Also, was she insinuating that the dogs make this their permanent home? "Are you trying to plant a seed here?" I joked.

"No! I swear Jeff," she said defensively, "I was just making an observation. I think the dogs really like it here, that's all."

"Okay…just wanted to make sure. This is a doggie motel, not their new residence."

"I promise. I'll tell Chris I'm taking them back. Just give me a few days."

"Sure," I smiled. When I thought about it, Anna did have a point. The dogs were happy. They all loved me. Anna's pets symbolized one of many things that were changing in my life, all having one common thread. All were bettering my self-esteem. The dogs, the Lovie Smith article, and, as much as I hated to admit it, *Hook, Line and Sink Him*. Even though I felt the business was morally wrong in a lot of ways, it was enabling me to act as a mentor and a teacher. I was helping people accomplish a goal. The biggest self-esteem lifter of all, however, turned out to be the woman sitting next to me on the couch.

Anna had a way of making me feel good about myself in ways I never had before. I couldn't quite put my finger on how exactly she did it, and I didn't even know if she was trying to or not. But something about when Anna walked into a room made me feel like I could fly. I know it sounds completely cheesy, but it was the truth. I think it was because Anna didn't look at me from the outside like every other girl did. Anna saw me for me. And she accepted me. In fact, she more than accepted me. She admired me, I think. No girl had ever made me feel respected and appreciated like Anna did. I wanted this girl. Badly.

"So, Anna…" I began my question as I poured myself another glass of liquid courage, "Tell me about Chris."

She giggled nervously. "What do you mean?"

"I mean, what's the deal?" Only alcohol could make someone fearless enough to use this tone. Anna did not seem to know how to respond, so I shifted gears. "How did you two meet?"

"In a bar."

"What bar?"

"Does it matter?"

"I guess not." I wasn't getting the information I wanted. Come to think of it, though, I didn't know what I wanted to find out. I probed some more. "Who approached who?"

Now Anna smiled confidently. "He came over to me and introduced himself."

"Did you like him right away?"

"Um…" she answered pensively, "I guess. Yeah."

That means no, I thought to myself.

"You know Jeff, Chris is a great guy. He's husband material," she said defensively.

"I'm sure he is, Anna," I said sarcastically as I gave myself another pour. "More wine?"

All of a sudden Anna stood up. "What's your problem?" she asked in a slightly raised voice.

"What?"

"You obviously have something to say, so say it."

I made a lame attempt at peace. "It's fine…I don't have anything to say." But I did. I had a lot to say, and unfortunately, I was buzzed enough to have the courage to speak my mind.

Here is where I turned into a complete asshole. I said in the most cynical voice I could muster, "Actually I do have something to say. Chris is an amazing guy. I'm sure you guys will live the next forty or fifty years together in bliss."

At this moment, Anna slammed her wine glass down on the coffee table so hard that I was shocked it didn't break. "See you later," she said, shooting me a bitter look. Then she headed for the door. I sat there watching her walk to my front door. Then I had an out-of-body experience and did something I would never do. I ran over to her, grabbed her, and kissed her hard on the mouth.

Anna kissed me back for around ten seconds before pushing me away and shouting, "What are you doing?" Before I knew it she was gone, leaving me standing there listening to six barking animals and watching the room spin.

# Chapter 22

The morning after the big kiss, I had a full agenda and no time for the pounding headache I woke up with, thanks to the two bottles of red wine I had polished off with Anna. I also could have done without the sick feeling in my stomach being caused by regret of my asinine behavior. Nonetheless, I had a very busy day. Here was my schedule in a nutshell (aside from canine duties):

9:00 Initial consultation with Jamie Lee, new client referred by Liz.

10:15 Take shower in men's locker room of Midtown Tennis club, befriend Simon, and find out why he's not getting engaged to Frieda.

12 noon Meet Mike for lunch and give him money we owe him for dinner with Liz.

12:30-3:00 Nap and/or take dogs for walk.

4:00 Cover Chicago Social Club volleyball tournament at North Avenue Beach for Pioneer Press.

5:45 Meet with Frieda to tell her what Simon said and to develop action plan.

8:00 Dinner with Jessica (the girl I slept with the night I met Anna).

I called Jessica shortly following my date with Jodi in an attempt to once again break away from my obsession with my business partner (obviously the female one.)

So this was how I was planning on spending my day, and I had no time to think about my pounding skull or how uncomfortable it was going to be to see Anna when the clock stuck nine.

Sure enough, I walked into our office at 8:45 feeling jittery as all hell. My venti coffee wasn't helping the matter.

My best friend could tell something was up. "Dude, what's your deal?" he asked.

"Massive hangover," I replied.

"Where did you go?"

"Nowhere. I was home."

"You just got drunk at home?" Then he put two and two together. "Wait a minute…you got drunk with Anna, didn't you?"

I nodded.

"Did something happen?" he asked excitedly.

"We kissed."

"What?"

I chuckled, "Yeah."

Dave was like a seventh grader. "Who kissed who first?"

"Let's not go there," I said sadly.

"Oh shit, sorry." Then Dave patted me on the back which brought a smile to my face.

Two seconds later, Anna walked in, and off my face went the smile. "Hi, guys!" she said in a cheery voice that sounded fake. Clearly, she was overcompensating for her unease.

Dave and I both said hello and then came the most awkward silence of my life. The three of us sat there without saying a word for at least twenty seconds till Dave, desperate to cut the tension, spoke.

"So Lori and I rented *The Departed* last night."

"I haven't seen that. How was it?" asked Anna.

"Great," replied Dave, "The best part about that movie is that there is absolutely nothing in it pertaining to marriage and/or weddings."

"Such a healthy relationship you're in, Dave," I said in an irritated voice.

"At least I'm *in* a relationship. You should try one. Maybe it would cure your judgmental attitude."

"What's that supposed to mean?"

"I mean, as the old adage says, don't judge a man till you've walked in his shoes."

Now I was getting pissed, although with my best friend I never really got pissed. I was half annoyed/half joking. "That's so original. Hey, I've got an old adage for you, Dave. How many times do you have to touch a hot stove before you realize you're going to get burned?"

Dave stood up and said, "Dude, what's your problem?" and I almost started laughing when I realized he was two seconds away from starting a fistfight with me.

Now Anna stood up. "Hey guys, easy..."

Dave shot Anna a look. "Stay out of this."

Now I was really going to crack up because Anna was in complete shock that Dave had just reprimanded her.

"Excuse me," said a voice at the door. The three of us turned and looked. "Is this *Hook, Line and Sink Him*?" a beautiful Asian girl shyly asked. Here stood our 9:00 client, Jamie Lee, and she had just witnessed our argument. If I were her and I saw and heard what she just did, I would have run out of there in a flash. After all, who would give their money to three idiots fighting with each other?

Anna was the first to recover. "You must be Jamie," she said, smiling and walking over to the girl. Anna held out her hand. "I'm Anna...and this is Dave and Jeff."

We all shook hands and Dave told Jamie to have a seat. She seemed scared, apprehensive. I wasn't sure if she was nervous about being here in general, or if she just felt anxious, because she had gotten a sneak peak at the quarreling individuals who were supposedly going to help her. I mean, seeing us getting ready to duke it out probably wasn't the best first impression.

"So how do you know Liz?" Dave asked Jamie.

"We work together."

We all smiled and nodded before Anna continued. "Tell us how we can help you, Jamie."

"Well…" Jamie was about to start talking, but something else happened instead. Her beautiful dark brown eyes filled up with tears and she began to cry. Hysterically and uncontrollably.

It reminded me of when Liz was in our office, telling us about Sam. She had pretty much acted the same way. Why the crying? I wondered. The only thing I could think of was that our clients probably had these feelings of wanting to be engaged bottled up so tightly in them for so long, that when they finally got the opportunity to release the cork the feeling of relief was overwhelming.

I wasn't sure how or why I knew this, but I suspected it was because of what had happened to me about twelve hours ago. Instead of crying, though, I forcefully grabbed Anna and kissed her as hard as I could. Maybe sobbing would have been more effective, I thought, as I watched the woman I was obsessed with hand Jamie a Kleenex and console her.

When Jamie finally stopped crying, I looked at my watch. It was 9:24 and I was on a tight schedule. I had to be naked in a locker room in an hour to meet Simon. That's why this chick needed to get it out quickly. "So tell us about your boyfriend. What's his name?" I asked.

Jamie looked up at me, mascara everywhere, and answered, "Ted."

"Tell us about Ted," Dave said, "What does he do?"

"Ted is a dentist." Jamie went on to explain that she and her beau had been dating for four and a half years. She swore on her nieces that she had no clue why Ted would not marry her. "We have the perfect relationship," she said. "We give each other a lot of space and we have often said that if we were married we would continue to do that."

"Have you talked a lot about marriage?" I asked.

"Yes, we have."

"Do you fight about it?" asked Dave, who wanted to know not only to get more information about Jamie's case, but for personal reasons.

"Not at all," answered Jamie, "And when we discuss marriage, Ted always says how much he loves me and how committed he is to us. He just says he needs more time."

Exactly eight minutes later, after we finished telling Jamie how we do business, there was a $500 deposit from her sitting on Dave's desk. *Hook, Line and Sink Him* had officially signed another client, and I had an 8:00 dentist appointment scheduled for the following week with Dr. Ted Baskin, D.D.S.

"Can I ask you guys why I'm the one doing all the work here?" I asked my business partners after Jamie was gone.

"Because I just had my teeth cleaned," said Dave, "And the dentist would know something was fishy."

"And no guy is going to open up to a woman and tell her details about why he won't commit to marriage," added Anna.

I nodded in agreement. I knew she was right. As for Dave, I disagreed, but I gave him a pass because I felt badly about our argument earlier in the morning.

We all stood up and left the room. As we walked through Dave's store and toward the door, I turned around and looked at my best friend. "No hard feelings?" I smiled.

Dave broke into a huge grin. "No asshole…no hard feelings." I walked back and hugged Dave while Anna stood there watching us and smiling.

"I'll call you after I meet Simon," I said as I opened the front door to leave.

Anna followed me out. "Bye, Dave!" she shouted.

"Ah, alone at last," was going through my head. I was just dying to hear what was going to come out of Anna's mouth. "Jerk," "asshole," or "dickhead" were a few words I thought were possibilities. As for my own mouth, I knew exactly what I wanted to say to Anna. The big question was, would I have the guts to say it?

This is what I rehearsed in the shower earlier that morning: "Anna, I just want to tell you that I'm sorry for acting the way I did last night. The truth is…I have feelings for you and I'm pretty sure, at least I hope, you have feelings for me too. Please reconsider marrying Chris and spend some time with me. If I thought you really loved your fiancé, I would not be saying all this, but I truly don't think Chris is your soul mate. I think I may be."

Then we would kiss, cancel our plans for the entire day (including my date with Jessica), and go back to my place and enjoy each other. Not just for sex, but for time together. I was crazy about this girl. It was time to face the truth. I took a deep breath and began. "Anna…"

"Jeff…" she said at the exact same time.

"Anna, I have to say something to you."

"Please let me go first," she smiled.

I nodded and she continued, "About the kiss and everything…let's just pretend it never happened."

"What?"

"Last night…I was drunk…and very stressed out…with the wedding planning and everything. I think I was being over-sensitive when you were just giving your opinion. Also, I realize…regarding the sarcastic comments…and the kiss…you were drunk, too."

"But Anna…"

"Let me finish. I consider you a good friend, Jeff, and I don't want to ruin that. Promise me we'll forget the whole thing and move on." Anna had a hopeful look on her face.

I was numb, especially when she kissed my cheek. "Okay?" she said with puppy dog eyes.

I nodded sadly, "Sure."

Then I hailed a cab for Anna and she got in. As I flagged down another one for myself, I felt as if my world had just fallen apart. Just when I was beginning to make money and was on my way to a better life, I suddenly felt crushed. I couldn't believe Anna was so quick to brush me off and move on. Either I had completely misread her, or she was refusing to acknowledge her feelings for me. Either way, it didn't matter. She had made her choice, and that was to go on with her engagement and step over the little roadblock that I had very temporarily placed in her path.

I went through the rest of my day on autopilot. It was a blessing that I had a lot to accomplish, because it forced me to work and not ponder the tremendous blow I had just faced. I told myself I would act like an athlete in a big game. I would put aside my personal feelings for a little while and perform. Only after the game was over would I allow myself to return to doom and gloom. But as any good coach would say, "During the game...only one thing matters: the game." And that thought is how I got through the remainder of my busy day.

Once inside the dressing area of the Midtown Tennis Club men's locker room, I placed my clothes and my unused tennis racket in a centrally located locker so that wherever Simon's locker was, I would not be very far. Then, I actually took my second shower of the day, since I had to look the part. I walked back into the dressing area, and a few seconds after I put my pants on I spotted Simon, based on the picture Frieda had supplied. He came out of the shower, towel around his waist, and headed to a locker just a few feet from mine.

Simon was completely bald but handsome. He had a good body for fifty-something, pretty lean and muscular, and he had a friendly look about him. He looked like a nice person. I waited for him to at least have his boxers on before I went in for the kill.

"How'd you hit em?" I asked.

Simon looked up. This guy was a talker, which made sense because so was his girlfriend. He answered my question about his tennis game for at least three minutes. Then he asked, "How about you?"

"Ah, not so good. I got a lot on my mind. Love troubles."

Simon's face lit up. He loved this. Unlike ninety-nine percent of the population, Simon wanted to hear more. "What's going on, buddy?" he said like he was my dad.

"You don't want to hear it," I said while slipping my shirt over my head.

"Well, I don't want to pry, so I won't press you."

Oh shit! Was he giving up on me? I had two seconds to save this. "Actually, my girlfriend just moved out because she wanted to get married and I'm just not ready."

"I'll be damned!" exclaimed Simon.

"What?" I faked.

"Why is it that women feel the need to pressure us into marriage? Can't we just leave well enough alone?"

"Sounds like you know what I'm talking about," I smiled, "Want to get some breakfast?"

Simon was like a kid in a candy store. "I know a terrific little greasy spoon close by."

"Perfect," I responded.

Twenty minutes later I was eating eggs Benedict. Seated across from me, Simon was enjoying an egg white omelet with a side of fruit and telling me all about Frieda.

"So, tell me, Simon, what would make you marry Frieda?"

"I would marry her in three seconds if…"

I held my breath. I was about to find out major info.

"If?"

"If Frieda were more thoughtful."

"How so?"

Simon did not answer right away. He was thinking carefully about what exactly he wanted to say. "Let me give you an example. My birthday is next Friday and it's a big one. Fifty-five…"

"Wow! Nice…"

"Now don't get me wrong. Frieda is fantastic. I'm sure she'll buy me a nice gift and go wherever I want…"

"That sounds good. So what's the problem?"

"Frieda would never think to have a surprise party for me. She would never just shock me, or do something really over the top."

I wasn't really getting Simon at this point. Wasn't that reason for not getting hitched a little petty and unimportant? "Is that really the reason?" I asked him.

He nodded his head slowly. "I know it sounds ridiculous, but that's really all it is. The funny thing is, I told Frieda I feel guilty getting married again because of my first wife who died a few years ago."

"And that's not true?"

"It's a bunch of crap!" Simon laughed.

Now I thought Simon was weird. He wouldn't marry his girlfriend until she has an "over the top" party for him, and now he was laughing about his dead wife. Another weird coincidence was that Simon used the exact same words about the situation as Frieda did. His excuse of feeling guilty about his deceased wife was "a bunch of crap." That's how I knew Frieda and Simon were on the same page. They were in sync. They thought alike, they talked alike, and they acted alike. It was sort of like they were already married.

Simon continued to laugh until his eyes got watery. Was he crying? I suddenly realized he was. He wasn't bawling or anything, but a couple of tears had formed. "Jeff, you have to laugh at these things. Otherwise you'll live life as a very sad person. When my wife died, I thought my life was over. And then time went by. And I kept living. And things got better. And then I met my Frieda. I do love her. But I think I will know when it's time to buy her a ring."

Now I was the one who felt like crying. Simon wasn't weird. He was a great guy who was still mourning the loss of his wife. "Well, Simon, laughter is a good dose of medicine for that kind of pain, I guess."

Simon gave me a big grin. "So tell me about your girlfriend. What's holding *you* back from ring shopping?"

I had to start making something up and I had to sound convincing, so I dug deep into my heart and pulled out what was ironically was the truth. I began my story with, "I really love her, Simon. She just doesn't love me back."

"Isn't it funny how you can just tell?" replied Simon, "Love is something you just can't fake."

As I went on and on spewing out the lies of my fake life, I realized Simon was right. You can't fake love. I wished right then that I could give that advice to Anna, who was definitely a love faker.

# Chapter 23

In my opinion, no one really participates in the Chicago Social Club volleyball tournament on a truly competitive basis. People play in the tournament for three reasons. One, to watch girls play volleyball in cute little bikinis; two, to watch girls play volleyball in cute little bikinis; and three, to watch girls play volleyball in cute little bikinis. And as for the girls in the cute little bikinis, they play because they know (and love) the fact that guys are watching them.

So here I stood on the beach with my pad of paper and pen, stopping passersby and interviewing them about why they were here, even though I already knew. I spoke with and got quotes from four participants and six spectators. Then I decided to watch a couple of games for the meat of the piece.

I took my shoes off and sat down in the sand, immediately digging my feet into it and enjoying the feeling in between my toes. The sun was beaming and it felt amazing. I put down the pad of paper, closed my eyes and held my face up to the rays. I realized right then that I did have the life, even though I was broke. Let's see...would I rather have little money and be doing this? Or be rich and sitting behind a desk in a cold, air-conditioned office building? Not a tough call. Plus, thanks to Anna there was a remote possibility that I could soon be able to do this without hurting for dough.

Anna...the girl who had gotten me out of my slump. But helping me with work was only a fraction of what she had done for me. Anna was the one who had brought love back into my life. She was the woman who had played a big part in changing me from a womanizing jerk to a guy who now wanted something more. Anna had helped me realize that not all girls were like Sheila, and that it was time to finally lay that whole nightmare to rest and start using my heart more and my sex drive less. I had to face it. I now wanted more than just a casual fling, more than just meaningless fun-filled nights. I yearned for a real relationship. Anna made me want to be a boyfriend three hundred and sixty-five days a year.

"Jeff?" I heard a voice call out. I looked over and standing above me was my date from a few nights ago.

"Jodi, hi!" I said smiling. I was actually glad to see her. Her petite little body looked so cute in her khaki shorts and her tight pink tank with the words "Rich Bitch" on it.

"How are you?"

I stood up. "I'm great. How are you?"

"Good."

"Are you in the tournament?" I asked her.

"No, just playing hooky from work to enjoy this beautiful day. You too?"

"Actually, I'm working. Covering the tournament for the Pioneer Press."

"Oh, right. I forgot. Well, that's a good thing. You're getting paid to hang out."

"Sort of."

Now we just stood in silence for a moment. Things were a bit awkward, probably because the last time I saw this girl we were about to have sex and then we weren't. At this moment, I could have easily said good-bye, stood up, and moved on, but I liked Jodi a lot and I didn't want things to be weird when we bumped into each other. That's why I decided to break the ice. "Look, Jodi. About the other night…"

"I'm totally cool with it, Jeff."

"Did you really mean it when you said you would like to be friends?" I asked her.

"Yes!"

"Because I would like that too. I mean it."

Jodi smiled, "Friends, then."

"Want to sit down?"

"Sure," she said.

The two of us sat with the sun in our faces watching the games and talking like two old chums. And it felt nice. This was a great girl. Had I been the old Jeff, I would never have given friendship with her a chance. I would have wanted either to sleep with her or nothing at all. But the new me was focused on what was inside of Jodi. I wanted to get to know her better, with no hidden agenda in the back of my mind. I was a stranger to myself and I liked the guy.

A half hour or so later, Jodi told me she had to go. She stood up and said, "Good to see you, Jeff." Then she smiled, kissed my cheek, and was off.

I called to her, "Hey, what's up with the boyfriend?"

Jodi turned around and shouted. "We're back together."

"Really?"

"For now, anyway!" she shouted.

I instantly knew Jodi would never end up with this guy, who she claimed wanted to marry her so badly. I had seen enough relationships in my life to realize, though, that people have to do their own thing and break up for good in their own sweet time. No one can tell them anything. They have to get to that point themselves. Just like Dave.

Hopefully he would soon realize Lori was not the girl for him. I just hoped he could get there without any unpleasant information from me. I was keeping the faith and waiting and being optimistic that he would wake up from his love-struck coma and realize who his girlfriend really was; a cheater, a liar, a nag, and my personal favorite, a psycho. I really hated that chick.

"Good luck!" I shouted to Jodi, who was now about twenty feet away.

She never looked back, she just put her arm up over her head and waved to me.

I smiled and then I had the strangest thought. Jodi was the perfect girl for Dave. What a pleasant surprise she could be, to mend his bruised heart after he ended things with the bitch.

I stayed at the tournament for a few more minutes and then jumped in a cab to meet Frieda back at the office.

"Your problem is pretty simple to solve," I told my cute little client, who looked more excited than kids at *Six Flags* to hear what I had to say, "Simon wants you to have an over-the-top surprise party for his birthday."

"What?" she asked, seeming confused, "That's it?"

"I think so," I said, "I think if you do this for him, that might be all it takes for him to go ring shopping. He really loves you, Frieda."

Upon hearing the strange request, the woman was so happy and so relieved that there was no insurmountable problem, that she jumped up off the couch and hugged me really hard. I found myself laughing and happy. I now thought that maybe helping these women truly was a good thing and that perhaps I should get the hell over the whole manipulation thing.

"Anna is going to help you plan the party," I told her, "She'll make sure it's really special."

"Wonderful!" exclaimed Frieda, "But does she have the time?"

"Let's call her and find out."

I dialed Anna on my cell.

"Hi, Jeff," she answered. God, I loved having this woman in my life.

"Hi."

"How was the volleyball tournament?"

"Good." I suddenly felt like Anna was my girlfriend. After all, wasn't this how serious relationships were? How was your day? Fine, how was *your* day? I had always thought this was so stupid. Now I loved loved loved it! "So…I'm sitting here with Frieda…"

"Oh! Tell her I said hi!"

"Anna says hi."

"Hi, honey!" said Frieda.

"So I told her you would help her plan Simon's fifty-fifth birthday bash. Is that cool?"

"Um, sure, I guess…" she hesitated, "But why me?"

I ignored the question because I wanted Frieda to feel like Anna said "yes" without wavering. "Okay so I'll give you guys each other's numbers and you can talk directly?"

"Sure but I asked you…why me?"

Again I ignored her. "Okay, I'll tell her!" I said, "Bye, Anna!" I hung up and told Frieda that Anna was excited and very much looking forward to helping with the party planning.

"That's sweet," said a gushing Frieda.

Our client left the meeting as happy as could be, but I remained cautious about her situation. I told Frieda as she was walking out that if Simon did not give her a ring within two weeks after the party, we would have to move to our three-step plan, which meant Frieda would have to break up with Simon, go on a date with someone else, and run into him.

"Well, hopefully it won't come to that," she said, "Then again, I wouldn't mind going on a date with a young hottie!"

I didn't tell Frieda this, but no way could we set her up with Mike as the patsy. It would be too far-fetched. We would have to find an older guy to go on a date with her to make Simon jealous. I decided not to worry about it until the time came, if ever.

The second Frieda was out the door, I called my business partner back. "Sorry, I couldn't talk openly with Frieda standing next to me."

"Obviously."

"I chose you to help her with the party for three reasons," I told her, "One, you're a woman. Two, you're in major party planning mode…" I wanted to add, "because of your upcoming wedding to the man you don't love" but I didn't. Instead, I finished, "And three, you're not really pulling your weight and you need to contribute some time and talent to *Hook, Line and Sink Him*."

With this, Anna just started giggling.

"You're laughing because you know it's true."

"Fine. I'll help."

The second I hung up with the party planner, Dave burst into his office, smiling from ear to ear.

"What are you so cheery about?" I asked him, holding my breath that it had nothing to do with his girlfriend.

"Guess what?" he said playfully.

"What?"

"We got another call this afternoon. A girl named Karen saw our flyer at one of the coffee houses. She's coming in tomorrow at 8:15. Cha-ching!"

I rolled my eyes. "I've got to go."

"Where?"

"Date."

"Who is it?"

"Jessica," I answered.

Dave nodded and smiled with approval. He followed me while I walked out of the store and shouted, "It's good to see you moving on!"

"Screw you!" I shouted back with a laugh. Then I waved good-bye, got into a cab, and thought about Dave the entire way home. His excitement about Karen didn't surprise me. My buddy was the definition of dedicated. He would do anything for anyone. His family…his friends…the girls we were trying to help…me, of course…and Lori. Maybe that was his problem. Maybe he was too devoted.

I would have a talk with him about being more selfish and un-committed. Of course, did I really have those qualities anymore? I realized right then how much my life had changed in such a short period of time. With six dogs at home, a business where I helped women, and a girl I would have been willing to die for, I was now anything but selfish and uncommitted. I too was a caring and dedicated man.

## Chapter 24

After my third shower of the day, I headed to El Jardin, home of the killer margarita, to hook up with Jessica. We decided to meet there versus me picking her up because she was coming straight from work and logistically it made more sense. I arrived five minutes early and sat down at the bar. Within a second, the bartender shouted from a few feet away, "What can I get you?"

"A margarita, I guess." When in Rome…

"On the rocks or frozen?"

"On the rocks, no salt."

As he made my drink, I sat there thinking about the evening ahead of me. Jessica was going to walk in here in the next five or ten minutes, and from what I remember she was basically a Barbie doll. We would end up having three things on this particular night: drinks, meaningless conversation, and sex. The thought of Jessica didn't really make my heart stop or anything, but did I mention we were going to have sex? I know I sound like a pig, and maybe I am, but the date with Jessica was about one thing: escape.

I found I was desperate to free myself from obsessing about my business partner/editor/real mother of my current houseguests. The only way for me to get Anna off my mind was to occupy it with someone else. And did I mention I was going to have sex? I needed this and I was going for it. Besides, I wasn't hurting anyone. I would make sure Jessica too had a lovely evening.

Halfway through my margarita, I glanced at my watch. Where was my date? I pulled my cell out of my pocket and checked to see if maybe Jessica called or texted me to tell me she was running late. One missed caller who turned out to be Dave. All of a sudden, I heard the front door of the restaurant open. It's about time, I thought to myself as I turned around to greet Jessica. But it wasn't Jessica. In fact, this was the last person on earth I expected to see.

"Hi!" Anna said, obviously as surprised to see me as I was her.

Our eyes were locked.

"Anna, hi," I smiled.

"Is your name, Jeff?" the bartender interrupted.

I turned around to face him. "Yeah."

He handed me a cordless. "Phone."

Anna stood there watching me. "Hello?" I said into the phone. The call was from Jessica, telling me she could not get away from work and that she had to cancel. As I listened to her explanation (which sounded true, by the way) I continued to stare at Anna, who stood there frozen. I then noticed an older couple walk in. Anna turned around and hugged them. I could tell they were Anna's parents.

"Don't worry about it Jessica...we'll do it another time...okay...yes...no...no problem..." I was now rushing her off the phone unsuccessfully.

I heard Anna's mother say, "Should we get a table?" Anna turned back to face me and again was standing there motionless and unsure of what to do.

"Uh huh...okay...no...I completely understand..." I said to Jessica while smiling at Anna, who was now giggling because she knew the person on the other end of the phone would not shut up.

"Okay, bye," I finally hung up. Thank God the girl got tired of apologizing.

"Jeff, these are my parents," Anna said, "Jane and Tom."

I stood up and shook their hands. "Nice meeting you." They were friendly, warm people who had a nice way about them. I added, "Congratulations on your daughter's engagement."

Their reactions spoke volumes. Jane's smile immediately disappeared. She said, "Thank you." Her tone was cool.

Tom's grin was also gone. "Yeah...thanks," he said almost like he was really saying, "Thanks for rubbing it in."

Everything had just become crystal clear. Chris did not like Anna's parents because Anna's parents hated Chris! Chris had told Dave and me that Anna's parents were "too nice" and "annoyingly nice." I now knew his real reason for disliking them was that he knew they couldn't stand him. It all made sense. Poor Chris. I had no clue why Anna's parents were so anti-Chris, but at the moment, I didn't care. I actually found it kind of funny. Plus, I must confess I was psyched.

I stood up to go. "Well, see you later," I smiled.

"Are you leaving?" asked Anna. Is she disappointed, I wondered. If I knew that for a fact I probably would have started doing cartwheels around the restaurant.

"Yeah, that was my date on the phone. She just cancelled."

Before Anna could even speak, her father exclaimed, "Well, have dinner with us!"

"Dad..." Anna scolded him like a teenager speaks to her parents.

"Thanks anyway, I think I'll just go."

I awkwardly walked past them. As I put my hand on the door to push it open I heard the sweetest voice in the world say, "Jeff...come eat with us." Now I seriously wanted to perform acrobatics.

We got a table and Anna's dad immediately ordered a pitcher of margs. Not five minutes later I found myself in a great conversation with him about how jinxed the Cubs are.

"Think about it, Tom," I said as I poured margaritas into everyone's glasses, "The Cubs have not won a pennant in more than a hundred years. Finally, they are inches away from going to the World Series and some schmo sitting in the stands blows it for them!"

"I have to agree with you, Jeff," Tom replied, "But I find there aren't too many true Cubs fans out there. Cubs spectators seem more interested in partying than they do in the actual team. Now…a White Sox fan…he is a true lover of his White Sox."

"Spoken like a true die hard Sox fan," I said, "Cheers!" I held up my glass and the three other people at the table followed suit. Then we toasted and sipped our drinks. I loved these people. They were anything but annoyingly nice. They were just nice.

"It is such a pleasure to meet a friend of Anna's who is so easy to talk to," said Jane.

Before I could respond, Anna jumped in. "Hey, what about Chris?!"

I had to try not to laugh when I watched Tom's expression. His smile turned into a frown at the mere mention of his future son-in-law. He tried to recover by saying, "We like Chris, honey."

"Yes, of course we do, dear," Jane added unconvincingly.

"Well, I should hope so!" Anna practically shouted, "He's going to be family!" Then she chugged her margarita faster than I have ever seen anyone chug any drink. When she finished gulping, she put her glass down and I immediately picked up the pitcher and poured her another.

While I was pouring, we locked eyes. "Chris is a lucky guy," I said softly.

"Thanks," she replied. A second later, I could have sworn I saw tears well up in Anna's eyes. She looked away quickly and I felt her overwhelming sense of sadness and confusion.

What was so hard about this for me, was that I could tell Anna didn't know how to get out of the engagement. I knew deep down she wanted to break it off but I couldn't say that to her. She had to figure that out on her own. I felt sorry for her, but I was also frustrated. Here was a girl who was engaged to a man she didn't love and she didn't have the guts to just end it.

All of a sudden I realized something else. Anna's scenario was sounding very familiar. She was actually acting a lot like Dave. My buddy was also in an undesirable situation, and he didn't have the balls to break it off either. The two of them were like two peas in a pod, exactly the same. And I loved them both, but they were also both driving me nuts. My two favorite people were both afraid and it pissed me off. But who was I to talk? I was afraid too. I wasn't trying to get out of a relationship, I was actually trying to get *in* one. And since I didn't have the guts to tell Anna how I felt, how was I any different than the two of them?

"So tell us about sports writing, Jeff," said Tom.

"Well, thanks to your daughter, my career is finally taking off." I looked at Anna with gratitude in my eyes and she gave me a sweet smile.

Anna told her parents all about the Lovie Smith article, how it had just come out, and how we were waiting for some type of reader reaction and stuff like that. I sat there munching on chips and salsa, listening.

Then Jane asked, "Is that how you two met? Through work?"

Anna panicked, "Uh…no…we…uh…"

I made the save. "We met through some friends, actually."

Anna breathed a sigh of relief. "Right…through friends."

Now I wanted to have some fun. "Hey, have you guys ever been to Arizona?" I asked Anna's parents.

Anna giggled.

"Once. A long time ago," replied Tom.

"You should take a trip out there," I said, trying not to laugh, "It's really nice!"

Anna's parents began discussing how right I was and how they knew some friends who had just moved out there. As they went on and on, I stared at Anna with a big grin.

"You're crazy," she said in almost a whisper.

I gave her a big wink and a smile, and I was thinking, yeah, crazy about you.

# Chapter 25

The next morning I was still on a high from my fantastic evening with Anna and her parents. I waltzed into *Hook Line and Sink Him*'s office ten minutes late, feeling like I didn't have a care in the world.

"It's 8:25!" shouted Dave, looking at his watch for dramatic effect, "Own a watch?"

"Sorry guys…traffic…" I said with a half-smile. Who cared? Why was Dave so uptight? One word. Lori.

My sweetie, on the other hand, (the one with the terrific folks) was sitting in her spot, smiling. Dave was in his spot, and my spot was empty. Seated across from them on the couch was a woman with an unfriendly look on her face. Physically, she wasn't bad. She probably could have been cute if she chose to wear make-up, get a hair style, and put on something other than a sweatshirt and old Levi's. I immediately thought, "When we talk to her boyfriend, what are the odds he's going to say the same thing?"

"Jeff, this is Karen. Karen, this is our other partner, Jeff," said Anna.

"Hi," I shook Karen's hand and tried to be as courteous and non-judgmental as possible, given the fact that something about this chick was seriously rubbing me the wrong way.

"Hello," Karen said in a very businesslike tone.

I sat down.

"Should we get started?" Dave asked. I suddenly felt like I was at a fraternity chapter meeting.

"Okay," Karen said.

"How may we help you?" Anna asked with sincerity.

Karen did something at this point that made me want to smack her. She sighed heavily as if she was annoyed by the question. Then she replied, "Well, obviously I have a boyfriend and I want to get married."

"What do you think is holding your boyfriend back?" Dave asked her.

Now it seemed as if we had stumped her. "Uh…I…uh…I don't know."

"Well, what's your hunch?" I asked.

"I really don't know. So tell me how this works."

"Here's what we do," Dave began, "We somehow run into your boyfriend and start up a conversation, without him knowing you've hired us, of course."

"Then we try to find out exactly what is holding him back. We aim to get specific reasons why he doesn't want to make the commitment," added Anna.

Dave finished off with his canned pitch, "After that, we guide you in our three-step program, which we will explain when it gets closer."

It was my turn. "We charge $500 up front and $2000 if you get engaged within six months."

Dave asked for the order. "Is this something you feel you would like to try?

We were all looking at Karen, who looked a bit like a deer in headlights.

Anna comforted her by saying, "I know it seems a little bit scary, but our method has already worked on two couples. You have to trust us."

"Can I ask you something?" asked Karen.

"Sure," Dave replied.

"What if I don't want the first part? I mean, what if I want to skip the talking to my boyfriend part? Can I just hear about the three-step program?"

"If you really want it to work," Dave explained, "you need to trust us and let us implement the entire program."

Now Karen started getting aggressive. "Look, it's my money. I'm the customer and I don't want you speaking to my boyfriend. I just want to hear what I can do to get him to marry me!"

Anna stood up and went over to the couch to sit next to her. She took Karen's hand and spoke softly. "Karen, I know this is a difficult and frustrating time. I was in your same position just a few weeks ago. Let us help you." I watched Anna with admiration. She had so much patience, when all I wanted to do was kick this miserable woman out of our office.

"You can," Karen replied sarcastically, "You can help me by realizing that I am the customer and that you should do what I want and just tell me the plan."

I finally couldn't take it anymore. "Fine," I said loudly, "Do what she wants. Tell her everything we do." Then I looked right at the witch and said, "Price is still the same."

"Fine," she said in her high and mighty tone.

"Karen, may I ask how you heard of us?" Anna asked.

"I saw your ad in that little coffee place--the one on Webster."

Anna responded, "I see."

I made a mental note to go in there and take our flyer down immediately.

"I've got to go," I said as I rose and headed toward the door, "I have to work." I had no interest in hanging around this horrible woman any longer.

"I have to go, too," Anna said, standing up. "Frieda and I have some appointments with caterers for Simon's party."

"I'll stay with Karen and tell her about the program, and about Mike." Dave said trying to be customer focused and cheerful.

"What?" asked Karen, "Who's Mike?"

"Mike is our friend who we would set you up with on a date."

"I don't get it."

"Well, we find out where your boyfriend is going and then we send you into the place with Mike to make him think you met someone else."

Karen seemed intrigued and happy, finally. She was smiling.

"Good luck, Karen," Anna said politely, "I hope you get all the information you need to get your guy."

"I'm sure I will," Karen answered sarcastically.

I didn't bother to say good-bye to our client from hell. I simply walked out the door, feeling relief that I would never have to see this person again. Something was bugging me, though. It almost felt like Karen was playing a part, like she was acting. Was she really here legitimately? Or was something going on that none of us had a clue about? I thought about charging back into the meeting and telling Dave not to reveal anything else but I felt maybe I was just being paranoid.

"Are you okay?" Anna asked, once we were outside. She must have sensed my apprehension.

"Did you feel like something weird was going on with that girl?"

"What do you mean?"

"I just think something isn't right. I can't put my finger on it."

"Here is how I feel. I think Karen is a very unhappy woman. And--like everyone else who comes in to see us, she's desperate."

"I guess you're right."

"Don't worry," she said with a smile, her eyes sparkling as they always did, making my heart pound like only a pussy-whipped dude's can. "So, where are you headed?" Anna asked.

It made me feel good to think she actually cared. "Home. I thought I'd take the dogs for a long walk. It's such a nice day."

"That sounds awesome. I wish I could do that."

"Why don't you?"

"What? Blow off work?"

"Yeah."

Anna looked at me and didn't say anything for a moment. Then she smiled and blurted out, "Okay! I think I will! Work can wait, right? I can't remember the last time I played hooky."

I smiled, "Good."

We went back to my place, and of course when the dogs saw Anna, they went nuts. After she fussed over them for a few minutes, we packed some doggie snacks and a couple of beach towels, rounded up the gang, and headed to the beach. The walk there took around twenty minutes, thanks to P.J, who took two poops, and Passion, who of course had to sniff everything in sight.

Once we got onto the sand, Anna and I took off the dogs' leashes and let them run around while we sat on the beach towels, enjoying the warm sun on our faces. We talked for a long time about writing, why we were writers, and who motivated us to become writers. I told Anna about how my mother had actually been the driving force in my majoring in journalism. Bringing up mom led to Anna's inquisition about my family. She wanted to know everything, so I told her.

I shared (surprisingly with ease) that my father had left us when I was nine and that my mother was a high school English teacher who also worked on Saturdays as a receptionist at a physician's office to earn extra money.

"My mom died a few years ago of Alzheimer's," I told her.

Anna looked at me, her big brown eyes filled with sympathy, and said, "I bet she was a good woman."

"She really was," I said with a sad smile. In an attempt to lighten things up, I added, "I think she was a big fan of *Today's Chicago Woman.*"

Anna giggled and then said, "Well, then...she would have been very proud of her son when she read this month's issue."

"Right," I smiled.

"Jeff..." Anna asked, capturing my attention.

"Yeah?"

"Do you think you'll ever get married? Have kids?"

I didn't have to think about my answer for very long. "It's funny. If you'd have asked me that question a month ago...I'd have said no way. But now...I would say...someday..." I looked out over huge Lake Michigan and finished, "I hope someday..."

Anna looked right at me. "Listen to me," she said firmly, "Only you have control as to whether or not you'll get what you want. Take the crappy hand you were dealt...your dad, and the Sheila cards, and get rid of them. Start fresh. Have the guts to believe in yourself as a good person...a worthy person...someone who can have the life he really wants. You deserve love...and to be loved."

It took everything in my power at this moment not to grab this woman and tell her how I felt about her. Instead, I took a deep breath and replied, "Thank you Anna."

She smiled shyly.

"So, let me guess. You had a really good childhood."

She smiled, "Guilty."

"You can tell." Now I looked straight into her eyes. "That makes me really happy."

"I had so much fun at dinner last night," she responded.

"Me too," I said with a smile. "Your parents are really nice people."

"I appreciate you saying that."

"I'm not saying it to be nice," I defended. "I really mean it."

"I know. I guess I'm just being sensitive because of Chris and everything. He and my parents just don't click. Never will."

"That must bother you."

"It does. A lot."

"But not a deal breaker when it comes to marrying Chris?"

Before Anna could answer, Poo-poo came over to her and jumped in her lap. "Hi, sweetie!" she said, just before kissing her dog on the lips and hugging him. She turned to me. "Can we not talk about it?"

"We can definitely not talk about it," I smiled, "But if you change your mind, I'm here."

Do you know how you know you're in love? This is a question I'd been wondering my whole life. Sitting here on the beach with Anna, I finally figured out the answer, so here goes. If the person you think you may love has a problem, all you want to do is take it from them and solve it or get rid of it. In other words, you want to take their pain, you want to take their suffering, you want to take the burden, and you want to carry it yourself, no matter how much it costs or hurts. That's what I wanted to do for Anna.

More specifically, what I wanted to do was to get into Anna's body, break up with Chris, and declare my love for me. Does that make sense? There was one small problem. I knew Anna did not love Chris, but the question remained, did she love me? She did kiss me back for ten seconds. Then again, she told me the next morning she wanted to forget about it. Nonetheless, here she was in the middle of a workday sitting on a beach with me.

All of a sudden, Anna blurted out, "I know my parents wish I was marrying you instead of Chris."

"It doesn't matter what your parents want, Anna. Only what you want. Do you love this guy or not? Because in case you forgot, backing out of the wedding is definitely an option."

Anna did not respond right away. She carefully thought about her next words, which turned out to be the kindest I ever heard. "I think you're the best friend I've made in a really long time, Jeff."

I smiled and then Anna held my hand. We sat there on that quiet beach with the sun beaming down. Neither one of us had any desire to speak for the next few minutes. All I could think was, this beautiful woman holding my hand was my friend, too. But she was also the love of my life and I had to do something to get her. I suddenly felt like one of our clients. Not that I wanted to marry Anna at this very moment, but I wanted her to be mine. Desperately. And I would do anything to get her. Since tricking and manipulating her in typical Hook, Line and Sink Him style was not an option, I realized I had to be honest with her and I had to let her know how I felt. I told myself to go for it. Then I took a deep breath and spoke.

"Anna, can I tell you something?"

"Sure," she smiled. Just then her cell phone rang. "Hold on," she said putting her index finger up, "I just want to make sure this isn't the office."

She let go of my hand and pulled her cell out of her bag. She seemed surprised after looking at caller ID. "Hi, honey."

Now I knew it was Chris. I had to have had the worst timing in the history of any declaration of love.

Anna continued talking to Chris. "Wow! Really? That sounds amazing!"

I now knew the conversation I wanted to have was not going to happen today.

Anna mouthed, "Sorry" to me and listened to the rest of what Chris was saying. "Okay, perfect! I'll see you tonight. Thanks, honey…I'm excited!"

She smacked her cell shut and told me the news. "Chris just surprised me and booked a weekend in Cabo," she said matter-of-factly, "We leave tonight." Anna spoke in the same tone she would have if she was saying, "That was work. They need me to come in." For a girl going on a weekend getaway with her fiancé, Anna did not seem very charged. I had a feeling that much like me, Anna would have preferred to sit on the beach like this forever.

I mustered up as much enthusiasm as I could. "That's great!"

"I'm sorry, Jeff. You were just about to say something. Go ahead. You have my full attention."

Oh, shit! What was I supposed to say now? I'd be damned if I was going to spill my guts right before Anna was leaving for a romantic weekend getaway with Chris.

"I...uh..."

She was smiling at me, waiting for something to come out of my mouth.

I continued, "The thing is..."

All of a sudden my cell rang. There is a God, I thought. I pulled out my cell and didn't even look to see who it was. Whoever was calling just saved my ass big time. "Yeah..." I answered.

"Dude, get this. We have two new clients coming in on Monday morning. One is a referral from Frieda, the other got us off our flyer."

I smiled as my savior and best friend went on and on about how much money we were going to make and how much work we had ahead of us.

"Thanks for the good news, Dave," I said, "Can I call you later? I'm on the beach with the dogs."

"Sure." Then he sang the theme song from "The Apprentice." "Money, money, money, money...money..." he crooned. Then he hung up.

I couldn't help but laugh.

"What was that all about?" Anna asked with a chuckle.

"That was Dave. We have two new clients coming in next week."

"Really? Who are they?"

I stood up. "Let's get going. I'll tell you on our walk back."

Now Anna stood up too. "Jeff?"

"Yeah?"

"I'm still waiting. Do you want to say something?"

"You know, Anna, I was just going to tell you..." I had to think of something. Think! Think! I told myself. Then I came up with something genius, although I really did mean it. "No matter who you marry, you'll make a great wife."

With this comment, Anna spread her arms out as wide as she could and wrapped them around me so tight that I felt like I was being squeezed. While she hugged me, I couldn't help but feel proud of my recovery, especially because what I said was sincere. Anna would make a great wife. Unfortunately though, probably not *my* wife.

# Chapter 26

The next morning was Saturday, and while my honey was probably on a beach having bad sex with Chris, I was headed as usual to Dave's store. Bagels in hand and dogs at home, I walked in expecting to have some time to hang out with my buddy and talk. Hopefully, Dave wouldn't bring up Lori. Hopefully, Dave wouldn't bring up Anna either. With any luck, current sporting events and only things that wouldn't cause any type of emotional reaction for either of us would be the topics of discussion this morning.

I would do my best to steer the conversation in this direction, but knowing Dave, three minutes into my visit he would use the "L" word (Lori). Even worse, it was only a matter of time before my buddy would grill me about Anna, and I was dreading it. Dave wouldn't ask me twenty questions, he would ask me fifty.

When I opened the door and entered *Be a Sport*, I was surprised to see him standing at the counter in a deep conversation with a guy who was leaning against a display counter a few feet away. I quickly surmised that the guy was a customer, because he had a bag in his hand and had obviously just bought something. But because of the way they were talking, I wondered if Dave knew this guy already.

"Jeff, what's up, buddy?" Dave said.

"Hi," I answered. Then I threw him one of the Einstein's bags as I walked toward him.

He caught it. "Thanks, man," he smiled. He turned to the guy and said, "Joe…this is Jeff. Jeff…Joe."

Joe eagerly stepped over to me and shook my hand. "Good to meet you."

"You, too," I smiled.

"You're not going to believe this one," Dave said to me, "Joe is in the exact same situation as me. His girlfriend wants to get married…he doesn't."

"Sounds like there's an epidemic going around Chicago," I joked.

Dave burst out laughing while Joe chuckled a little bit. He then continued what he must have been telling Dave before I interrupted their talk. "So Michelle asked me the other day…straight out…if I'd prefer Maui or Aruba for our honeymoon."

"No, way…" said Dave.

"Swear to God," Joe continued, "And I'm like honey, I'd prefer if you'd back the fuck off and let me…the *guy*…get down on one knee and ask you to marry me before you start planning where we're going after our wedding…which isn't even in existence yet and may never be…since you're completely turning me off right now!"

Joe was hilarious. Both Dave and I were cracking up. I couldn't believe this guy. This was good. Maybe his attitude would rub off on Dave.

Dave responded to Joe, "Dude, did you really say that?"

"Not those exact words," Joe chuckled, "Pretty close, though. I don't think I said 'fuck.'"

"Well, I wish I had the guts to say that to Lori. She actually booked a band for some weekend next July for us."

"Dude…you better nip it in the bud," said Joe, "Otherwise, next thing you know you'll be walking down the aisle in a tux wondering what the fuck just happened and how you got there."

I wanted to hug this guy. How did I get so lucky to have such a great guy land in *Be a Sport*? This guy was really giving Dave the talk he desperately needed.

"So mind if I ask you...why don't you want to marry Lori?" Joe asked, "What's holding you back?"

Now I had déjà-vu big time. I felt like Joe was me and Dave was Chris or Sam or Simon or the dentist I was scheduled to meet with the next week (Jamie's boyfriend). It was weird but interesting, because now I wanted to hear what Dave would say.

He didn't answer right away. He thought about it for a moment. Then he looked at me. I was so nervous, I had to stop chewing my bagel with the veggie schmear. When Dave finally answered, I wanted to throw up my bagel with the veggie schmear.

He took a deep breath, looked at Joe, and said, "I think Lori's cheating on me." Then he looked at me.

I froze while Joe said, "Oh man, that sucks. I don't even know what to say."

"Neither do I," I finally managed, "How did you find out?"

Dave looked sadly at the ground and said softly, "I didn't. I just had a hunch. I mean, I'm her boyfriend. I can tell."

"Look..." I began but Dave interrupted me.

"Jeff, I don't want to know any details. Just keep it to yourself. I want to talk to Lori first. I'll let you know when I want to talk about what you know."

"Anything you say," I told Dave.

Joe walked up to the counter and shook Dave's hand. "Listen, Dave...I hope it works out for you...either way. You seem like a great guy and you don't deserve some bitch cheating on you."

Dave smiled sadly and shook Joe's hand. "Thanks, man. Hey, come in here anytime. You can have my friend discount...twenty off on anything you see."

"Will do," replied Joe, "I have my eye on that Gayle Sayers helmet, which I may need the next time the subject of marriage comes up with Michelle and me. If she decides to beat the crap out of me, at least I'll be protected."

Dave and I couldn't help but crack up. "Joe, great to meet you, buddy," I said, shaking his hand, "Call the store if you ever want to hang out with us."

"Definitely," he said, "See you."

The second Joe was gone, I looked at Dave and said, "Dude…I'm really sorry."

"What are you sorry for, Jeff?" he asked, "You didn't do anything wrong. You did everything you were supposed to. I told you this before. I just have to deal with this my own way. Let me talk to Lori."

"Cool," was all I could say.

Before I knew it, Dave moved onto another uncomfortable subject. "So okay, I've held my tongue long enough. Are you going to tell me about Anna in this lifetime or what?"

"I wish Joe was still here," I joked.

"Joe's gone and if you don't start talking, I'm going to beat the shit out of you."

"I'm scared," I said with a chuckle.

"Shut up Jeff and tell me what's going on."

I sat there unable to finish my breakfast and completely incapable of putting all of my feelings into words.

So Dave said only what was necessary. "Just tell me…are you in love with her?"

I looked up at him and answered, "Like you can't believe."

Dave gave me a sympathy smile and a huge pat on the back. We ate in silence for a few moments.

"Can I tell you something that may make you feel better?"

"Sure…"

"Liz told me the other day that Anna told her she had sex with Chris and pretended he was Brad Pitt."

I chuckled. "Really?"

"Yeah."

"That does make me feel better, actually."

Dave gave me a very serious look and said, "Jeff, you have to tell her how you feel."

"I will…"

"No, I mean soon. What are you waiting for?"

"The right time."

"Don't wait too long," said Dave, "She just ordered her wedding invitations."

"You think I look anything like Brad Pitt?"

"No…I'd say more like Ben Affleck."

I was pleased with that response.

"What about me?" asked Dave, "Who do I look like?"

Giving my best friend shit was one of my favorite things to do, just because I loved the guy. "George," I replied.

"Clooney?" he said, his voice filled with hope.

"Costanza."

"George Costanza?!"

I burst out laughing.

"Fuck off," Dave said with a laugh.

# Chapter 27

The following week was completely nuts. Monday morning, two new potential clients visited "Hook, Line and Sink Him" and surprisingly both were guys. The first prospect was Kyle Henricks, thirty-four, gay and very upset that his boyfriend of seven years did not want to marry him until gay marriage in Illinois became legal.

"He knows that's never going to happen!" cried Kyle, "All those damn Republicans!" Kyle reminded me of a soap opera star. Based on his good looks and colorful expressive personality, he probably would have done well in that field. "Please help me," he continued.

Anna, with her sun-kissed Cabo face, asked, "Well, I have to ask you, Kyle, what is your definition of marriage, since you can't have a legal license anyway?"

"I want a wedding. I want a huge effing wedding with flowers and a wedding party and two hundred guests who can witness us exchanging our vows. I don't care about a piece of paper. I want a commitment in public."

"I can work with this. I really don't see any difference, do you guys?" Dave asked us.

"I'm fine with it," I said. I liked Kyle and I didn't believe *Hook, Line and Sink Him* should discriminate. I believed we should manipulate and plan and scheme and fool and trick people of any race, religion, ethnic background, gender, and sexual orientation. So after we got a bit more information, we signed Kyle on as an official client.

Our next appointment was Eric Malone. Eric was straight, but if someone put Kyle and Eric next to each other in a room and asked me which one was gay, I would probably have chosen Eric. He had a very feminine way about him. Eric was one of those straight guys who everyone thought was gay, based on the way he dressed, his mannerisms, his love of shopping, his familiarity with brand names like Jimmy Choo and True Religion, and the fact that he had credit cards from Neiman Marcus and Pottery Barn. He also waited in line for eight hours to get tickets to The Spice Girls reunion tour.

Eric came to us because his on and off again girlfriend of two years refused to get engaged to him. "She says she just isn't ready," he said. I was actually in the middle of a yawn when Eric dropped the bomb. "But I really love Jodi..."

Jodi? Pizza place Jodi? As my business partners sat there with their heads nodding and listening to Eric go on and on, I was suddenly in panic mode. If Jodi was the Jodi I had gone on a date with two weeks earlier, I already knew all the answers! I knew precisely why Jodi did not want to marry Eric. There were several reasons. One, he called her "honey bunny." Two, he wasn't into sports. Three, he always insisted they hold each other for at least an hour after sex. There were a few more, but these were the big ones that Jodi had mentioned the night we went to dinner. I had to make sure Jodi was Jodi, so I asked Eric, "Tell me...what does Jodi do?"

Eric replied proudly, "She's a stockbroker for Morgan Stanley." Bingo.

"Financial advisor," I instinctively corrected.

The second it came out of my mouth, I realized I may be blowing my cover, and everyone in the room was giving me weird looks.

To save myself, I added, "Isn't that what they call themselves? I mean, I'm just guessing." Luckily, no one thought twice.

This would be such easy cash. I didn't even have to do anything. There would be no finding Jodi and pretending to meet her by chance. It had already happened. I just couldn't let Eric know. Eric would have to tell me where to find Jodi. Then I would tell him I went there and met her. Meanwhile, I would do no such thing. Great, I told myself, Now I was not only manipulating clients' spouses, I was being dishonest to the clients themselves. But who cared? We were still going to give Eric what he wanted. Plus, we were going to make some easy money.

"I think we can help you, Eric," I said. My partners agreed, and believe it or not, Eric told us we could find Jodi at noon at guess where. The pizza place.

"I'll be there today at noon," I said, smiling as I took the $500 check out of Eric's hand.

After he left, Anna and Dave were both suspicious. "What's up with you?" Dave asked me with a smirk.

"What do you mean?"

"You seem very into this case," Anna answered.

"Well," I said in an extremely cocky manner, "It just so happens that I know Jodi."

"What?" exclaimed Anna.

Dave picked up on it right away. "Is she the same Jodi you went on a date with last week?"

"You went on a date?" Anna acted almost hurt by the news. Miss Engaged seemed a bit territorial when it came to me, which made me realize there was justice in the world. Maybe a good dose of old fashioned jealousy was exactly what Anna needed to get her to cross over the line and admit her feelings for me.

"Yeah. We only went out once," I said with a smile. I wanted to add, "Don't freak out. Say the word and I'll never date another woman ever again." I didn't, though.

"Oh," she responded, "Was it fun? I mean…is she nice? Is she pretty?"

"Both," I said. This was great! Anna really cared! I couldn't feel sorry for her, though, because less than forty-eight hours earlier she'd been sipping margaritas and having sex with Brad Pitt.

"Great," she answered in her very bad acting voice.

"So when we went out, Jodi told me she had just broken up with Eric because he wanted to get married and she didn't. She even gave me the reasons she doesn't want to marry him!"

"What are they?" asked Dave.

"He calls her honey-bunny…"

"Yuck!" said Dave.

"He makes her cuddle after sex…"

Dave had a disgusted look on his face while Anna asked, "Is that bad?"

I finished, "And…he's not into sports."

"And she is?" asked my buddy, the ultimate sports lover.

"Yeah. Actually, Dave, I was thinking you and Jodi might hit it off."

"Dave has a girlfriend, Jeff."

"Yes," said Dave, "Thank you, Anna." He turned to me. "I have a girlfriend, dickhead."

"Sorry," I said in a cynical voice.

"So, since you know the reasons already…are you still going to the pizza place?" asked Anna.

"What's the point?" I responded, "Let's wait a couple days…get Eric back in here…tell him the reasons, and then set him up for the big date."

Dave added, "With…"

All of a sudden, my buddy and I, at the exact same time started to laugh.

"What's so funny?" asked our female business partner.

"Perfect…" said Dave.

I nodded in full agreement.

"What's perfect?" Anna asked.

I looked at her and said, "You're going on the date with Eric."

"What? No way."

"Yes!" exclaimed Dave, "You're our female Mike!"

"I'm not doing that."

"Anna...you are part of this business. You owe it to your partners," I said with a chuckle.

I walked out of Dave's store smiling. *Hook, Line and Sink Him* did have its positive moments. It was fun sometimes. Plus, some clients really were benefiting from our services. Not Anna, and certainly not that Karen chick, but Liz was still happy, from what I had heard, and Frieda would no doubt be engaged very soon. But something was a little bothersome about Eric and Jodi. Jodi was my friend. How could I do this to her?

After a quick trip into Starbucks, where I got a double shot grande skim latte, I finally won the argument with myself. Jodi really did care for Eric. After all, they had been together on and off for two years. That had to mean something. So if I could help change him for her, would I be doing such a bad thing? Satisfied that I had won my own case, I sipped happily and headed to the bank to deposit the two checks from the morning's business.

That afternoon, while on the couch watching ESPN, Passion on my lap, of course, I got a call from Anna requesting my immediate presence at the Casino Club, a posh and very prestigious men's club. Apparently, Frieda had decided to have Simon's surprise bash there, and for unknown reasons, the women wanted me there to help them make some decisions.

"Anna, party planning is an area in which I clearly have no expertise. Trust me...if you're going to ask me to choose between grilled sea bass and filet mignon...I'm going to tell you I prefer a good hot dog and some fries."

Anna giggled, "Just come here, Jeff. We need a guy's opinion for a few things. After all, the party *is* for a guy..." She finished her sentence in a whisper, "And all the guys who work here are gay."

"See you in a few," I said before hanging up. Only my Anna could drag me away from ESPN to go meet with a caterer and make decisions regarding tablecloths, chair covers and party favors.

I spent the entire cab ride trying to remember a name, the name of a girl I attended some charity ball function with at the Casino Club years earlier. For the life of me, I could not recall this chick's name. It was driving me crazy. Sandra…Shawna…no…that wasn't it.

I was surprisingly taken aback when I walked into the empty round ballroom of the club. Either I was really drunk or just plain oblivious the last time I'd been in this room for the charity ball with what's her name, because I didn't remember how beautiful and grand and spectacular it was. The walls were painted forest green with gold trim, giving it a dark, elegant supper club feel. It had a big, round, vaulted ceiling with several gold chandeliers hanging from it. Gold pillars stood all around the room, spread out about every six feet or so. And in the back was a big stage, obviously for bands or other performances, whose backdrop consisted of dark red satin curtains trimmed with gold fringe, tied back with thick gold ropes and framed on top, with huge valences. I'm not a party planning expert, but I had to admit this was an amazing, take your breath away kind of ambiance, and absolutely perfect for Simon's shindig.

"Jeff!" Frieda called to me from the other side of the room, "Come here! We need you!" She and Anna and some guy were standing over a table and looking down at something that I assumed was a menu.

I walked over to them, and sure enough they were deciding whether they should go with passed hors d'oeuvres or a few appetizer tables. "What do you think?" Frieda asked me.

"I say go with the tables. More food." When I looked up at the guy, who I surmised was the chef, he looked thoroughly disgusted by me. I thought it was kind of funny.

"So what do you think of this place?" Anna asked me, "Isn't it perfect?"

"Yes, Anna…" I said, looking into her sparkling eyes, "It's perfect."

We held our gaze for a few moments, interrupted by our cute client, who seemed bubbly, happy, and very enthusiastic about throwing the man she loved a fabulous party. "Anna dear...you should have your wedding here." End of gaze. Anna quickly looked away from me, almost in shame. "Don't you agree?" Frieda asked me.

"Actually, Anna's wedding is going to be at the Ritz Carlton," I responded. Then I looked at the unhappy bride-to-be. "Right?"

"Yeah," she said absentmindedly. Then she turned to the chef. "So let's go over the dinner menu."

"I have a great idea for Jeff," exclaimed Frieda, "Let's let him do the wine tasting."

"I love you, Frieda," I said cheerfully, "I'd be happy to help." Again, the chef had a look on his face as if he was appalled by my lack of culinary sophistication. And again, I found humor in it.

"Let me take you back to the kitchen," the chef said to me in a condescending voice, "Andrew has the wines."

He looked at the girls, "I'll be back, ladies."

"Sure..." said Anna.

"Thanks, dude..." I said to the chef. Then I actually patted the guy on the back, and believe it or not that got him to crack a little smile. Suddenly, as I was walking out of the grand ballroom, it hit me. "Sierra!" I shouted.

"What?" Anna shouted.

"Sierra! That was her name!"

"Whose name?"

I chuckled. "Forget it. It doesn't matter."

Minutes later I was standing in front of a chopping block sampling wines and enjoying myself perhaps a little too much. I decided to text Dave to rub it in, but when I reached for my cell in my pocket, I realized I'd left it back in the other room.

"Be right back," I said to Andrew, "I forgot my phone."

When I reached the ballroom, I heard my girls, Frieda, an older, wise woman and Anna, Miss issue-ridden chick who had no clue how to get out of her majorly undesirable situation, talking. I don't know what made me do it, but I decided to eavesdrop. I ducked behind a pillar and listened to their conversation.

"I'm so excited about this...you have no idea!" Frieda gushed to Anna.

"I'm glad for you."

"Simon is going to go crazy when he walks in here! I can't wait to see the expression on his face!"

Anna had a sad look on her face. "Frieda, can I ask you something?"

"Sure, honey."

"How did you know Simon was the one?"

Now Frieda caught on. I could tell she hadn't sensed Anna's doubt about her engagement until now. She answered, "Well, you know I'm divorced."

"Right..."

"So I already made one mistake...and I would never marry someone I wasn't a hundred and ten percent sure about because the last thing I ever want is to be divorced again."

"I can understand that."

Frieda then shifted gears and asked her marriage coach a startling question. "How's the sex with Chris?"

"What?!" Anna responded.

"Am I getting too personal? I'm sorry. It's none of my business."

It took everything I could not to burst out laughing, and at the same time the anticipation of hearing how Anna would respond was killing me. Just like she told Liz, would she tell Frieda about Brad Pitt?!

"No," said Anna, "It's just..."

"What?" Frieda responded, "You think older people don't have sex?"

"I didn't mean..."

"The thing is," Frieda said proudly, "people my age actually have better sex than younger people, and the only reason I know that is from personal experience." She put her arm around Anna and continued, "See...when you get to a bit older, you don't look as good...things start to hurt you all the time...you start to worry about getting cancer and other diseases...and death...and those are the things that aren't so good. But what's great about aging is that you become really smart. You know what you want and it's crystal clear. I know for a fact, with absolutely no uncertainty, that Simon is the man I want to grow old with. I mean *really* old with."

Anna attention was captivated beyond belief, her wide eyes fixated on this woman she now looked up to a great deal.

Frieda went on, "And the sex...well...I think when you're older, you're less inhibited...more relaxed...more sure of yourself. You make love not just with each other's bodies but with your minds and your souls. The whole experience is much richer in so many ways. And that makes the physical part incredible."

It was at this moment Anna dropped the bomb. "Sex with Chris is really bad."

I actually had to put my hand over my mouth, so as not to gasp, revealing to the ladies that their nosy wine taster was hunched behind a big pole and intently listening to every word of their very private chat.

Frieda lifted up Anna's chin and said, "Who's the guy who really loves you for *you*? Who's your best friend? Who's the guy who makes your heart stop when he walks into a room?" Tears welled up in Anna's eyes.

Please say Jeff...please say Jeff, I prayed silently.

"He's the one you should be with," said Frieda, "Then...I guarantee...no questions asked...you will have good sex."

"What am I going to do, Frieda?" she asked, a tear rolling down her cheek.

I prayed again, Please say "Tell Jeff how you feel" Please say "Tell Jeff how you feel".

Frieda hugged Anna and said with a sad smile, "Only you can answer that question."

## Chapter 28

Anna didn't even say hello when she called me the next day. After I answered the phone, she said, "We're looking for a feature piece and we want to call it 'He Loves Sports More Than He Loves Me.'"

My response: "That is the gayest thing I've ever heard." I have to admit, though, that I was extremely psyched because I now knew my Lovie Smith piece was getting great reader feedback, and that the magazine editors wanted more of me and my writing.

"Well, if it's too gay for you," Anna responded playfully, "I'll get one of our other freelance writers who are lined up to write for us to work on it for eighteen cents a word."

"You mean I got a raise already?! Three whole cents a word?!"

"Do you want the job or not?" she asked.

"Yes!"

Anna told me I was to interview couples whose relationships were being plagued by the guy's obsession with watching sports, so I began doing some preliminary research on the internet and making a list of people to interview. As I surfed the net, Passion on my lap of course, my cell phone rang again.

"Sup?" I answered.

"Lori broke up with me."

I thought I had heard wrong, so I stopped everything I was doing except for rubbing Passion's tummy. "What?"

Very slowly, Dave repeated, "Lori…broke…up…with…me."

Now there was silence for about ten seconds. Was Dave waiting for me to say something? What I wanted to say was, "Great! Congratulations! Your life just got a million times better!"

"Hello?" Dave said.

"I'm here."

"She said she can't wait anymore for me to marry her."

"Oh."

"What am I going to do?"

"I'm sorry, buddy. I know you must feel like shit. But, maybe this is for the best. I mean, Lori does have a point."

"You're taking *her* side?"

"Dude…how can you ask me that? You're my best friend."

"Look…I've got to go…I'm going to close the store and go talk to her."

"Are you crazy? Listen…don't do anything stupid. Let's go out tonight and talk about it. We'll do sushi or something."

"Okay," Dave said sadly.

"Dave…" I said like I was trying to talk someone into not jumping off a building, "Seriously…don't do anything today. Just let it be. We'll talk about it tonight, okay?"

Dave didn't answer me.

"Okay?" I repeated.

"Yeah, okay," he finally said.

When I hung up the phone, I felt extremely happy. Dave was rid of the psycho cheating bitch from hell! He was free! I felt sorry for him and I knew that he was hurting. I couldn't help but think, though, that Lori had just given him a huge gift in the long run. She had made it possible for Dave to meet the girl of his dreams. A girl like Jodi, perhaps. Although, thanks to me, Jodi was probably going to be engaged in the next few weeks. In any event, this whole nightmare relationship had come to an end. At dinner tonight I would talk to Dave and set him straight.

And eight hours later that is exactly what I was trying to do over some California rolls. Unfortunately, though, my buddy was a wreck. I was surprised when I realized how devastated he really was. Didn't he feel any sense of relief? After all, he knew Lori was cheating. He had come out and told me that. Wasn't he happy now that he had an easy out? Not in the least. He couldn't eat anything, he ordered a diet coke, and he was the most quiet I had seen him since the day he told me his parents were getting divorced ten years earlier.

"Dude, tell me what I can do to make you feel better," I said, "Want to hook up with a chick or something? I can make it happen."

"Nah...thanks anyway."

"Want to go somewhere this weekend? Vegas maybe?"

"No, thanks."

We sat in silence for awhile while I ate and Dave pretty much stared into space. But after a few minutes, I couldn't take it anymore.

"Dave...listen to me..." I began, "You and Lori, you had a good thing. But the best part of it ended a long time ago and over the past year or so, all you two did was argue. She wanted to marry you and you didn't want that."

"I didn't want that *yet*," Dave defended, "I wanted it eventually."

I put my chopsticks down. "I don't think you did."

"Are you saying you don't think I ever wanted to marry her?"

"That's what I'm saying."

"You have no clue."

"Fine. I have no clue. But let's forget about all that for a second and remember what you told Joe. Do you not recall telling him that you knew Lori was cheating on you? How about that?"

"Well, I just suspect it. I don't have proof."

I couldn't stand it anymore. "Well, I do!" I said almost shouting. People at neighboring tables began to stare.

"Don't tell me!" Dave shouted, "I don't want to hear it!"

"Why?"

"Because you have never liked Lori and whatever you have to say is going to be skewed."

"Listen to yourself!" I shouted, "Can you say denial? Why don't you want to see the writing on the wall? I'm looking out for you. I'm trying to help you, damn it! You're my best friend!"

The second the words "best friend" came out of my mouth, I noticed two people walk into the restaurant out of the corner of my eye. I looked up and my jaw dropped. Walking to a table right by ours were none other than Lori and some guy I had never seen before. Dave must have noticed that my mouth was wide open, because he followed my gaze. In an instant, I watched my buddy go from pissed at me to suicidal. I literally thought the guy was going to start sobbing right then and there.

Now Lori saw us. She looked surprised, but something told me she wasn't. After all, Lori knew this sushi place was Dave's favorite. If she had to go on a date, why would she choose here? "Hi, guys," Lori said sadly.

"Are you fucking kidding me, Lori?" Dave practically shouted.

"Dave..." Lori said calmly, "We broke up."

"I'm going to sit at our table and leave you guys so you can talk," the date said.

"Good idea," I responded.

"I'll be over in a minute," Lori smiled to him.

The guy walked away.

"We've been broken up for like seven hours! You're already dating?"

"Look...I'm sorry this happened. I didn't think you would be here tonight or I never would have come."

I couldn't help butting in. "But you knew there was a chance."

Lori gave me a dirty look.

"I don't want to hurt you, Dave. I love you. And this guy...it's nothing serious. He's just a friend."

"Have you been seeing him behind my back?" Dave asked.

"Of course not!" she defended. Then she said something so unbelievably unethical I couldn't even deal. "Dave...I swear to God...I would *never, ever* cheat on you! You have my word. *Never*...when we were together...was I *ever* with another man."

I stood up and pointed my finger in her face. "That is such bullshit. Do you have any morals whatsoever?"

"Shut up, Jeff," she said, "This is none of your business."

I pointed to Dave and answered, "*He* is my business so you shut up."

Dave didn't try to break up our fight. He simply stood up and threw a twenty down on the table. "I'm out of here." Then he walked out leaving Lori standing there with her head down. I felt like a proud father at this moment.

"See ya," I said coldly. Then I followed my poor buddy out.

# Chapter 29

If someone gave me the choice of sitting in Cook County jail (general population) or sitting in a dentist's chair, I would hands down choose incarceration. My fear of the dentist began very early in life when my mother took me to a guy who did not believe in anesthesia. With a mouthful of cavities at five years old, the sadist filled my teeth sans pain management and I never forgot the feeling.

So the fact that I agreed to go to Jamie's boyfriend for a checkup and a cleaning was admirable in my opinion. I didn't have dental insurance, so Dave and Anna agreed to split the bill, since I was the one investing my time, doing the work, and drudging up some pretty horrifying memories.

I made it through the cleaning without incident, except for the fact that my shirt was soaked with sweat. After the hygienist was finished, Ted came in to do the exam. He seemed like a pretty nice guy, tall, thin, well dressed. He shook my hand and immediately got down to business. I hadn't thought about how hard it was going to be to carry on a personal conversation while my mouth was wide open.

So as Ted banged his little instruments on my teeth and looked at each of them with his teeny tiny mirror, I carefully thought about what I would lead with to get this guy to open up to me about Jamie.

"Okay, Jeff," he said, "There's one tooth in the back that may be a little iffy, so I'm going to have my nurse take an x-ray. Other than that, things look good. By the way, how did you hear about us?"

Shit! Hadn't thought about this question. "Uh…Yellow Pages?"

"Really? I don't advertise in the Yellow Pages. I do Money Mailer and Val-pack."

"Val-pack!" I interrupted, "That was it."

"Well, good." He got up off his little stool. I panicked. Was that it? Was he about to book out of here?

I quickly thought of something and sat up in my chair. "Hey Dr. Baskin, can I ask you something?"

"Sure."

"Did a girl named Heather Adams come in here for a cleaning?"

"Hmm...Heather Adams..." After a moment he answered, "No. Doesn't ring a bell."

"Oh...just thought I would ask. I gave her your name because she's looking for a dentist too. Heather is my..." Now I let the drama begin. I put my head down like I was going to start crying and continued, "Heather..." Now I put my face in my hands. I was thinking I could actually produce tears if I wanted to.

"Are you okay?" said Dr. Baskin.

I looked up at him. "I'll be fine. Heather is my ex-girlfriend. We just broke up."

"Oh...I'm so sorry to hear that."

I looked down at my lap sadly. "Heather...she wanted to get married...and I just couldn't do it. I just don't feel like I'm ready yet. Still, it hurts so much that we're not together anymore." Then I looked up at Ted. "I'm sure you think I'm an idiot. You're married, aren't you?"

"Actually, it's funny you bring it up." Now Dr. Baskin sat back down.

My face was still showing extreme sadness, but inside I was laughing because once again I couldn't believe how easy people were to trick.

He continued, "The tension is thick in my arena right now. I feel like I should get engaged to my girlfriend but I'm just not ready."

"Why?"

"I love Jamie. I really do." Now Dr. B. was the one with his head down.

"Well, what is it? What's holding you back?"

"I'm not really at liberty to say."

"Okay, that's cool," I said, faking my respect for Ted's wishes. I began getting out of the chair, holding my breath that the good dentist would throw me a bone. As luck would have it, (really I should say predictability) Ted decided to fess up.

"Okay, I'll tell you. But you can't say anything to anybody."

"Doc...I don't know one person you know," I lied, "I'm actually the perfect person for you to tell."

I anxiously waited for him to spill. After a moment of silence and a deep breath, Ted came clean (no pun intended.) The next thing out of his mouth was completely shocking. "I'm seeing someone else." I tried to hide my amazement, but judging by the way Ted looked me, I could tell it showed. "I know...I know..." he said, "it's horrible. I couldn't feel any worse about it. It just kind of happened. I met this other woman...her name is Sheila..."

After Ted said "Sheila," the room began to spin. I was absolutely sure it was *my* Sheila. Don't even ask me how I knew. I hadn't seen my ex-girlfriend since that fateful day in Briscoe Gucker dorm at Indiana University, when I'd punched her new guy and he'd pummeled back at me. So I had no clue where she was living or what she was doing or if she was married or single. Add to that fact, there were probably about a million Sheilas running around Chicago and the odds were pretty slim that Ted's piece on the side was the same woman who had broken my heart so long ago. Still, my gut told me that Ted's Sheila was my Sheila.

"I think I may be in love with both girls," he continued. "I definitely love Jamie...but I have really strong feelings for Sheila too. And I don't know what to do. Sheila knows about Jamie, but Jamie has no idea about Sheila. So I continue to ask myself which girl I'm meant to be with. Jamie Lee…or Sheila Brooks…both beautiful, wonderful women."

And there it was. Confirmation of what I already knew. I sat there, trying to act relatively normal, when in reality I felt like I was in some kind of bad dream. What I had just heard was way worse than any non-Novocain cavity filling experience I had ever had. I didn't know what to do. Sweet, beautiful Jamie was the victim of a two-timer, his other girlfriend being an immoral heartless creature with a history of infidelity. I felt sick to my stomach with grief for my client and felt the pain I knew Jamie would endure from this whole thing. It was the same pain her boyfriend's other girlfriend had caused me twelve years ago. At that moment, I didn't hate Sheila. I didn't even dislike her. I felt sorry for her. And I felt lucky to be free of her. As for Dr. Baskin, I wanted to hold the guy down, take his drill, and shove it into his mouth, drilling into a tooth and causing him the physical grief and torture I knew so well.

When I called Dave from the cab to tell him about our old high school classmate and the guy she was dating, his response was, "Forget about it for right now. I need your help!" Dave was in panic mode, which I was actually relieved to hear because it was better than the "nothing to live for" mood he was in the night before.

"What's wrong?" I asked.

"Kyle's boyfriend is coming in here in like five minutes. Kyle told the guy he wanted a Bears jersey he saw in here for their anniversary. He thought it would be a good way to get him into the store so we could find out why the guy doesn't want to get married."

"So? While you're showing him the jersey, just start talking to him. Somehow figure in a way to tell him you have this girlfriend who wants to marry you and that you aren't ready to commit." The minute those words came out of my mouth I knew I just screwed up huge.

"But I'm not in that situation anymore!" Dave shouted, "My girlfriend, who wants to get married to me so badly, is out dating someone else! Wait a minute! She isn't even my girlfriend anymore! She's my ex-girlfriend!" Dave seemed like he was really flipping out and I did not know what to do because I was still pretty far away.

"Okay, get a hold of yourself," I told him, "For the next few minutes you have to be an actor. Just play the part with Kyle's boyfriend. Get some info out of him. Ask him why he doesn't want to marry…I mean…you know…have a big wedding with Kyle. I'll be there as soon as I can."

"Please hurry."

"I will. You can do this buddy!" I said to Dave, sounding like my old high school football coach at halftime against Glenview North my senior year. We were losing 49 to 3.

"I'll do my best," Dave recovered.

And that he did. When I walked in, I found Dave in a serious conversation with Kyle's boyfriend, who was standing at the register with the jersey Kyle supposedly wanted in hand. Dave introduced me. "Jeff…this is Steven. Steven…this is my best friend, Jeff."

I shook hands with my client's boyfriend. He was pretty much who I saw Kyle with, tall, handsome, nice smile. For some reason, they seemed like a couple who really fit together.

"We were just discussing the fact that Steven here wants his partner to convert to Judaism," said Dave. Then he turned to Steven and added, "You don't mind if I tell Jeff, do you?"

"No," Steven smiled.

"Dave is Jewish," I said.

Both of them looked at me as if to say, Who cares? And what does that have to do with anything?

Steven explained, "It would just be really nice to be able to celebrate the Jewish holidays with Kyle…and him actually knowing what's going on…and wanting to practice the traditions…like lighting Hanukkah candles and having a Passover Seder…not just for me but for himself."

"I can understand that," said Dave, "My ex-girlfriend is Jewish and that was a big plus."

My buddy looked at me to see how I was going to react but instead of giving him a sympathy look or saying something like, "Don't worry, Dave, you guys will get back together," which is what the guy was dying for, I simply ignored the comment and instead spoke to Steven. "Have you told this to Kyle?" I asked.

"Actually, no. I'm afraid he may not want to do it. If that's the case, we'll end up broken up...which is what I don't want."

"Why wouldn't he want to convert to Judaism" asked Dave, "Is he really into his religion?"

"Not at all. He's a non-practicing Lutheran."

"My advice would be to bring it up and see what he says," said Dave.

Now I pretty much wanted to strangle my best friend, because if Steven actually took Dave's suggestion and went back and asked Kyle to convert and Kyle said no, that would be it. We needed to talk to Kyle first and see how he felt about becoming Jewish. And now, because of Dave, I felt like I had to rush to speak to Kyle before Steven saw him.

Dave semi-redeemed himself when he asked Steven, "So...besides the Jewish thing...what else is holding you back from taking the next step with Kyle?"

Now Steven blushed. I could actually see his cheeks turn red. He gave us a big grin and asked, "Can I trust you guys?"

"Yeah dude...for sure!" Dave exclaimed.

I hated myself big time when I smiled and added, "Dude, you can totally trust us. Who are we going to tell?"

Now Steven ran his fingers back through his hair and took a dramatic deep breath. "Okay...here's the thing."

My heart was pounding because I knew what he was going to say next was going to be extremely personal. I wasn't sure if Dave had actually caught on to that, because he said, "What's the big deal? How bad can it be?"

"It's just embarrassing, but here goes," said Steven. Then he blurted out something I seriously could not believe he said. "Kyle talks too much during sex."

The first thought in my head was, Is there anyone on this planet that does not have a problem with their sex life? Think about it. Almost every single person we'd interviewed as to why they didn't want to get engaged had told us they had an issue that was somewhat sex-related. Chris basically told us Anna wasn't into it, Sam said Liz never initiated sex, Jodi said Eric held her too long after, and now Steven!

It was actually really sad to me that people were so unhappy in the sack. Then again, who was I to talk? I wasn't even *in* the sack anymore, thanks to Anna. I had taken myself completely out of the love game. What was I doing? I asked myself. Yes, I felt sorry for Steven and Kyle and all the other unhappy lovers, but at least they had someone. I suddenly felt completely alone and it was a horrible feeling. Were there any girls I could call to help me get rid of this empty hole in my heart? Maybe I'd call Jessica again and see if we could hook up. She'd been calling or texting almost every day since she cancelled at the Mexican place. She'd for sure want to get together. "No, thanks," I answered myself. There was only one girl I wanted.

"Aren't you going to say anything?" Steven asked, bringing me back from my trip to Pityland. I realized I had to get a grip, get over the self-torture, and continue doing my job manipulating and conning people. After all, Kyle was my client and he had just paid me to help him. So that's what I ended up doing.

I put my hand on Steven's shoulder and said with a chuckle, "Dude…the talking thing…that doesn't really work for me either."

# Chapter 30

Steven wasn't out the door for two minutes when I dialed Kyle. "How do you feel about being Jewish?" I asked him.

"Oh, my God! Is that what he wants?" he responded, "Why didn't he just ask me?"

"I think he was scared you'd tell him no and I guess for Steven, that would be a deal breaker."

"So should I bring it up to him? Suggest it, maybe?"

"Later. We need to talk about something else."

"Is it bad?"

I cleared my throat. How the hell was I going to break the news to this guy that the love of his life thinks he's too chatty in bed? *Hook, Line and Sink Him* was now starting to bug me big time. What did I need this for? Didn't I have enough going on in my life without getting involved in the bad sex lives of other people?

"Kyle, listen, please don't get upset by this…"

"Oh, my God…" said Kyle, bracing himself.

Dave was now standing next to me and I could feel his wide-eyed stare, as if he was in disbelief that I was actually going to finish my sentence.

"Steven thinks you talk too much during sex." A bottled water appeared in front of me at this moment, compliments of my best friend. I opened the lid, took a huge gulp, and waited for Kyle's response, which came after a seemingly lengthy pause.

His tone was very formal when he finally spoke. "Well, no need to belabor the subject any further. I get it. I'll see what I can do, I guess."

"I'm sorry, Kyle. Just so you know, everything with us is confidential. The information we get stays between us and our clients."

"Thanks, Jeff. You're really cool." Kyle seemed happier. "Hey...at least you didn't tell me he was cheating on me!"

I immediately thought of poor Jamie and slutty Sheila and felt nauseous. Again, why did I need to be in this business?

I didn't think it was possible to feel any lower or anymore like the scum of the earth until Kyle and I moved on to another subject, which was how, where, when, and why he would falsely end his relationship with Steven. Shortly after the break up, Kyle would of course be running into Steven while on a date with someone else. The date: none other than Mike.

"Fine, but I want double the pay," Mike demanded when I asked him how he felt about going out with Kyle, "And no hand holding or anything."

I chuckled at his response. Mike wasn't a homophobe or anything. He was just a guy trying to make a buck, just like myself and Dave. And even though I was currently not a huge fan of *Hook, Line and Sink Him*, we did have quite a business here. A part of me felt like we were similar to an executive search firm trying to place people in jobs. We had good candidates who were just looking to better themselves in life. And their partners were like the prospective employers. They needed to be sold on the candidates. That is how we were operating, and I found myself really conflicted, because a big part of me thought nothing was really wrong with this. Money was coming in and we were helping people obtain happiness. What was so wrong with that? Sure, there were some unpleasant moments, like telling people they weren't up to par under the sheets, but maybe the good outweighed the bad. I was feeling optimistic all of a sudden; that is, until Eric called me later in the day.

"I just broke up with Jodi," he said sadly, "Now what?"

Upon hearing this news, I felt guilt beyond belief. Jodi...my friend...was in all probability now hurting thanks to me and my manipulation. Even worse was the next step I was about to take. I picked up the phone and dialed her.

"Hello?" Jodi answered her phone.

"Jodi? Hi, it's Jeff."

"Hi, Jeff."

"How's it going?" I asked.

"Not so great. Eric broke up with me again today."

"Oh, I'm so sorry. But that's actually really strange. Did you say he broke up with you today?"

"Yes. Why?"

"Because I am actually calling to ask you if I can set you up on a blind date."

"Really?"

"Yeah. I have this friend...his name is Mike..." I went on and told Jodi about him and how I thought for some reason they would click, and that I had this weird feeling, yada yada yada. The plan was, set them up to go on a date so they could run into Eric and Anna, and Jodi would think her ex had a new girlfriend. Genius, huh?

I realized it was scary how talented I was at exploitation and con games. But the truth was, I couldn't give myself too much credit, because tricking people wasn't that difficult. Our basic formula of "jealousy plus insecurity equals commitment" was simple and basically the same for every situation. We just had to tweak and personalize it a little bit for each couple.

So three days later, on a Saturday around four p.m., Mike met Jodi at Caribou Coffee. I chose Caribou because I had a buddy who worked there and he agreed to let me stand in the back, therefore allowing me to peek my head out and watch the unfolding scene, just like I had with Anna, Mike and Chris.

Mike arrived first. When he saw Jodi, our prey, enter the place, he freaked. He sent me a text. "Is this her? If so, she's hot!"

"Just do your job," I texted back.

As I watched Jodi enter the coffee shop and look around for her date, I have to confess that I really did think she was an attractive little package. She had the looks, the body, the brains and the sports-loving mentality. Plus, I felt like she had a good heart, something that I'd never cared about before, and something that now really mattered to me.

I poked my head out and watched what was shaping up to be more suspenseful than any James Patterson novel I'd ever read. "Are you Jodi?" Mike asked.

"Yes…" she said as she exhaled. It was obvious she was nervous. "You must be Mike."

They shook hands and then ordered their coffees. "Why don't you go sit down?" Mike said to his date, "I'll get the drinks and bring them over."

"Sure," said Jodi. Then she pointed to two velvet purple chairs by the window and asked Mike, "How about over there."

"Perfect," he said.

Now I sent a text to Anna. "They're here, sitting by window" was all it read.

"Be there in five," she texted back.

A few minutes later, Anna and Eric walked in. They were holding hands and pretending to be in a conversation. My text had helped Anna, because she was able to pinpoint where Jodi and Mike were sitting immediately, without having to look around. As for Eric, she must have told him not to look around, because he never took his eyes off his fake date.

I saw Anna look at Jodi and Mike, who were making polite conversation. Then I saw Jodi look up and notice Eric standing in line. What I witnessed next sparked a multitude of feelings in me. I found it both hilarious and incredibly sad. And then there was the insanely jealous part of me. Anna grabbed Eric's face. No one heard her say softly to him, "No tongue…got it?" I then saw Eric nod, just before Anna kissed him hard on the mouth. They stayed embraced for a few moments, at which point Jodi stood up and walked over to them.

"Eric?" she said softly. Jodi wasn't psycho angry, she seemed more sad and hurt.

Eric pulled away from Jodi and exclaimed, "Jodi! Hi…"

"Hi," she said softly.

The three stood there in awkward silence till Anna introduced herself. Jodi shook her hand and then looked at Eric. "Have you been cheating on me? Is she why we're broken up?"

"No! I promise."

Anna just stood there, looking like she wanted to hug Jodi. I wished I could tell her to act more territorial, like she was the new girlfriend who didn't care a thing about the ex. But Anna looked like she was going to cry. Thankfully, Jodi didn't notice.

"Look…I need some air," said Jodi, her eyes filling with tears, "Good luck, Eric. I hope you find what you really want." She walked back to Mike and explained that she wanted to leave, and then Mike walked her out. At this point, I had a pit in my stomach that was bigger than the empty space in my heart, the space I had reserved for Eric's pretend new gal.

I walked out from my hiding place and put my arm around Eric, who looked more miserable than Dave did the night we ran into the wench and her new dude. "Eric, trust me, you'll be fine. It's all going to work out."

"I sure hope so, Jeff," he said sadly.

"Anna thinks so, too," I said proudly. Then I looked at Anna and said cheerfully, "Right? Everything's going to fall into place for Eric. Don't you agree?"

Anna did not answer me, not with words anyway. Her response was a complete and utter meltdown, tears flowing down her face and that sound of hyperventilation that girls make when they're crying so hard they almost can't breathe.

"Oh, my God!" Eric panicked, "She totally doesn't think so! I know it!"

"Yes, she does," I urged, "Right, Anna?"

Anna nodded.

"Then why are you crying?" asked Eric.

Anna looked up at him. She had stopped blubbering, but tears were still streaming down her face. "You don't want to know," she said sadly.

"I want to know!" I wanted to shout, but I didn't. Instead, a reflex took over. I grabbed Anna and hugged her as hard as I could. She hugged me back, and we stood there gripping on to each other for a long time.

Eric didn't know what to say or do, so after a few minutes, he said something just to fill dead air, I think. "By the way, you're a really good kisser."

Both Anna and I, still in each other's arms, began to laugh. And as I held this woman I loved so deeply, I was thinking about how right Eric really was.

# Chapter 31

Diamonds are a girl's best friend. That may be true, but from a guy's perspective a diamond is something you have to drop ten grand on to make your girlfriend, who's about to be your fiancé, happy. When choosing the ring, the question then becomes, do you go for size or quality? Probably a little of both, but how do you know how big you should go and how good the stone really needs to be? Hopefully, you have a jeweler with some integrity who knows what the hell he's talking about, which is what I was thinking when I first walked into Brinkman Jewelers.

Standing at the counter looking at some stones through a glass case was none other than my best friend, who had called and asked me to meet him here. When he heard the door of the store open, he turned around and greeted me. "Hey, Jeff," he said with a nervous smile.

"Please tell me we're here for one of our clients," I answered with an uneasy chuckle, "Tell me we're choosing a ring for Frieda…or Kyle…or even Karen!"

Dave turned back around and continued to gaze into the display. He didn't look at me when he spoke. "Dude…I have to do this."

"Do what?" I asked, although I already knew what was coming next.

Now he looked up. "Look, I love her and I don't want to lose her."

This was so pathetic to me that it was frustrating. "Dave," I said calmly, while grabbing his shoulders so he would be forced to give me his full attention, "You are my best friend. I can't stand here and watch you ruin your life."

"Ruin my life?" he said, almost shouting. "By marrying the girl I love?"

I did not answer right away. Instead, I looked around. There were no other customers in the store, but I could tell the three people working here were becoming extremely uncomfortable. One of them disappeared into the back of the store. I think the other two wanted to hear the scoop despite the awkward atmosphere. Finally, I took a deep breath and said softly, "You don't love her."

"What?"

"You heard me."

"I don't love her?"

"Right."

"Oh yes...I love her," Dave said angrily, "You're the one who doesn't like her...in fact, you hate her."

I finally admitted my true feelings for Lori and said, "Fine. I hate her, okay? But I also don't care about her. I care about you."

"Look, Jeff...I'm buying Lori a ring today and nothing you can say is going to stop me."

"Don't be so sure."

"What does that mean?"

I took a deep breath and dropped the big one. "A few weeks ago, I saw Lori with another guy. They were all over each other, groping one another and making out like crazy."

Now I had silenced my buddy. He just stood there looking at me. The two employees were doing the same. One's jaw looked like it was on the ground.

"I'm sorry, Dave," I continued, "I know you didn't want the details, but I thought it was time you knew the truth." There. I'd said it. And even though I felt horrible for being the bearer of bad news, I was relieved that my secret was finally out. If Dave was going to marry

Lori, he needed to know what she was all about, whether he wanted to or not.

Unfortunately, when Dave responded to my bomb, it made me realize that nothing I knew or said was going to stop him from his intentions. "Lori and I talked it over and she told me about it," he said. "She also said nothing else happened and I believe her."

"So it's okay for your girlfriend to tonsil swap with other guys?"

"I'm done with this conversation," he said, "Do you want to support me on this or not?"

I looked at Dave for a moment before answering and wondered when he had become so desperate. When had his self-esteem gone down the toilet? When had he decided to sell his life short and marry the first good lay he ever had? Finally, I spoke some very difficult words. "Dave…if you do this…I don't want any part of it."

"What does that mean?"

"That means…don't tell me…don't talk about it with me…and don't expect me at the wedding." Then I sadly turned away and began to exit the jewelry store.

"So, that's it?" I heard Dave ask when I reached the door, "The guy who's supposed to be my best man isn't even going to come to my wedding?"

I stopped but I didn't turn around. "Nope."

"Well, that's great, Jeff. Thanks. But while you're busy blowing off my wedding, why don't you take a good look at yourself. You are such a hypocrite. You spend all your time plotting and scheming for engagements to happen and you're raking in the bucks doing it. Meanwhile, your own life's a mess. You know what you are?"

I finally turned around. "What am I?" I asked sarcastically.

Dave delivered harshly, "You're a pussy."

"Am I?" I asked, gritting my teeth.

"Yeah. You're too afraid to go after the girl you really love. That's why you don't want me to do it either."

"Are you for real?" I asked, "You actually think I don't want you to be with Lori because I'm not with Anna?"

Now I think Dave felt stupid because he just stood there speechless. What Dave had just said infuriated me beyond belief. How could my best friend say something so demeaning? Did Dave think I was that selfish? All I wanted was for the guy to be happy. I was trying to protect him, to save him from destroying any chance he had at being happy in life. But for some reason, he was choosing to ignore my good intentions.

I realized right then there wasn't a person on earth who could talk Dave out of getting engaged. He had made the decision and that was that and he wasn't going to believe me or anyone else that marrying Lori was the worst idea in the world. In the twenty some years I had known my best friend, I could never remember the two of us speaking to each other like this. And it was bumming me out big time.

What was equally upsetting was that he was correct in one thing he said. I really was a pussy, too chicken to go after Anna. And I hated myself for the simple reason that I could no longer blame Sheila for my phobia of gold wedding bands. The traumatic effect of being deceived by her was dormant now, probably permanently, so I had no excuse for not having the balls to tell this wonderful woman how I felt about her. Me, Jeff, the guy who could get any girl he wanted, the guy who had women lined up at the door, the guy who refused to give anyone his heart, was letting fear of rejection stop him from taking a chance on someone with whom I knew I could find true happiness.

I had been lucky enough to meet a person whose radiant eyes made my heart stop, whose cute little laugh made me feel weak in the knees, and whose sheer lack of sports knowledge made me grin every time I thought about it. And to seal the deal, Anna and I were friends, too. I somehow knew I could trust her and be myself around her without being judged. The bottom line, I could no longer imagine my life without Anna being a major part of it. Yet I wasn't doing anything to let her know how I felt.

I was too afraid to make a move, too afraid she may prefer to settle for a life with Chris and ignore the place in her heart where I stood. I was a true coward who had chosen to keep my feelings silent. If I told Anna how I felt and if she rejected me, the price was too high. I wasn't sure I could cope with losing her. Not speaking up at least gave me the hope that someday things would turn out for us. But what was I waiting for? The clock was ticking and Anna was going to be walking down the aisle soon. Still, I was letting risk rule my actions (or I should say lack of actions).

"Look," Dave said, "I didn't mean that."

"Yes, you did," I said coldly. Then I turned around and walked out of the store.

I spent the remainder of the day at the park with my six best friends, all whose names began with the letter P. These were the friends I could rely on not to judge me, the friends who liked me unconditionally, the friends who didn't criticize me for my shortcomings, and the friends who would ultimately go back to live with their mother, perhaps my best friend of all.

"What should I do, Pita?" I asked the little pooch, who happened to be sniffing my leg at the moment, while her brothers and sisters were roaming around elsewhere. "Do I risk everything and just tell her how I feel?" Not surprisingly, Pita ignored me. Did I think he was going to answer me? Perhaps give me advice?

Next to come by and visit was Pretty Boy. "Hey, dude," I spoke to the dog, probably sounding like an escapee from the nuthouse. "What do you think? Should I sit her down and just tell her I love her?" Pretty Boy actually looked at me and for a split second I thought she may speak. Wrong. She began wagging her tail and barking, which meant she wanted a treat. After I obliged, she was off.

Asking for advice made the most sense when Passion walked up. "Hey, Passion…you feel my pain…don't you, buddy? Do you think your mother loves me?" Talk about a sign. This sweet, very dramatic, romantic little dog practically jumped into my arms and began licking my face.

# Chapter 32

The next morning, a new client named Fatima Parikh had a consultation with *Hook, Line and Sink Him* at 8:45. The only reason I showed up was because I had to see Anna afterward to review the second draft of my new article, which was due a couple days later. Otherwise, I would have chosen to stay in bed and forego yet another opportunity to screw up some poor guy's life.

Fatima was beautiful. Being of Indian descent, she had dark skin, and dark eyes that made her exotic. The woman was glamorous. That was the bottom line. Even better, she seemed like a sweetheart.

"What do you think is holding your boyfriend back?" Dave asked her.

I felt like punching him for two reasons. One, I was still extremely pissed about his very harsh words the day before; and two, I was tired of hearing this bullshit question. It was so canned. I was sick of the whole thing. I could not help what came out of my mouth next. "Obviously, she doesn't know or she wouldn't be here," I said sarcastically.

Anna tried to keep things normal and minimize the tension. "Fatima..." she said gently, "The first thing we do is talk to your boyfriend..."

"Without him knowing you've hired us, of course," Dave added in his usual fashion.

What I said next was very unusual, though. "Right... because we're conniving manipulators and if you work with us, you'll be getting engaged based on complete bullshit. Is this something you would like to try?"

Everyone, including our sweet innocent client, was looking at me like I was nuts.

"Excuse my partner, Fatima," said Dave.

"Yes," Anna added, "He doesn't mean that." She shot me a look.

I looked at Fatima and stood up. "I'm really sorry Fatima," I said, "You seem like a really nice girl." Then I looked at Anna and said sadly, "I can't do this anymore."

I walked out of the room, and once I got outside Dave's store I knew our business was coming to an end. That was it. This whole thing, it all had to stop. It had messed up our lives and the lives of dozens of other couples whose relationships were now based on lies and secrets and manipulation.

I took a deep breath and was about to hail a cab when I heard Anna call, "Jeff!" I turned around and there she was. "What is it?" she continued, "What's wrong?"

I was about to say "nothing" when it occurred to me that "nothing" was the last thing I should say. This was not *nothing*. It was something, and it was time to face the truth. All of a sudden, I was fuming. I was livid with *Hook, Line and Sink Him* and all of its employees. Mostly, though, I was outraged at myself. So instead of answering Anna's question, I simply looked at her. Without saying a single word, I stormed off down the block.

Anna followed. "Please...talk to me," she pleaded after a few steps.

I finally stopped and turned to her. "What we are doing in there is wrong. All of those people...Liz...Frieda... Jamie...Kyle...Eric...even that bitch Karen...it's wrong. It's wrong! Eventually all of our couples are going to get engaged based on fabrication and deceit."

"That may be true," Anna responded, "but even if things started off as a lie, they could turn out for the best. We may have tricked the guys, but no one is holding a gun to anyone's head when they go out and buy a ring. They are coming to that decision on their own."

"That's not true! They aren't coming to any decision themselves! We are playing with fate! With people's lives! I have to go call a girl right now...Jamie...and tell her that the reason her longtime boyfriend won't get engaged to her is that he has another girlfriend! My ex-girlfriend! Try living with that kind of guilt!"

"Well, maybe you're doing her a favor. If I were her, I would want to know."

"But that's not your decision to make!" I shouted, "Or mine! Her world is about to crumble, and I caused that!"

"It would have crumbled anyway," Anna pleaded, "Just later rather than sooner."

"That doesn't matter. Don't you see? I can't play God anymore. I'm finished controlling people's lives and playing with their hearts."

Anna and I stood in silence for a moment, and I actually thought she was going to side with me until she said, "And what about Liz? She's doing great. Sam is so into the engagement. He actually told her he felt a great sense of relief and that he didn't know what took him so long and why he had been afraid to commit. He said, and I quote, 'I should have done this years ago.'"

"I'm happy for Liz, but knowing that doesn't make me feel any different."

"What about me? What about Chris? We're happy."

Now I couldn't take it another second. I was completely furious. I didn't want to get into a huge fight with Anna, so instead of responding I turned around and continued storming down the block.

Again, Anna followed, but this time I could tell that by not responding, I'd struck a nerve. "Hey..." she shouted from a few feet behind me, "I'm talking to you. Don't walk away from me!"

I finally stopped, turned around, and pointed my index finger in Anna's face. "You and Chris will never be happy!"

Anna gasped. "How dare you say that!"

I went on, "You and Chris will never be happy because you don't love Chris!"

"Yes, I do!"

"No you don't. You know who you love?" Now I pointed my finger in my own face. "You love me!"

Another gasp from her.

"That's right," I continued. I was shouting now. "You love me, Anna. And I love you. I love your dogs…I love your parents…and I love your hair! I even loved it when it was big and streaked five different colors! I love you, okay?" It was only when I stopped yelling and the long silence began that I realized what I had just declared. After about ten seconds of the two of us standing there looking at each other, I realized we both had tears in our eyes. I was waiting. And waiting and waiting. Finally, I said softly, "Say something."

As tears rolled down Anna's cheeks, she said, "But I'm engaged."

"Well, get un-engaged!"

"Where were you, Jeff?" she shouted, "Where were you all this time?"

"Why does it matter?" I said with a smile, "I'm here now."

I waited for a response, but Anna just stood there staring into my eyes. And after a few more moments of silence, tears rolling down her sweet round cheeks, she whispered, "I can't, Jeff. I could never do this to Chris. I'm sorry." Then she turned around and ran off.

I shouted after her, "Great! Tell him I said hi!" Again I had turned into the asshole. Why didn't I run after her and tell her again to break it off? Instead, I gave up. At that moment, I felt completely helpless. I sadly turned around and continued slowly down the street.

And just when I thought things could not possibly get any worse, I heard another female voice call my name. I looked up and saw a very angry Jodi walking quickly toward me. Eric was a few steps behind her. "How could you?" she shouted at me.

"Jodi…I…"

"Don't you dare even speak! I am flabbergasted by what you tried to pull! You tried to trick me into getting engaged! Do you have any morals whatsoever?"

As Jodi continued to rant and rave, I noticed Eric standing behind her, mouthing "Sorry..." to me. Apparently, Eric could not go through with the full-fledged plan so he had confessed everything to Jodi that morning. I felt like punching the guy, but in a way I had some new-found respect for him.

Speaking of punches, though, I never saw the left hook coming toward my right cheek. Jodi's punch hit me so hard that I actually fell on the ground! Little petite Jodi had knocked me down. On our date, she had told me she took kickboxing classes on Mondays and Thursdays. Now I wondered if she'd ever missed a class! Jodi's punch made Sheila's college dude's seem like a light tap. After getting a sample of Jodi's boxing skills, I realized that if Jodi and the guy were in the ring, fighting for the heavyweight championship of the world, I would put money down on Jodi.

As I sat there in some dirt, several passersby stopped to ask if I was alright, as Jodi and Eric had walked off immediately after the assault. I stood up and announced to the world that I was okay. And as I walked down the block, I could tell some of the spectators were trying not to laugh.

## Chapter 33

The next day, since I was in a fight with my best friend and in a very weird place with my boss/business partner/love of my life, I decided to forego covering the Maine South cross country meet. I wasn't too worried about blowing it off, because "He Loves Sports More Than Me" had turned out great, and I was confident that more work would be coming.

It was ironic. Left with a black eye, a broken heart, and the guilt of being one of the owners of *Hook, Line and Sink Him*, at least I got a consolation prize, which was no small thing. Thanks to Anna, I truly had found my niche. I had always loved two things, sports and women. Now I was writing sports for a female audience. How perfect was that?

The combination, though shocking to myself and to everyone who knew me, really worked, and the quality of the writing showed on paper. I had received numerous e-mails and letters from female fans, and I knew it was only a matter of time before *Today's Chicago Woman* would offer me a full-time writing position. Even more exciting, managers from other publications had begun contacting me, and I already had some assignment offers on the table. Finally, my career had been born. And coincidentally, at the same time, my love life had just died. I got the job but I couldn't get the girl.

"That's life," I could just hear Dave say with a smile. But in reality, I wouldn't hear Dave say anything, with or without a smile, because we weren't presently speaking. I wondered when he was planning on giving Lori the ring, and I wanted to call him and once again urge him not to do it. However, I knew he wouldn't listen to me, so I decided to butt out and let Dave do his thing. As for me, I would spend the day enjoying myself as much as I possibly could with my sore eye and bruised heart.

I took the dogs to *Wrigley Field* that morning and I let them stay there as long as they wanted. I wondered when Anna was going to take them home; and with the latest drama between us, how was that going to work? Would she just never speak to me again and forget about her kids? Highly unlikely. Maybe Anna would finally tell Chris she was taking the dogs back and come over one last time to get them. The whole thing was so unpredictable.

I mean, after declaring my love for her, could she really call me and say, "Jeff, can you just keep them for a few more days?" Probably not. At any rate, I realized that when I told Anna I loved her dogs, I was being sincere. I had come to care about her little pets and I would have been willing at this point to keep them forever. But I knew Anna would want them back soon, so I decided to have quality time with them until then.

After the doggie morning I headed out solo, down to Michigan Avenue. My first stop was to Banana Republic to buy some new clothes. Because I would soon be having meetings with editors on a regular basis, I figured I needed to upgrade my wardrobe a little bit. I ended up spending almost five hundred bucks on two pairs of pants, four shirts, a belt, a pair of shoes, and thanks to the persuasive (and very attractive) saleswoman who helped me, a leather jacket.

Walking down Michigan Avenue with three huge Banana Republic bags, and feeling very metrosexual, I realized I was starving, so I stopped at Mickie D's and ate. After a Big Mac, large fries, and a biggie Coke, I decided I needed the new Kanye West CD, so I headed to Borders, where I found myself leisurely browsing around the store. I came upon a new display that featured all kinds of sports books. Naturally, I was like a kid in a candy store, and spent the next half hour leafing through at least twenty different books. I decided to buy four of them. "Sports Illustrated: The Football Book," "Amazing but True Sports Stories," "The Best American Sports Writing of the Century," and just for fun, "Sharp Sports Betting." A cute little blond rang me up. "That'll be $93.81," she flirted.

I handed her my credit card and stood there wondering if I should start up a conversation. Why not? I was a free man. Then again, I was a new man. I didn't want to converse and then date and/or sleep with the cute little blond. She deserved more. And I realized (without spending a dime in therapy, mind you) that I deserved more, too. I had really grown as a person over the past couple of months and I was proud of the new me. Yes, I could thank Anna for changing me, but I also had to give myself credit because I had become a better person. Not just for the woman I loved, but for Jeff.

All of a sudden, don't ask me why, but I glanced over to the entrance of the store on my right. What I saw sent me into deep shock. There was Lori talking and giggling with two other people. One was Karen, the other was Joe. Karen! Our rude client! And Joe! Dave's customer, the one we'd clicked with. A moment later, I watched Lori hand each of them some money. Within seconds, I put two and two together and figured out what was going on. *Hook, Line and Sink Him* had been reeled in big time. The great manipulators had just been manipulated. It all made sense.

Lori must have somehow found out about *Hook, Line and Sink Him*. She then offered a decoy, Joe, money to go into Dave's store and pretend to be a customer, when in reality, he was there to find out why Dave didn't want to marry her. She then offered Karen money to call us and come in for a consultation.

After hearing our advice, Karen went back and told Lori what to do and she did it. Lori broke up with Dave and shortly after, she went out on a date with someone and purposely ran into us at our favorite sushi place. When I thought about what she had said to Dave, I wanted to throw up all the greasy food I just consumed. "I swear to God...I would *never, ever* cheat on you! You have my word. *Never*...when we were together...was I *ever* with another man," she had said to Dave in her most sincere voice. Lori had said that because she knew what Dave wanted to hear, thanks to Joe. The owners of *Hook, Line and Sink Him* had been fooled by our own game, and in the next day or so, Lori was about to cash in her winnings and collect a diamond engagement ring from my buddy.

Quickly, I signed the credit card slip and ducked behind a bookshelf until I saw all three leave. Apparently, Borders was their meeting place for the payoff. As I watched them walk out the door, all I could think of was how stupid I was for not figuring out the whole scam. How could I not have known? Lori's moves were so predictable. Dave and I had made them up, for God's sake!

When I thought about Joe in the store and how much Dave and I had both really liked and trusted him, it sickened me. And Karen... Here was a woman who acted almost mechanical, showing no emotion and getting right down to business. How could I have overlooked that? At the time, I had told Anna I thought something was fishy, but I had chalked it up to paranoia. And now I was paying for it, or I should say Dave was paying. I, Jeff, the biggest con artist I knew, had been tricked by Lori the bitch! I had to admit she was a lot smarter than I had ever given her credit for. Well, this time she had gone too far.

The good news was, I'd witnessed the three conspirators and found out the truth in time (hopefully). I had to get to Dave. I had to warn him about what was going on before he gave Lori the ring. I called his cell and it went right to voice mail, which meant it was off. Desperate to find him, I decided to go look for him. I headed to *Be a Sport*. When I got there, I pushed the door open pretty aggressively and found Mike standing behind the register.

"Hey, where's Dave?" I asked him.

"Hello to you too, dickhead," Mike answered with a chuckle.

"Sorry, dude. I just really need to talk to Dave."

Mike answered, "He took the day off. Said he had a lot to do."

"Any idea where he might be?"

"No. Did you try his cell?"

"Yeah. Thanks, man." Then I rushed out.

"Hey, how did you get the black eye?" Mike shouted.

I tried not to get too pissed off by his question, because it wasn't his fault that I got beaten up by a woman. By going out with Jodi, Mike was just doing his job. I will say, though, I was getting very irritated by people asking me constantly, "Hey…what's up with the black eye?" and "Dude…who did you get into a fight with?" How long did it take for a shiner to heal? How long would I have to lie and tell people I got into a bar fight with one of the Chicago Bears?

Next, I stopped at Dave's apartment, but he wasn't there either. From the outside of his building, I called his home phone and then his cell again. Still voicemail. I left a message. "Dave…buddy…it's me. Call me. It's really important. Call my cell, okay? Call as soon as you get this." I hung up. What more could I do? I thought about going to see Lori and telling her everything, but I really did not want to interfere that way, because I felt Dave deserved the satisfaction of sending his girlfriend into shock by telling her he knew her dirty little secret. It was making me feel all warm and fuzzy thinking about Dave dumping Lori for good. I fantasized about Lori being inches away from getting the rock of her dreams, and then being called out on her scheme. That's how much I hated that chick.

It was now 5:00 and time was passing by. Where the hell was Dave and why was his cell phone off? Not knowing what else to do, I started to walk home. I was two blocks from my apartment when my cell phone rang. Thank God, I thought, Finally.

I answered without even looking at caller ID. "Where the hell are you, Dave?"

A voice that wasn't my buddy's answered, "Jeff? I have to talk to you!"

"Who is this?"

"It's Kyle!" he said in a panicky voice.

"Kyle, what's up?" I asked, "Is something wrong?"

"Majorly. Steven found my diary and read it!"

"And?"

"He knows everything. He knows about *Hook, Line and Sink Him*, he knows he was set up when he went into Dave's store to buy my jersey, he knows I was planning on breaking up with him tomorrow!"

My first question was, "Jesus, Kyle...how long is your diary?" Then I asked, "And who has time to keep a journal these days? And on paper!"

"I'm sorry, Jeff," Kyle whined, "I didn't mean to get you in trouble."

"So what now?" I asked my client. I wasn't sure what to do at this point. Do we give him back his money? Come to think of it, I was sure we were going to have to give Eric back his money, too. The two $500 checks were the least of my worries right now, though. I was more concerned with getting punched again, this time by a presumably very pissed off Steven. And maybe he would not stop with a simple punch. For all I knew, he could murder me! Especially if he knew where I lived, which, thank God, he did not.

"Well, he stormed out of here and he's on his way to your apartment. I wanted to warn you."

"What? How does he know where I live?"

"He made me tell him your last name," Kyle said like a little boy confessing in a principal's office, "and then he looked in the White Pages."

I stood there for a second wondering how I never realized I was listed in the White Pages. I had actually never thought about it before, but it made sense. You want to find someone, you look in the phone book, right? "Is this guy going to kill me or what?" I asked Kyle.

"Actually, no. He's not a violent person."

Major relief. "Then why is he coming over?" I asked.

"He's going to sue you," answered Kyle.

"He's what?" I asked. This was a new one for me.

Kyle repeated, "He's going to sue you…serve you with papers."

"Kyle, I'll give you your money back."

"Listen, Jeff, I don't want my money back. This is the best thing that could have happened to me. This whole thing forced Steven and me to talk like we never have before. I am converting to Judaism…and he's agreed to let me plan a big wedding next summer. Two hundred people!"

"That's great, Kyle," I said semi-sarcastically, "I'm happy for you."

"You know what else?"

"What?"

"Sex without talking is really good!"

"More info than I really need, Kyle," I said with a laugh, "But I'm happy for you." I actually was psyched for Kyle. Things had all turned out for the best. Except for the fact that in about three minutes, when I reached my building, some guy was going to be waiting for me and he was going to serve me with legal papers. "So if everything is so great, why does he still want to sue us?"

"Because he's a lawyer."

"Well, that makes sense," I said as turned the corner onto my block. Sure enough, there was Steven. He was wearing a suit and pacing back and forth on the walkway that leads to the front door of my building. "Thanks for the warning, Kyle," I said sadly. Then I snapped my cell shut and prepared myself. I was about to be severely berated and threatened. The truth was, I deserved it.

"Are you looking for me?" I asked him.

He looked up at me with a cold stare and said, "You better believe it."

"Steven…I'm really sorry…"

He interrupted, "How could you? I told you things…I put my trust in you and the sports store owner…"

"I know and the thing is, everything is confidential. I swear, Steven, I would never say a word about…you know…"

"My sex life?" he shouted.

I looked around to see if anyone was listening and then whispered, "Yes."

"My sex life couldn't be better right now!"

"Good!" I said with lots of enthusiasm, "So we helped you!"

"Maybe you did, but the way you went about it was wrong." He handed me some papers and finished, "And illegal. I'll see you in court." His voice was calm but icy. This guy was good. He scared the shit out of me without any violence at all.

I walked into my building without even looking at the legal documents. I realized right then I was completely exhausted. All I wanted to do was collapse on my couch. Between getting punched in the face, seeing Lori and her cohorts, trying to hunt down Dave, stressing over my fight with Dave, stressing about my love confession to Anna, feeling guilty about Jodi, worrying about Frieda, worrying about Liz, very much worrying about Jamie, and the latest, having a lawsuit filed against me, needless to say I was worn out.

The second I hit the sofa, I literally was out like a light, in a deep sleep coma, complete with snoring and everything. And it wasn't until four hours later when Pita jumped on me to let me know she and all her brothers and sisters had to go take a leak, that I was forced to get up.

While waiting for the dogs to pee at this late hour on my quiet street, I called Dave's cell again. Again it went straight to voice mail. I then texted him: "Dude, call me. Very important." I snapped my cell shut and looked up at the stars. Dave was most likely engaged now, and there was absolutely nothing else I could do.

# Chapter 34

I was dreaming. Anna and I were sitting on the beach talking. Actually we were in the exact same spot where we had sat in real life when Anna told me I was the best friend she'd made in a really long time. And then, just when I was about to tell her I loved her, her cell phone rang. It happened differently in my dream.

In my dream, Anna told me I was the best friend she'd made in a really long time. Upon hearing those words, I leaned over and gently kissed her lips. Anna kissed me back, and we began passionately embracing each other. I knew from her kisses that I finally had my girl. She was all mine. It was exciting, electrifying. Yet at the same time I felt calm and relieved, like I could finally exhale and release the pent up stress I had been carrying around for weeks, constantly worrying about how I was going to get my Anna.

A few moments, later her cell phone rang. In real life Anna had answered it, learning Chris had just booked a spontaneous trip to Cabo. Not in my dream. In my dream Anna ignored the ringing cell, which was lying on the towel next to us, and kept on kissing me. All of a sudden, one of her dogs (I think it was Poo-poo) took the phone in his mouth and ran into the lake with it. Anna and I were both aware of what was happening but neither of us stopped the dog. We were too wrapped up in the moment to care. Then, Anna's dad walked up.

"Anna, what are you doing?" he asked.

She broke away from the kiss and looked at her father. "Kissing," she said with a giggle.

"I can see that," said her dad, "But what about Chris?"

She responded, "I'm with Jeff now."

"Well, what a nice surprise!" he exclaimed. A pitcher of margaritas suddenly appeared in his hands. "Now I don't have to move to Arizona," he said with a smile.

"What's going on?" Anna's mom asked. She had now magically appeared as well.

"Anna dumped Chris," said Anna's dad, "She's in love with Jeff now."

"Wonderful!" Anna's mom responded.

"Is that true, Anna?" I asked her, "Are you in love with me?"

Anna did not answer. She sat there silently and I had no idea why.

"Anna, let me make it easy for you," I suggested, "If you love me, press this button." I then pulled out a doorbell and handed it to her.

She stared at it for a moment, still unable to utter a word. Then, to my pleasant surprise and delight, Anna smiled and pressed the button. It made a buzzing noise that sounded exactly like the buzzer of my front door. Anna pressed it again. Another buzz. And again, another buzz. And again, more buzzing. I was thrilled. Anna loved me! She actually loved me so much that she kept pressing the button over and over again. The buzzing got to be so repetitive and loud that it woke me up.

I sat up very quickly and realized the buzzing noise was real and that someone was at my front door, ringing me furiously at what I imagined was a very early hour. I got out of bed and ran to the intercom. Of course, all the dogs followed me and began barking and jumping on me. They seemed panicked. I wasn't. I was annoyed. Probably some drunk ringing the wrong apartment. "What's up?" I yelled.

"Jeff...it's Lori!" she shouted.

What? Bummer number one, Anna's buzzing was just a dream. Bummer number two, Dave's lying, cheating, scheming, manipulating girlfriend and most likely now his fiancé was paying me a visit! "Lori, what are you doing here?" I asked, "And what the hell time is it?"

"It's 8:30. Please, Jeff, can I come up? I need to talk to you."

I buzzed her in. Then I rubbed my eyes in an attempt to become fully awake and I began showing the dogs some affection to calm them down. They were the only living creatures to whom I planned on being not only civil but also nice to this morning.

A moment later I heard Lori knock on my door. I opened it and couldn't even bring myself to say hi.

"Hi," Lori said.

I motioned for her to sit on the couch and she obliged. It was a bit strange. Lori seemed scared of me (with good reason, I guess) and was acting tentative, as if she was uncertain about how much information I knew.

"So, what's up?" I asked coldly.

I looked at her for an answer, but Lori was unable to utter a word. She just sat there silent.

I waited. Moments later still nothing. "Are you going to speak?" I asked.

Lori nodded but she didn't say anything. Instead she began to weep.

Shit! I thought. As much as I despised this woman, I never enjoyed seeing a girl cry. It just wasn't right, no matter what. "Lori, what's wrong?" I asked softly, while trying to get a glimpse of her left ring finger. I got a tinge of excitement when I realized there was no ring on it. Not that one had to be a rocket scientist to figure out that if she was here in my apartment bawling, obviously she hadn't gotten engaged.

As Lori continued to cry, the dogs began coming up and surrounding her, each one sniffing and licking her in different places. Only Passion stayed with me. The rest were trying to console the stranger. After a minute, Lori looked up at me. With tears in her eyes and a little giggle, she asked, "Jeff...when did you get all these dogs?"

I smiled, "It's a long story. Then I said with sincerity, "Lori, tell me why you're here."

Lori composed herself and began explaining how the night before, Dave had taken her on a carriage ride down Michigan Avenue. "It was the perfect evening…stars in the sky…sixty degrees…no wind for a change. I knew Dave was going to ask me to marry him." After speaking these words, she began to cry again.

I waited for her to stop, but she kept on sobbing and the dogs kept on licking, sniffing, and rubbing up against her--all except for Passion, who continued to lie happily in my lap. I was surprised that she chose not to join in, since she was the most loving of all the dogs. But maybe she could sense Lori's character and didn't feel any pity for the weeping cheater.

"Sorry…" said Lori through tears.

"It's okay," I said, "Take your time."

"Anyhow…Dave said to me, 'You know how much I love you' and I thought he was going to pop the question right then."

"But he didn't?" I asked, trying not to sound too hopeful.

"No. He didn't," she said, shooting me a dirty look, "'Try to understand what I'm about to tell you,' he said. Then he told me he was planning on asking me to marry him and that he had a ring and everything."

"But?" I asked her.

"But he said he just couldn't do it. He said he would be getting engaged for all the wrong reasons." Now Lori began semi-crying again. "He said he didn't think he loved me enough to spend the rest of our lives together and that he didn't realize how he felt until right then."

"Yes! Yes! Yes!" I was screaming in my head. At this moment I stood up, excused myself, and headed to the bathroom. I wasn't trying to be rude, but the adrenaline running through my body was just too intense and I had to release my pent-up energy.

I walked into my john, closed the door, and then I actually did a cheer. "Go Dave...go Dave...you're the man...you're the man..." I chanted while furiously shaking my fists in the air. Believe it or not, I hadn't been this excited since Michael Jordan's three-pointer in the last second of the 1991 championship game against the Lakers. Dave had come to the conclusion on his own that Lori wasn't the right woman for him. Even without knowing that his girlfriend had tried to trick him into it by sending decoys into *Hook, Line and Sink Him*, he had reached the right decision and decided against giving her the ring.

I walked back out to the living room, looked at Lori, and said as sincerely as I could manage, "Sorry..."

"Are you okay?" she asked with cynicism.

"You have no idea!" I wanted to shout out. Instead, I sat back down on the couch, nodded my head, and feigned sadness. Passion jumped up on my lap. Then my buzzer rang again.

"Oh God!" she exclaimed, "I bet that's him."

I picked up Passion, carried her over to the intercom and answered, "Who is it?" even though I already knew the answer.

"Me," Dave said.

I buzzed him in and turned to face Lori. "What do you want me to do? Should I leave so you guys can talk?"

"Actually," she said, "I came here to see if you could talk to Dave and change his mind. I love him, Jeff, and I want to be his wife."

I could not believe this chick! Did she have no shame? I responded, "Lori...the bottom line is...of course you want to be his wife. Not because you're in love with him but because you want to be a wife. Anyone's wife. In fact, I don't even think you love Dave. I think your clock is ticking and you just want to get married."

Now Lori gave me the ultimate death look. Her sad little victim act ended and now she looked like the witch who had just given Snow White the poison apple. "Well, you know all about that, don't you Jeff?" she said, "You're an expert. Hook, Line and Sink Him, right?"

Now I was pissed. Who was *she* to judge *me*? I looked at her with disgust. "Yeah...maybe I do know about some things about tricking guys into marriage. But I also know that *you* do too."

"What?" By the look on her face, I knew now that she had no idea that I knew about her little scheme.

"That's right, Lori...I know all about Karen and Joe."

Lori now knew she was busted big time.

"Such a shame...I loved Joe. I had no clue he was your hired help."

Before Lori could respond, Dave knocked on the door.

"It's open," I said loudly.

"Hey..." said Dave as he walked in. He immediately saw Lori.

"Hi, honey..." she said to him.

"What are you doing here?"

Before Lori responded, I said, "Let me get out of here and give you guys some privacy. I'll go walk the dogs."

"No, thanks, Jeff," he said, "You can stay." He looked at Lori, "I think we said everything we needed to say last night. By the way, I just came from that little park off Michigan Avenue--you know--the park where you threw the diamond ring."

"You found it?" Lori asked.

Dave pulled a one and a half caret solitaire platinum set ring out of his pocket. "Of course I found the fucking thing. I've been searching for it in the grass since the sun came up!" Dave turned to me and explained that after he had told Lori he couldn't marry her, she had asked him to see the ring. "In my stupidity, I gave it to her," he went on, "And after giving the diamond a quick look she tossed it off of the horse and buggy and it landed somewhere in the park."

I tried really hard not to, but I couldn't help cracking up a little bit. Both Dave and Lori gave me dirty looks.

Dave turned to Lori. "So, may I ask what you're doing here?"

Now Lori began to cry again. "I'm sorry about throwing the ring," she managed through tears, "I was just really hurt."

I was getting extremely tired of all the drama, so I rolled my eyes to Dave, who ignored me and rushed over to Lori to comfort her.

"I can't believe this!" I blurted out, "She just threw a five thousand dollar ring in the grass and you're feeling sorry for her?"

"Six thousand," Dave corrected, still consoling his girlfriend--or ex-girlfriend. I wasn't sure at this point.

"You know, I just don't get it," Lori sobbed, "I did everything right. I followed all the steps."

"What are you talking about?" Dave asked her.

"I broke up with you...I ran into you while I was on a date..."

Now Dave began to put the pieces together. "Oh my God! Are you talking about our business? How did you find out?"

Still sobbing, Lori explained that she saw our ad at the Teeny Beeny café and recognized the phone number. "So I paid this guy I know, Joe, to come into your store and find out why you didn't want to marry me."

"Joe? He was your decoy?" Dave asked, "I actually loved that guy."

"Me too," I added.

Lori continued, "And then I sent Karen into *Hook, Line and Sink Him* to find out how it worked."

"Karen came in for *you*?" Dave asked.

Lori nodded, tears continuing to flow down her cheeks.

Dave took Lori's hand and held it. "Lori...the business worked for some couples. And for me...it almost worked, till I tried to imagine having kids and growing old with you. I just couldn't. I do love you. I just don't think we belong together for life. And I'm so sorry, Lori, because I think you're a good person. You're just not *my* person."

Lori's sadness suddenly turned to rage. Wiping her tears she shouted, "I'm not *your* person?" Before Dave could even react she went on, "Well, guess what? You're not *my* person either!"

"Lori, please..." Dave pleaded. Leave it to my buddy to be kind to the very end.

Lori headed for the door. As she opened it and just before she walked out of my apartment and out of our lives forever, she turned around to deliver one final blow. "By the way...I cheat on you all the time!"

In unison Dave and I said, "We know."

Lori slammed the door shut and that was that. The dogs were a good distraction as they immediately began to jump on Dave and shower him with licks.

Dave turned to me and said with a smile, "Did you know that you tried calling me thirty-two times yesterday?"

"Plus I texted you."

"Eight times," Dave said with a smile.

"Isn't that what friends do?" I asked.

As Dave filled me in on more details from the previous night, I thought about whether I should tell my best friend about the martini guy, Karl, and about seeing Lori with Karen and Joe at Barnes and Noble. Eventually I would tell him everything I knew, but for today I decided to do the guy a favor and give him a rest. I realized he'd been through enough in the past twelve hours, especially when he showed me his grass-stained pants, the result of spending hours on his knees looking for his diamond.

A little while later, I decided to update him on my love life. "By the way, I took your advice," I began, "I told Anna I loved her."

Dave had the same excited look on his face as he did the day I told him I got us front row tickets for the Bruce Springsteen Born to Run concert. My buddy was so happy for me.

"Don't get too excited," I said sadly, "She shot me down."

"Oh..." he said, "I'm really sorry. I'm also really surprised."

"Thanks. Here's the thing. I have to let Anna go. Spilling my guts was a good thing, and now I feel like I can live with the fact that I did everything I could to try to get her. Eventually I'll have peace with the whole thing."

I didn't share this with Dave, but I realized something very cool about the Anna situation. For the first time in such a long time, I had taken a chance with someone. And even though it didn't work out I knew now that I was capable of love. This was a huge accomplishment for the commitment-phobic womanizer who never let anyone into his heart. Loving Anna made me feel vulnerable and scared, but I realized those feelings were normal and healthy and that they made me come alive. Anna would always be special to me for that reason.

"I think we're both going to be okay," said Dave. Then he joked, "By the way...how's your eye?"

"Fuck off," I laughed.

## Chapter 35

Standing outside the lion house at Lincoln Park Zoo waiting for Jamie to arrive, I found myself extremely nervous and fidgety, understandably so since I was about to relay to this poor woman the information I had received while getting my dental exam a week ago. I had to tell Jamie about Sheila and it was not going to be an easy pill for her to swallow. The reason I had the luxury of putting off this meeting was that Jamie had been on a business trip and today was the first time she was able to see me.

I chose to meet her in a big open public place because I felt like Dave's office was too confining. The thought of the three of us sitting across from her telling her the bad news in such a tiny environment was just way too close for comfort. I also chose to see Jamie by myself. Dave and I had talked about him being here with me, but we both agreed that Jamie would be better off hearing the news in a one-on-one situation. Also, Dave decided he would be better served working in the store and fielding and returning calls for *Hook, Line and Sink Him*. Our business was now getting tons of calls, and with all three of us out of commission for the past few days, there were several people who needed callbacks.

As for Anna's whereabouts on this particular Saturday morning, I had no clue. I assumed with Chris, probably snuggling under the covers and discussing honeymoon destinations. We had temporarily lost contact and had not spoken in three days. No calls asking, "How are the dogs? Are you paying enough attention to Passion?" Is Pretty Boy getting enough to eat?" Are P.J. and Pepper fighting a lot?" No calls about my article, either. The final draft was now finished and I was waiting for feedback. Most importantly, though, no call to clear the air about the big love declaration. At some point, Anna and I were going to have to try to move past our one-sided love affair and have the whole "let's just be friends" talk. So until she decided to get up the guts to show her face again, Dave and I had to run the business.

I realized that calling Anna was an option. "Be the bigger person," I could hear my mom's voice from the early eighties. Sorry, mom. No way. I wasn't about to call some chick whose response to the outpouring of my heart and soul was, "I could never do this to Chris. I'm sorry."

"Jeff!" I heard Jamie's voice and turned around to see her excitedly walking toward me and waving. Nausea was setting in.

I mustered up a smile and a cheery face. "Hi, Jamie, how was your trip?"

"Fine," she answered, "Oh my God! What happened to your eye?"

The hits just kept coming. "I'll tell you about it later," I said, "Let's walk around."

"Okay, sure."

We walked a few steps before either of us said a word. Finally Jamie blurted out, "So? What did he say? I'm dying to know."

"Well...this is really hard for me."

Jamie stopped walking and turned to me. We were standing in front of the sea lion pool, where the animals were gliding gracefully in and out of the water. At that moment I wished I was one of them.

"What is it?" she asked urgently.

I put my head down as I could barely look at this poor girl. "Ted has another girlfriend. He said he's in love with both of you."

"Really?" she asked softly.

Slowly I nodded my head. Then I pulled out my wallet, took out some bills, and handed them to Jamie. "Here's your money."

Jamie looked at the money and then looked at me, tears now rolling down her cheeks. "I don't want the money back."

"Please, just take it."

Her voice began to rise, "I don't want the money." Now she shouted, "I don't want the money! I want Ted!" She buried her face in her hands and began to sob.

The moment could not have been any worse. Not really knowing what to say, I managed, "I feel horrible about this. Is there anything I can do for you?"

She looked up at me and said through tears, "There's nothing!" Then she put her face right back into her cupped hands.

At that moment, I knew she was right. There was absolutely zero I could do. I had ruined this person's life. I had crushed her by meddling into something that was none of my business. What was happening to Jamie was all my fault. And I loathed myself. "I'm really sorry…" I whispered, "really sorry."

Two seconds later, Jamie looked up at me and suddenly something felt strange. The reason I say that is because all of a sudden Jamie wasn't crying anymore. The look on her face had turned from devastation to concern. What is Jamie so worried about all of a sudden? I wondered. I got my answer when I realized I myself was crying. Me. Jeff. Mr. Tough Guy, Mr. Hard Ass. I was sobbing now. Tears were streaming down my face, and I was making these strange sounds and breathing funny. I could not remember how long it had been since I cried.

"Are you alright?" Jamie asked me.

All I could do was start laughing, which made Jamie start giggling.

Through laughter and tears, I said, "I'll be okay." I chuckled some more, tears still trickling down, "To tell you the truth, I have a broken heart too," I confessed.

Now Jamie hugged me tight and we stood there, both continuing to semi weep.

When we finally broke away from the hug Jamie asked me if I would mind walking around some more.

"Sure…" I answered, "Let's go see some giraffe." We turned and headed toward them.

"You know, Jeff…" Jamie said, "Please don't feel badly about what you did. Remember, I came to you."

"Thanks, but I can't help feeling really guilty about this whole thing."

"The thing is, you just found out for me what I would have found out later anyhow. And better now than in another year or two, right?"

"Maybe, but who am I to play with fate like that?"

Jamie stopped walking, turned to me, and smiled. "You're just a sweet guy with a good heart who gave me a little push to get out of a bad situation." Then she gently kissed my cheek. "I think I want to go home. I have a lot to do."

I smiled, "Like break up with Ted?"

"Yes, like break up with Ted and start living my life."

I shoved the five $100 bills into Jamie's coat pocket and said, "For what it's worth, Ted's other girlfriend's name is Sheila Brooks."

"Do you know her?"

I grinned and nodded. "Sheila and I go way back. For the record…it'll never last."

"Why do you say that?"

"Two reasons. One, because Sheila will always be a cheater…"

"Yeah…"

"And there's no doubt in my mind that Ted will regret screwing it up with a girl like you."

She kissed my cheek. "Thanks, Jeff. How about you? Will you be okay?"

"I'll be fine. I'm going to see the giraffe, and then I'm going home to do the same thing as you; start living my life." I held her hands and asked, "Keep in touch?"

"You bet," she grinned and then she was gone.

When I reached the home of my tall friends, I watched them for the next few minutes, admiring their beauty and gracefulness. I wondered what kinds of troubles a giraffe may have. I once read somewhere that male giraffe compete for access to females by wrestling with their necks to determine who is stronger. The giraffe who wins gets his girl. Not a bad way to get chicks. I thought to myself, Maybe I should go over to Chris's and neck wrestle for Anna. That concept made much more sense to me than the way humans try to win over the people they love.

A little while later, I began walking home from the zoo and my cell phone rang. I looked at it. Dave. Who else? "Hey, buddy..." I answered.

"Hey. How did it go with Jamie?"

"It was okay. She'll be all right. How do you feel?"

"Me?" asked Dave, "Like the guy from the Shawshank Redemption who broke out of jail. Like a free man."

I chuckled.

"Hey, I was wondering. Would you come by the store...like at 5:00?"

"Why?"

Dave seemed hesitant. "Well," he said cautiously, "We have a client coming in."

"Are you kidding me?" I shouted, "Dave...haven't you learned your lesson yet? No more clients. I'm done."

"Jeff, listen...just one more. I promise. This woman...she really needs our help. I swear...I know what I'm doing."

Dave...the most good-hearted person I knew, always trying to help people. The guy who had such a hard time with his own life, but who never neglected to lend a hand or give advice or try to save someone. So Dave agreeing to take on one more client made sense. The woman had probably touched some part of him, and with his giving, caring soul, he couldn't find it in his heart to say no. I loved this guy. That's the only reason I agreed to the meeting. Plus, I have to be honest. *Hook, Line and Sink Him* had actually helped a few women. What was the harm in helping just one more?

## Chapter 36

I walked into *Be a Sport* having a silent argument with myself regarding Dave's decision to take on one last client. Hadn't he realized enough was enough? I had a black eye, we were being sued, Jamie had a broken heart, Dave's relationship was over, and Anna... Well, no matter how much she was fooling herself, *Hook, Line and Sink Him* hadn't done her any favors.

Then there was Liz. And Frieda. Plus, Dave had been through so much the past couple of days. If he wanted me there, I needed to be there for him. But this was it. After this client, I was calling it quits, and no one was going to talk me out of it.

"Dave!" I shouted, "Where are you?" I looked around the store but no Dave.

"In here!" I heard him shout to me. I headed toward the office. When I entered the little room, I found Dave cleaning off his desk and putting some files into a big cardboard box.

"What are you doing?"

"Per your wishes, I'm closing up shop," he said with a sad smile, "After this last client...that's it."

"Cool," I said, "I really thought you'd go kicking and screaming."

"No. I agree with you, Jeff. Time for us to retire."

I nodded and began helping Dave clean out *Hook, Line and Sink Him*'s office. We boxed some more things and cleaned up a little bit, which took about ten minutes, a heck of a lot less time than it did to set up our little venture. We worked in silence, each of us with a lot on our minds. A little while later, Dave looked up and said, "So do you really think we're getting sued?"

"I don't know," I answered, "Based on those papers Steven gave me, it seems pretty serious."

Dave chuckled, "I told you...the small businessman always gets screwed."

We both started laughing and finished packing up, until all the remnants of our little business were in boxes.

"I think that's it," Dave said while closing up one of the boxes, "You know, I really did have a good time with this, didn't you?"

I smiled and reflected for a moment. "Yeah. I guess so. It's funny...for me this started out as a gig to make money and to get my article in Anna's magazine."

"Which you did..."

"Which I did. But you know something Dave? You know what *Hook, Line and Sink Him* did for me? It forced me to listen to women." I stared past Dave and continued, "For the first time in my life, I really get them. I've spent most of my adult years trying to get women into bed, and now, I see the inner beauty. You know?"

When I looked back at my buddy, he was looking at me like I was from outer space.

I continued, "I understand them better now. Not just their bodies and their lips but their hearts."

"Wow," Dave said, "Just when you think you know someone..."

"Shut up."

"You've done like a complete 180."

"So, asshole...let me see that ring again," I said in an attempt to drastically change the subject.

From his jeans pocket, Dave pulled out the diamond engagement ring he had bought for Lori and handed it to me.

"Did this really cost six grand?"

"Let me tell you about this ring," Dave sold me, "This ring is a one point two solitaire, with VS1 clarity, and graded F in color."

I put the ring down on Dave's desk and said with a smile, "Money well spent."

"You're such an asshole," Dave joked.

Two seconds later, we heard the front door of the store open. Dave nervously jumped up and said, "Wait here a second. I'll be right back." Then he left the office and shut the door behind him. I realized our final client had just arrived. I knew nothing about her.

A minute later, Dave came back into the office and said nervously, "Okay...she's here."

"Well, tell her to come in. Let's see if we can help sucker her boyfriend into a lifetime commitment."

"Nice attitude, Jeff."

Dave left again for a few seconds, and when the office door swung back open I got a huge shock. Standing in the doorway was none other than Anna. "Hi," she smiled.

"Hi," I said. Surprise, confusion, nervousness, and excitement were all happening in my body.

Dave cleared his throat. Very formally he asked her, "How may we help you?"

Anna sat down in the chair where our clients usually sat and answered Dave's question. "There's a guy...I haven't known him for very long..."

I stood there with a puzzled look on my face, trying to figure out what was happening. Anna was acting. She was semi-smiling, as if she was playing a role.

"This guy..." she continued, "I broke off my engagement because of him."

"Anna..." I said.

Like I wasn't even there, Dave responded to Anna. "Well, if you want to work with us I think we can help you." I could tell Dave was trying not to crack up. He went on, "Let me explain our three-step program."

Now Anna was holding back laughter too.

"Is someone going to tell me what the hell you guys are up to?" I said with a chuckle.

My heart stopped when Anna stood up and walked toward me. Out of the corner of my eye, I saw Dave smile and leave the room. Anna put her arms around my neck.

Before she had a chance to speak I told her, "We charge $500 up front…$2000 if you get engaged within six months. Is this something you'd like to try?"

"Oh yeah…" she smiled. Then she kissed my lips softly, passionately and most important, lovingly.

I whispered, "I love you, Anna," and my sweet girl instantly said it back.

A few moments later, she gently pulled away from me and said, "You know, Jeff…don't worry about me putting pressure on you to get married." She smiled, "I can live without being a bride…I just want to be your girlfriend."

"That may be a problem," I said. Then I took her hands in mine, "Because I don't want you to be my girlfriend."

"You don't?" she asked, worry in her voice.

"No, I want you to be my wife. Will you marry me?"

Anna nodded and smiled, tears filling her eyes.

I walked over to Dave's desk, and picked up the diamond solitaire ring. "Will you wear this temporarily till we trade it in for yours?"

"Sure," Anna giggled, through tears.

As I placed Dave's ring on Anna's now bare left ring finger, something popped into my head. I was getting engaged, without ever having gone to bed with my future wife. Wow! "What am I thinking?!" I asked myself. The answer was as clear as day. I was thinking that I had found true love. Not that sex wasn't important to me, trust me, sex would always mean something. But somehow I knew that Anna and I wouldn't have any problems in the bedroom. She was my girl. And that's what made me so sure.

I kissed her again and everything was finally perfect. I now realized that the guy who was so intensely afraid of marriage had to start a marriage business to learn about love. And now, instead of being the guy who "Hook, Lined and Sank Him," I was soon going to be a husband. I was going to be one of those guys I had always called "suckers" or "poor bastards." But the way Anna felt in my arms at this moment made me recognize that before all this, I was the sucker. I was the poor bastard. And now...I felt like the luckiest guy on earth.

# Client Follow-up

## Liz and Sam

Since Anna and Liz were best friends and Anna and I were now a couple, we wondered how we were going to explain the coincidence to Sam. After all, wouldn't Sam be suspicious that the same guy who befriended him at the pizza place turned out to be his future wife's best friend's boyfriend? How does this stuff get so complicated? I wondered.

Here is how we dealt with it. Anna and I sat Liz down one night and told her we thought she should tell Sam the truth.

"Are you crazy?" she shouted, "Absolutely not!"

"If Sam really loves you, he won't care," Anna pleaded.

I added, "And do you really want to hide all this from the man you're going to spend the rest of your life with?"

Reluctantly, Liz agreed to come clean with Sam. All of us (Liz, myself, Anna, and Dave) took Sam out for drinks one night and told him the whole story.

Naturally, he was furious. He felt betrayed, deceived. "It's over, Liz!" he shouted. Then he stood up and stormed out of the restaurant. We all ran after him, but he refused to speak with any of us.

Liz spent the night at Anna's place (with me there, of course) and cried for hours. Eventually, we all crashed on Anna's couches. Around 2 a.m., Liz's cell phone rang.

"Hello?" she answered.

We could tell it was Sam. They talked for a few minutes, and when she hung up, Liz told us Sam was on his way over. A few minutes later, he showed up at Anna's apartment and told Liz that for her to go to the extremes she did to get him to marry her, he had no doubt she would make a loving, loyal wife. So just like that, he wanted the engagement back on.

However, Liz did something that shocked me. She did not accept Sam's re-proposal. Instead, she decided to make the same deal with Sam that he had made with her four years earlier. "If you want to marry me," Liz told him, "I think you should call me in six weeks."

"Are you joking?" Sam asked.

"Liz…what are you doing?" asked Anna.

Liz ignored her friend. "Look Sam…I really love you. But you have to figure out on your own if you really, truly, sincerely, want to marry me."

I tried to step in and take control. "Look, Liz…I think everyone here would agree…Sam's in."

Liz paid no attention to me either. She continued speaking to Sam. "I tricked you into it. Now it's up to you to come to the correct decision fully on your own."

She looked at the calendar on her watch, "Six weeks from today is around October 31, Halloween. If you still want to marry me on Halloween, give me a call."

Sam was flabbergasted that Liz would use the same tactic as he had years earlier. Nonetheless, he knew she felt strongly about it and he therefore had no choice but to play by her rules. As for Liz, she was pleased with herself for letting Sam go. She felt confident that if he did come back, her marriage and their love would be completely genuine and would last forever.

Sam called me a few times during the six weeks to check in and to see how Liz was doing.

"Don't worry, Sam..." I would tell him each time we talked, "It's cool." I would always end the call on a positive note. "Just do your time" I would smile. I realized right then that I would always be good at hook, line and sinking people, even though we were no longer in business.

Six weeks later on Halloween, Liz and Sam were officially engaged (again). They invited Anna and me over for dinner to celebrate. Liz cooked us a fantastic meal, thanks to the cooking classes she had taken. During dessert (caramel crème brule), Liz informed Sam that she would not be getting a boob job and that he would just have to live with her breasts the way they were.

"But if you know anyone who's interested, I would highly recommend Dr. Carmine Bongio," Anna joked.

Liz and I giggled. Sam didn't get it, but it didn't matter.

"As long as you continue the cooking classes and initiate sex once in awhile, I'm totally fine with your boobs," Sam joked, "In fact, I love your boobs!"

Liz was gleaming. Her love for Sam was truly evident, especially moments later when she did something extremely romantic and sweet. She handed Sam a beautifully wrapped present with a big bow on it.

He smiled and opened it. Inside the box was Liz's remote control. "I completely relinquish control," she smiled.

Sam hugged his fiancé tightly. "I love you, Liz," he said.

"I love you, too."

The following spring, on a beautiful cool crisp night, Liz Sullivan married her longtime boyfriend. As promised in high school, Anna was the maid of honor. The wedding took place at the Ritz Carlton, which was recommended by Anna, who had gone to see the caterer while engaged to Chris, if you recall.

## Frieda and Simon

Simon walked into his fifty-fifth surprise birthday bash and saw the dimly lit, gorgeous ballroom and a hundred and fifty of his closest friends. To say he gasped is an understatement. He looked so stunned, Frieda was secretly afraid he was having a heart attack.

After the initial shock wore off, he was able to relax and truly enjoy himself. "Frieda...my Frieda..." he said happily, holding out his arms to hug and show gratitude to his girlfriend. "This means so much to me...you have no idea."

While hugging Simon, Frieda thought to herself, yes, I do. But the fact that she had used our services to find out what her guy really wanted didn't bother her at all. All that mattered now was that the man she loved was thrilled, flattered, and ecstatic beyond belief. And Frieda found great joy in this. Simon's wife's death had been tragic and unbelievably heart-breaking, and her guy deserved happiness. And that's all Frieda had been trying to do--make Simon happy. And that's why she felt at peace with hiring *Hook, Line and Sink Him*.

The party guests dined on foods from Simon's three favorite countries: Italy, France, and America. Stations were set up for each country, each with an elaborate buffet. Frieda spared no expense as she went for the open bar, huge floral arrangements at each table, and a massive dessert table.

Anna attended the event. Frieda introduced her to Simon as "Anna the party planner," which was actually true since Anna had been instrumental in most of the decisions. One moment, when Frieda wasn't occupied dealing with details of the party or talking to guests, Anna found her window to talk to her lovely client and friend.

"You look so beautiful, Frieda..." Anna said, kissing Frieda's cheek. Her compliment really was sincere. Frieda, though well into her fifties, looked stunning. Her face had lots of age lines and her cheeks were a bit sunken in, but her face radiated happiness and light, so much so that tonight, years seemed to have been erased from her physical appearance.

"Same to you, sweetie," she smiled.

"I'm really happy for you, Frieda," said Anna, "Simon seems like a wonderful man."

"He is..." she gushed. "So what about you? How are things?" Frieda gave Anna a hopeful smile.

"Well..." Anna declared happily, "I'm finally having good sex."

Frieda gasped. "That's wonderful! What changed it for you?"

Tears welled up in Anna's eyes when she answered, but she also had a huge grin on her face. "Actually...it's *who* changed it for me. I'm finally with the person I love. I'm with the guy who loves me for me...and the guy who's my best friend."

"So you and Jeff finally worked things out, huh?"

Anna looked at Frieda like she was a tarot card reader who had just predicted something major.

"Don't be so shocked," Frieda giggled, "I'm a pretty perceptive lady...except for when it comes to my *own* guy!" They both burst out laughing.

A moment later, the band began to play again. It was *The Late Night Band,* actually, the band Lori wanted to hire for her and Dave's wedding. Apparently, they weren't as booked as Lori had made them sound.

Everyone, including Simon and Frieda, danced up a storm until it came time for the cake, which was the final kicker as to why the party was officially "over-the-top." Frieda had spent over $1000 on a Ron Ben-Israel designer cake, which looked more like a wedding cake than a birthday cake, especially since it had beautiful fresh flowers on it. On top of the cake stood a figurine of Simon, tennis racket in hand.

"I am completely and utterly wowed by this evening, my darling," the birthday boy told Frieda at the end of the night. "The fact that you did this for me is a sign." And the rest is history.

A week after the party, Simon went out and bought his longtime girlfriend a two carat sapphire engagement ring. He decided to forego the traditional diamond and go with the bright blue gem because sapphires are the stone of destiny, according to the Greeks, and the fact that Frieda had thrown an amazing party for him was fate.

Simon never found out the truth about *Hook, Line and Sink Him* and how the party actually came about, but he and Frieda moved in together and planned their wedding and both were blissfully happy. Simon taught Frieda how to play tennis and Frieda ended up changing her license plate from "Was His" to "Got M."

## Kyle and Steven

Steven ended up dropping the lawsuit against *Hook, Line and Sink Him* at the urgings of his fiancé. Kyle and Steven were married in Connecticut a few months later and are now a legally married couple.

A few months ago, they had a totally fun, crazy reception with two hundred friends including myself, Anna and Dave. In my entire life, I can't ever remember getting as drunk as I did at their bash. I vaguely recall doing the Michael Jackson Thriller dance while lots of people clapped. Anna told me the next day that she thought I actually had a hidden talent and that if things didn't work out for me at *Today's Chicago Woman,* I would have no problem getting a job as a Chippendale's dancer.

Kyle still writes in his diary.

# More Client Follow-up

## Jamie and Ted

Just shy of a year after I told Jamie about her two-timing dentist boyfriend Ted, she attended a Cubs game with a few friends. Not a huge sports fan in the first place, Jamie wasn't looking forward to sitting in the bleachers in hundred degree weather around a bunch of loud, obnoxious, beer-drinking guys. But she knew that if she wanted to actually have a life, she needed to give new things a chance.

During the fourth inning, she got up to get a hot dog and noticed a very attractive guy in line in front of her. He seemed kind of goofy, but in a really cute way, and he had beautiful eyes. The fact that she was actually interested in someone thrilled her. Jamie could not remember the last time she had even looked at a guy. This was huge.

The guy turned and noticed her. "Hi," he said with a nice smile, "I'm Mike." Mike turned out to be our Mike.

The two of them decided to hook up after the game at *Murphy's*, the greatest post-Cubs game spot in town. They had some appetizers and drinks and talked for a long time. Jamie told Mike about her break up with Ted.

"He didn't want to marry me and I couldn't understand why. It was driving me nuts!" she told Mike as she gulped down the rest of her third beer.

"So you finally dumped him or what?" asked Mike, pouring her another glass out of the pitcher.

Now Jamie began to giggle.

"What's so funny?"

Suddenly she was laughing. Hard.

Mike just sat there, wondering why this seemingly normal girl had just gone psycho.

Jamie composed herself finally and came clean. "Actually...I have to tell you something, but please don't judge me. I've never told a soul about this, but for some odd reason I want to talk about it with you."

"Okay."

"So since I couldn't understand why Ted wouldn't marry me, I hired this company...it was called *Hook, Line and Sink Him*."

Mike freaked. "Oh my God! No way!"

"What?"

"I worked there!"

"What?!"

"Jeff and Dave...they're my friends..."

"No way! I love Jeff!"

Now both of them were smiling and giggling, amazed at what a small world it was. After a few moments, Jamie asked, "So, what did you do for them?"

Mike smiled proudly, "I was the guy who went on the dates with the girls to make their boyfriends jealous."

Jamie took another big gulp of beer and flirted, "Well, looks like they chose the right guy."

Now Mike really liked this girl. They ended up kissing for hours outside of Jamie's apartment, exchanging numbers, and going out pretty much every night after that for months. In fact, they're still dating.

Ted ended up marrying Sheila. Trust me...it will never last.

## Karen

This is a really hard story to believe, but it's the truth. One day, several months after we'd met her, Anna actually got stuck in an elevator with Karen. Anna was visiting friends who lived in Karen's building. While the two rode up the elevator in uncomfortable silence, both realizing who the other one was, the car stopped. They were between the fifteenth and sixteenth floors, trapped for more than an hour.

So with time on their hands, they ended up talking. "Can I ask you something?" said Anna.

"Sure," Karen said unenthusiastically, sitting down on the elevator floor.

"Why are you so unhappy?"

Karen looked up at Anna and said, "Look at me. I'm plain. I'm nothing. How can someone like *you* ask me that? It's so condescending."

"Look, Karen," said Anna, taking a seat next to her, "I don't think I'm better than you. I think I just try harder."

By the time the maintenance guys got the elevator going again, two girls had bonded. And when the doors opened, they exchanged numbers.

Karen called Anna the next day and the two of them went out on a mission. Their first stop was at Elizabeth Arden, where Karen got a new hairdo. They spent the next five hours on Michigan Avenue, where Anna helped her spend thousands of dollars on new clothes, shoes, accessories, and make-up. The girl had never spent a dime on herself and the funny part was, she was a very wealthy woman. Karen had made a lot of money as a computer consultant for two major accounting firms in Chicago and had stashed it all away. Until now.

"This is the best investment you've ever made," exclaimed Anna when she saw Karen walk out of the dressing room in Saks, "You're gorgeous!"

Karen hugged Anna tight. "Thank you so much."

When they said good-bye Karen, giggled and joked, "If and when I get a boyfriend…and if he's dragging his feet on proposing…be prepared to hear from me."

A new look was just what Karen needed to brighten up her personality and find her self-confidence. Lori left Karen eight messages and seventeen texts before she realized Karen wasn't interested in being friends with her anymore.

# Fatima

Dave called Fatima and told her that *Hook, Line and Sink Him* was no longer in business and that he was sorry to have wasted her time. In true Dave style, though, he ended up talking to her for more than an hour, listening to her problems, and giving her advice on how to get her boyfriend to marry her.

Dave basically told her the *Hook, Line and Sink Him* philosophy, which was break up with him, run into him on a date, and change everything he doesn't like about you. Dave didn't realize something important: Fatima was taking notes.

She ended up breaking up with her boyfriend and heading to India for one of those quickie arranged marriages that are so popular now. The guy freaked out and followed her across the world. But by the time he got there, it was too late. Fatima had fallen head over heels for a guy to whom her parents introduced her. She was married within two weeks.

She called Dave when she got back to the states to tell him the story. When he asked her how she knew she did the right thing, she said, "My husband told me he knew he wanted to marry me right away…in the first ten minutes, in fact. That's what I'd always wanted and what my American boyfriend couldn't give me."

Fatima's pregnant, by the way.

# Jodi

Looking through the window and watching all the girls in Jodi's kickboxing class made me nervous. I could tell that every woman in there could pretty much kick my ass, just as Jodi had a few weeks earlier. My plan was to wait outside the studio till the class ended and talk to Jodi when she came out. And I was scared, because if she was still as pissed at me as she was when she punched me, she might actually ask one of these athletic and powerful women to uppercut or speed bag my face. Still, I had no choice but to brave it out, because I truly felt the need to clear things up with her.

When the class finally finished, the door swung open and women began walking out, towels and bags in their hands, sweat dripping off their bodies. It was very loud as all the kick boxers chatted with each other, shouting things like, "Call me!" and "See you Thursday!"

When I finally saw Jodi I was nervous--borderline panicky, in fact. Not because she had punched me harder than Sheila's guy had (or any other man ever had, for that matter) but because I cared so much and I didn't want to blow my chances of winning her friendship.

"Jodi..." I called.

When she looked up and saw me, her face turned to stone. "What do you want?" she asked coldly.

"I want to apologize. Please...would you let me explain?"

"There's nothing to explain, Jeff. It's pretty obvious. You tried to trick me. You tried to con me into marrying Eric."

"You're right, I did. But here's the thing. There was a part of me who knew you really cared for Eric and I believed that if I got him to change some things for you, maybe you would be happy with him."

"Very convenient for you since you would have made $2000 off the deal."

"Actually, $2500."

"Are you looking to be punched again?" she asked. I knew she was still very angry, but something told me she was lightening up.

"Listen, Jodi…I never meant to hurt you. I really like you. I mean that. You're adorable…and you're smart and you're a good person."

Now I saw a smile begin to form.

I went on, "And your best qualities are that you like sports and Jimmy Buffet."

Now I got the full-fledged grin. "I'm really mad at you, Jeff, even though I'm smiling. But I will admit…you may have done me a favor. I mean…Eric and I are not good for each other. So maybe you just accelerated the end of us."

"Well, maybe I should charge you for my services then," I joked.

Jodi put her fist up like she was going to punch me and I actually flinched. She immediately noticed I was scared of all five feet of her. "Sorry I hit you," she giggled.

"It's okay. I deserved it. Friends?"

Jodi smiled. "Friends."

"Because…" I got into a boxer's ready position before continuing, "I want to set you up with someone."

"Are you trying to get into a fight with me?" she asked with a giggle.

"You have to trust me on this one." I then walked her to her car and told her all about Dave. "He's a huge sports lover," I explained. Then I joked, "Plus, he'll never call you 'honey bunny.'"

This sent Jodi into hysterics. By the time we parted ways, she agreed to meet my best friend. Before they went out, I made sure to tell Dave the inside scoop that when Jodi was with Eric, she hated the fact that he made her hold him after sex for at least an hour. Dave and Jodi ended up going out and hitting it off. They're still dating.

*Hook Line and Sink Him*

A few weeks ago, Anna and I went out on a double date with them. We headed into *The Burwood Tap* for a couple of beers. It was strange. I hadn't been there since the night I'd seen Anna, the night I'd met Chris, the night my world changed, and the night I fell in love.

We all sat lined up at the bar, my good friend Jodi, my best friend Dave, myself, and on my other side, my sweet, adorable, non-sports loving, and, I might add, hot, fiancé, Anna, who was wearing her brand new cushion cut diamond on a platinum band.

All of a sudden, I heard a woman shout, "When?"

The guy she was yelling at shouted back, "I don't know! Soon!"

"I can't wait forever for you to marry me, Brian," she said.

This is where Dave elbowed me and began to laugh.

"Leave it alone," I warned.

"Are you sure?" asked my buddy.

"We might be able to help her," Anna chimed in.

"Yeah," added Jodi, "She seems really nice."

I smiled at the three of them and repeated myself: "Leave it alone."

We all continued sipping our beers.

## *The End*